A NIGHT
IN THE CEMETERY

A NIGHT
IN THE CEMETERY

AND OTHER STORIES OF
CRIME & SUSPENSE

ANTON CHEKHOV

TRANSLATED BY PETER SEKIRIN

PEGASUS BOOKS
NEW YORK

A NIGHT IN THE CEMETERY
AND OTHER STORIES OF CRIME AND SUSPENSE

Pegasus Books LLC
45 Wall Street, Suite 1021
New York, NY 10005

Translation copyright © 2008 by Peter Sekirin

Interior design by Maria Fernandez

ISBN: 978-1-933648-86-6

Printed in the United States of America

CONTENTS

PREFACE ix

A NIGHT AT THE CEMETERY 1

WHAT YOU USUALLY FIND IN NOVELS 6

THE SWEDISH MATCH 8

A NIGHT OF HORROR 35

WILLOW 45

A THIEF 51

THE ONLY WAY OUT 57

AN EXPENSIVE DOG 61

CURVED MIRROR 65

A COURT CASE 69

THE BROTHER: A SLICE OF LIFE 73

A CONFESSION 76

IN THE DARKNESS OF THE NIGHT 81

THE INTENTIONAL DECEPTION 83

ON THE SEA: A SAILOR'S STORY 88

IVAN THE CABMAN 93

PERPETUAL MOBILE 97

EVILDOER 107

DEATH OF AN OFFICE WORKER 113

75 Grand 117

At the Cemetery 124

The Conversation of a Man with a Dog 128

The Wallet 132

A Dead Body 136

Too Much Talking! 142

Conversation of a Drunken Man
with a Sober Devil 148

Psychopaths 151

Assignment 158

Fire in the Steppe: An Evil Night 167

Ignoramus 175

Task 181

Dreams 190

A Crime: A Double Murder Case 201

Drama 208

An Ambulance 216

Bad Business 223

Misfortune 230

The Man Who Wanted Revenge 239

Thieves 246

Murder 266

Criminal Investigator 278

The Drama at the Hunt 285

A NIGHT
IN THE CEMETERY

PREFACE

While the plays and novellas by Anton Chekhov are known and loved the world over, it will come as a surprise to many to learn that he actually began his career as a crime and mystery writer. He had always been fond of the genre, and during his mid-twenties, he began writing suspense stories as a hobby while still in medical school at Moscow University. His first story, "What is Met in the Novels," was published shortly thereafter in *Dragonfly* magazine. As befitting Chekhov's exceptional style and sensibilities, the letter he received from the editors at *Dragonfly* on January 13, 1880, began his writing career in an equally absurdist way: "This isn't bad at all. We will publish the material you sent us. Best blessings to you and your future work." He continued to write suspense stories as a young doctor, eventually segueing into the more "literary" forms that cemented his place in literary history, returning to the crime and mystery genre at the end of his life.

From 1881 to 1883, Chekhov lived in Moscow and continued to study medicine at the university. He wrote many humorous crime stories for *Dragonfly, Spectator,* and *Alarm-Clock* magazines, including "The Swedish Match" and "Night of Horror." His stories were very popular, and a close friend mentioned in his memoirs that since Chekhov was so prolific, his writing was the main source of income for his entire family. His attention to his formal studies, however, never wavered, and he continued to excel in the classroom and clinic. (M. Chelnov, "Chekhov and Medicine." *Russian News,* 1906) If anything, Chekhov was able to use his medical knowledge to supplement his literary pursuits—his thorough knowledge of anatomy recurs again and again throughout this collection as various police officers and detectives sort their way through every kind of murderous mystery.

Chekhov graduated from medical school in 1884 and moved to the countryside outside Moscow as a practicing family doctor. In January 1885, he wrote to his brother, Mikhail Chekhov, betraying mixed feelings about his current profession. "Medicine is all right. I continue to treat sick patients. . . . I have a lot of friends, many of whom also seem to need medical care, and of course I treat half of them for free." In another letter later that month, he writes: "Sick patients bore me to death. I had several hundred patients this summer, and made only one ruble." Fortunately, life soon became more interesting out in the villages, as Chekhov began to accompany the local police on criminal investigations and perform autopsies for them. Many of stories from 1884 to 1886 feature a doctor or medic assisting the detective as the main protagonist, most notably in "Drama at the Hunt," "The Dead Body," and "Double Murder."

In 1886, Dmitry Grigorovich, a prominent writer then in his mid-seventies and a close personal friend of the literary luminaries Ivan Turgenev, Leo Tolstoy, Nikolai Nekrasov, and Fyodor Dostoevsky, wrote a letter to Chekhov, expressing admiration for his literary talents. Grigorovich passed Chekhov's stories around to his various acquaintances, and Chekhov's star continued to rise in the Russian literary world, with the *St. Petersburg Daily,* a prominent national paper, publishing several more of his stories.

As his reputation grew, friends and critics encouraged Chekhov to move away from these short crime and suspense pieces and focus on "big" literature. In a letter dated August 9, 1886, the journalist M. Remezov wrote: "I think the time has come for you to write serious, lengthy stories, and claim your place in literature." Taking this advice to heart, Chekhov became more and more entrenched in literary society, establishing close friendships with Leo Tolstoy and composer Peter Tchaikovsky. He staged his first play, *Ivanov,* later that year. But he was not quite ready to give up the mystery genre entirely. He published three collections of his crime stories between 1886 and 1889, and wrote twenty more new stories. Most of these stories were scattered throughout a variety of periodicals (see Annotated Table of Contents), and until now have managed to escape the notice of contemporary translators and editors.

The year 1889 was a watershed in Chekhov's life and career. Following the deaths of his father and his brother Nikolai, Chekhov traveled throughout Siberia, visiting Russian prisons and observing village life in the easternmost parts of the country. His travels took him through the Volga Valley, Perm,

Tiumen, Tomsk, Krasnoyarsk, Irkutsk, Khabarovsk, and Sakhalin. He kept an extensive diary, complete with detailed sketches and interviews of hundreds of officers and inmates from the notorious Sakhalin prisons. Upon his return, this diary was serialized in the newspaper *The New Time* under the title "From Siberia," and was his darkest published piece to date. In a letter to his publisher, Anton Suvorin, he wrote: "I have been in northern Sakahlin for two months. . . . I don't know what will come of this, but it will be big. I have enough material here for three books. Every day, I got up at 5 a.m. and went to bed late and stressed, as there are many things I have yet to do. . . . There is not a single prisoner out of the several thousand here, nor is there a settler in Sakhalin, with whom I haven't spoken." In December of 1890, following his return to Moscow, Chekhov wrote several more, and darker, crime stories, but these were the last of such stories for many years, as he turned his focus to theater and more literary short stories.

Needless to say, Chekhov's plays, novellas and short fiction pieces were met with great success, and it is for these that he is best remembered. As he neared the end of his short life, Chekhov spent more and more time writing longer novellas. He married the actress Olga Knipper and won several prestigious literary prizes, and as he wrote his novellas, he came full circle and turned back to the mystery and suspense genre that had started his career. These crime and suspense stories are an important part of Chekhov's literary journey, and even at this early stage in his literary career, his unique absurdist sensibilities, so beloved in his plays and novellas, are evident in raw form and are a compelling addition to the Chekhov canon.

A NIGHT AT THE CEMETERY

⊷ ⊷

P lease, Ivan Ivanovich, tell us something scary!"
Ivan Ivanovich stroked his moustache, cleared his
throat, smacked his lips, moved closer to the inquiring
ladies, and began to tell his story.

My story begins, as do most traditional well-written Russian
stories, with the phrase "I was drunk that day."

It happened after the New Year's Eve party where I celebrated
with one of my best friends, and I got as drunk as a fish. In my
defense, I should say that I had a good reason for getting drunk
on that night. I believe it is a worthy pursuit for people to feel
happy on New Year's Eve. Every coming year is as bad as the
previous one, the only difference being that in most cases it is
even worse.

I think that during our traditional New Year's Eve parties
people should fight, be miserable, cry, and attempt suicide. One
must remember that each new year leads you closer to death,

the bald spot on your head spreads, the wrinkles on your face grow deeper, your wife gets older, and with every new year you have more kids and less money.

As a result of my misfortunes, I got drunk. When I left my friend's house, the clock tower struck two o'clock in the morning. The weather outside was nasty. Only the devil himself could tell whether it was autumn or winter weather.

It was pitch black around me. Although I tried to look as far ahead as I could, I could not see anything. It was as if someone had put me in an enormous can of black shoe polish. It was also raining cats and dogs. The cold, sharp wind was singing terrible, horrifying notes—howling, moaning, and squeaking, as if an evil being were conducting an orchestra of nature. The mud stuck to my shoes with every slow step. The few streetlights that I accidentally encountered on my way resembled the crying widows one would see at funerals.

It seemed the weather itself felt like vomiting. A thief or a murderer might rejoice to have such weather, but for me, a drunken civil servant, it was very depressing.

"Life is boring," I philosophized to myself as I tried not to fall. "This isn't a life, but an empty, dull existence. Day after day, year after year, all the while still the same inside, no different than when you were young. Many years pass while you still only drink, eat, and sleep. In the end, they dig a grave for you, bury you, and have a party after your funeral with free food, telling each other, "He was a good man, but he didn't leave enough money behind for us, the scoundrel.' "

I was walking from one end of town to another, which was a very long walk for a man who had just had too many drinks. As I made my way through the dark and narrow side streets, I did not meet a single living soul, nor hear a single sound. At first, I walked on the sidewalk, as I was trying not to wet my boots, but despite my good intentions, my boots became soaking wet. So, I began walking in the middle of the street. This way, I had less chance to hit a lamppost or fall into a ditch.

My way was cloaked with cold, impenetrable darkness. At the beginning of my trip I came across several dim lampposts, but once I had passed a couple of small streets, even those small lamps disappeared from view. It was then that I began trying to find my way by touch. I was trying hard to see anything through the pitch dark, and as I listened to the wind's howl, I hurried. Little by little, I became filled with an inexplicable fear, which turned to horror as I realized that I had lost my way.

"Hey, taxi," I cried, with no reply. I then decided I should walk in a straight line, reasoning that sooner or later, I would get to a big street, where there would be lights and taxis.

Without looking back, being afraid to look even to my sides, I started to run . . .

Ivan Ivanovich paused, downed a shot of vodka, and stroked his moustache, before continuing on.

I don't really remember how long I ran. The only thing that I remember is bumping against something, badly hurting my knee, and extreme pain.

I remember sensing it was a strange object. . . . I could not see it in the darkness, but felt with my fingers that it was cold, wet and smoothly polished. I sat on it, while I rested. I won't take advantage of your patience, but I can tell you that after a while, when I lit my match to light a cigarette, I saw that I was sitting on a tombstone!

Around me, I could not see anything but darkness, nor hear a single human sound. Then, I saw a tombstone! In horror, I closed my eyes and jumped to my feet. I took a step away from the tombstone, and stumbled into something else! Imagine my horror as I encountered a wooden cross from the cemetery!

"Oh my God, I am in a graveyard," I thought, covering my face with my both hands, as I sat back down on the marble tombstone. Instead of the Presnya District Cemetery, I usually went to the Vagankovo Cemetery. As a rule, I am afraid neither of cemeteries nor of the dead. I am not prejudiced, nor do I believe in fairy tales. However, after finding myself among these silent graves in the middle of the night, with the wind howling and dark thoughts filling my mind, I suddenly felt my hair stand on end as a cold shiver went up my spine.

"This cannot be," I spoke aloud to try and calm myself. "This is just an illusion, a hallucination. It's all in my imagination, especially since I have recently read a book about spiritualism."

At this moment, lost in my nightmarish thoughts, I heard some very weak and quiet footsteps. Someone was walking toward me, but they didn't seem like human footsteps, for they were too light and way too frequent.

"A dead man walking," I thought.

Finally, this mysterious someone drew close to me, touched my knee, and heaved a deep sigh. Then I heard a howl. It was a terrible, deadly howl coming from a grave, pulling at my nerves. If as a child you were scared of your nanny's fairy tales, and stories about dead men, imagine how I felt as I heard the howl from somewhere near me!

I instantly became sober as I froze in horror. It seemed to me that if I opened my eyes, I would see a pale yellow bony face, covered in half-rotten cloth.

"Oh God! I wish morning would come faster!" I prayed.

However, before morning came, I went through another

inexpressible horror, a horror impossible for me to describe. As I sat on the tombstone, listening to the howling of the grave dweller, I suddenly heard new steps.

Someone was coming straight toward me, with heavy rhythmic footsteps.

As soon as he came to me, the creature from the grave let out a deep sigh, and a moment later a cold, heavy and bony hand rested heavily on my shoulder.

At that moment, Ivan Ivanovich had another shot of vodka and cleared his throat for the second time.

"And what then?" the ladies asked him.

I woke up in a small square room. The dawn could hardly shine its light through the small barred window. "Well, well," I thought. "This must mean the dead men pulled me deep into the graveyard."

Suddenly, I was filled with joy, for I heard human voices behind the wall.

"Where did you find him?" a low but loud bass voice questioned.

"Yes, sir! I found him in front of the Mr. Whitehead's Monument Store, sir!" another hoarse voice answered. "Right next to the showroom with tombstones. I saw him sitting there embracing the monument, with a dog howling next to him. My guess is he had quite a few drinks, sir."

In the morning, when I was completely awake, they released me from the police station.

WHAT YOU USUALLY FIND IN NOVELS

A duke, a duchess who used to be a beautiful woman, a rich man who lives next door, a left-wing novelist, an impoverished nobleman, a foreign musician, various servants: butlers, nurses, and tutors, a German estate manager, a gentleman, and an heir from America.

All the characters are unremarkable, yet sympathetic and attractive people. The hero saves the heroine from a crazed horse; he is strong-willed, and he shows his strong fists at every opportunity.

The sky is wide, the distances are vast, and the vistas are broad, so broad that they are impossible to understand. This, in short, is Nature.

Friends are blond. Enemies are red-headed.

A rich uncle: a liberal or conservative, according to circumstances. His death is more useful to the protagonist than his advice.

An aunt, who lives in a remote provincial town. A doctor with a concerned expression on his face, who gives people hope for the coming health crisis. He has a walking stick with a bulb, and he is bald. And where there is a doctor, there are illnesses; arthritis caused by overwork, migraines, inflammation of the brain. A man wounded in a duel, and advice to go to the spa.

A servant who worked for the old masters and is ready to sacrifice everything for them. He is a very witty fellow.

A dog that can do everything but talk, a parrot, and a nightingale. A summer cottage near Moscow and a mortgaged estate, somewhere in the South. Electricity, which is stuck into the story for no reason.

A bag of the best Italian leather, a china set from Japan, an English leather saddle, a revolver that fires perfectly, an order on the lapel, and a feast of pineapples, champagne, truffles, and oysters.

Accidental overhearing, as a source of great discoveries. A huge number of interjections, and of attempts to use technical terms whenever possible.

Small hints about important circumstances. Very often, no conclusion.

Seven mortal sins at the beginning, a crime in the middle, and a wedding at the end.

The End.

THE SWEDISH MATCH

━━◆━━

PART ONE

On the morning of October 6, 19__, a well-dressed young man came into the office of the Second Police Precinct of the City of S. He made a statement to the effect that his master, a retired officer, Mark Ivanovich Banks, had been murdered.

The young man was very excited while he was making his deposition. His hands were trembling, and his eyes were glazed with horror.

"To whom do I have the honor of speaking?" the chief of police asked.

"I am Mr. Post, Banks's manager. Horticulturist and mechanic."

The chief of police and two witnesses, who arrived at the scene of the murder together with Mr. Post, discovered the following: a crowd of people was standing next to the house where Banks was killed. News of the murder had dispersed instantaneously across the neighborhood, and because it was the weekend, people from all the neighboring farms and villages had come to have a look. People in the crowd were talking noisily. There were several pale and crying faces. The door to Banks's bedroom was found to be closed. The key was stuck in the lock from the inside.

"It is obvious that the thieves came into the room through the window," said Post, when he examined the door.

They went into the garden to have a look at the bedroom window. The window looked gloomy and sinister. It was covered with a faded green curtain. One corner of the curtain was folded back a little, so they could look inside the bedroom.

"Did any one of you look through the window?" asked the police chief.

"No, sir," said the gardener Efrem, a short, gray-haired man with the face of a retired drill sergeant. "How could we? It is none of our business, sir! We were all afraid."

"Oh, Mark Ivanovich, Mark Ivanovich!" The police chief sighed as he looked at the window. "I told you that you would finish badly. I told you, my dear, but you did not listen to me. Dissipation is no good."

"We have to thank Efrem," said Mr. Post. "He gave us the idea. Without him, we would never have realized it. He was the first to notice that something was wrong around here. This morning, he came to me and said, 'Why has our landlord been asleep for so long? He has not left his bedroom for this whole week.' He told me this, and I became dumb as if someone had struck me on my head. It dawned upon me that he had not appeared since last Saturday, and today is Sunday. Seven days, I am not kidding!"

"Yes, poor man." The police chief sighed again. "He was a

clever young man, well educated and kind, with good manners. He was such good company, too! But he was a dissipated man, let him rest in peace! I had expected so much more from him. Hey, Stepan," he said, addressing one of the witnesses. "Go to my office right now, and send little Andrew to the police precinct. Tell him to file a report! Tell them all that Mark Ivanovich has been murdered. And then go to the prosecutor's office, tell the man, Why is it taking him so long? He should be here already! And then, as soon as possible, you can go to the detective Nikolai Ermolaevich, and tell him to come here. Wait, I'll write him a note."

The police chief put guards around the house, wrote a brief note to the detective, and went to the manager of the estate to have a cup of tea. For the next ten minutes he sat on a stool, carefully biting a lump of sugar and sipping the boiling hot tea.

"Yes," he said to Post. "There you are. Rich and famous, a really well-off young man. 'A man loved by the gods,' as the poet Pushkin used to say. And what happened to him? Nothing! All he did was drinking and womanizing . . . and, as a result, he is dead."

"Two hours later, the detective arrived. Nikolai Ermolaevich Rusty (this is the detective's name) was a tall, strongly built man of about sixty years; he had worked in his profession for nearly a quarter of a century. He was well-known in the local county as an honest, clever and energetic man who loved his work. He arrived at the scene of the crime with his constant companion and assistant, the junior officer Dukovsky, a tall young man of about twenty-six years old.

"Is it true, gentlemen?" started Mr. Rusty, as he entered the Post's room and hastily shook hands with all of them. "How is it possible? They killed Mark Ivanovich? No, I can't believe this! It's im-pos-si-ble!"

"Well, that's about it." The police chief sighed.

"Oh my God! I saw him a week ago. Last Friday, I saw him at the local country market. I have to admit, I had a shot of vodka with him!"

"So there you are." The police chief heaved another deep sigh.

They sighed a few more times, said the few words which people usually say in such cases. Each had a cup of tea, and then they stepped out of the manager's house.

"Make way!" the police sergeant cried into the crowd. When they entered the landlord's house, the detective started his investigation from the bedroom door. It was made of pine, painted yellow, and it was not damaged. There were no signs or outstanding marks which could assist the investigation. They decided to break in.

"Gentlemen, please stay outside. Those of you who are not officers, please do not enter!" said the detective, when, after a long period of knocking and cracking the door was opened by dint of axe and chisel. "Please do not enter—this is in the interests of the investigation. Sergeant, don't let anyone in!"

Rusty, his assistant, and the police chief opened the door and finally entered the bedroom, walking in an undecided manner, one step at a time. There they saw the following. A huge wooden bed with a thick feather mattress stood in front of the only window. A wrinkled blanket lay on the wrinkled mattress. The pillow, in a nice cotton pillowcase, also very wrinkled, lay on the floor. A nickel coin and a silver pocket watch lay on the bedside table. There was a box of sulfur matches next to them. There was no other furniture—only the bed, the table, and one chair. The sergeant looked under the bed and saw about twenty empty liquor bottles, an old straw hat, and a quart of vodka there. There was a boot covered with dust under the table. The detective cast a glance at the room, frowned, and then blushed.

"Scoundrels," he mumbled, pressing his fists together.

"And where is Mark Ivanovich?" asked Dukovsky quietly.

"I told you not to interfere!" Rusty responded rudely. "You'd better study the floor. This looks like another case in my practice. Evgraf Koozmich," he addressed the sergeant in a lower voice, "I had a similar case, it was about twenty years ago, you should remember. The murder of merchant Portraitov. The same thing: the scoundrels killed him and dragged the dead body through the window."

Rusty went to the window, pulled the curtain aside, and carefully lifted the windowpane. It opened.

"It opens. This means it was not locked. Hmm. There are some scratches and traces on the windowsill. Do you see them? Here, a trace from somebody's knee. Someone came from the outside. We should make a detailed examination of the window."

"I don't see anything special on the floor though," Dukovsky said. "No spots, or scratches. I found only one bruised Swedish match. Here it is! As far as I remember, Mark Ivanovich did not smoke and as a rule, he used safety sulfur matches, not the Swedish ones. This match could be material evidence."

"Oh, shut up please!" the detective shook his head. "You and your matches! I can't put up with these clever fellows. Instead of looking for matches, you'd be better off to examine the bed."

After the examination of the bed, Dukovsky reported:

"I found no blood, or any other suspicious spots. No torn linen either. I saw the signs of somebody's teeth on the pillow. Besides this, on the bed, I found the remains of a strange liquid, which smells and tastes like beer. The arrangement of the objects on the bed suggests to me that some struggle was going on there."

"I know without you that there was a struggle! Nobody is asking you about a struggle! Instead of looking for a struggle, you'd better . . ."

"One boot is here, the other one is missing."

"Yes, and what?"

"This means that he was strangled when he was taking off his boots. He did not have enough time to take off his second boot, but they . . ."

"What are you talking about? How do you know that they strangled him?"

"Because there are traces of teeth on the pillow. The pillow itself is very scrambled and thrown two steps away from the bed."

"You talk too much, you're like a chatterbox! Go to the garden. You should have a good look at the garden instead of staying here, and I can examine the room better than you."

When the investigators came into the garden, they searched the grass. The grass under the window was flattened. A patch of thistles under the window was smashed. Dukovsky found several broken branches and a piece of cotton cloth on them. On one of the upturned heads of the flowers, he found a dark-blue woolen thread.

"What color were the clothes he was last seen wearing?" Dukovsky asked Post.

"Yellow."

"Excellent. This means that they wore blue."

Several of these thistle blossoms were cut, and carefully wrapped in paper. At that moment, two more people arrived at the scene: the court officer Svistakovsky and the doctor Tutuev.

The court officer greeted them, and at the same time started to satisfy his curiosity. The doctor, a gaunt and slim man with fallen eyes, a long nose, and a sharp chin, sat on the stump of the nearby tree, greeting none and asking nothing. He sighed and said,

"And the Austrians are excited again! I don't understand, what do they want? Well, Austria, again Austria! This is the sphere of your political influence. I hold you responsible for this tension, for this state of affairs . . ."

The examination of the window brought no results. But the examination of the garden and the bush next to the window gave many useful clues to the detectives. For example, Dukovsky managed to trace a long dark line on the grass. It consisted of a series of spots, and stretched for several steps in the garden. The line ended at the lilac bush with a big brown spot. It was where they found a boot, which matched the one in the bedroom.

"This is old blood," said Dukovsky, examining the spots.

The doctor, when he heard the word "blood," stood up lazily, and cast a fast sliding glance at the spots.

"Yes, this is blood."

"This means that he was not strangled, if it's blood," said Rusty, looking mockingly at Dukovsky.

"They strangled him in the bedroom, and here they became afraid that he might come back to life. Therefore, they hit him here with a sharp object. The blood spot under the bush indicates that he was there for a rather long time, while they were looking for means to remove his body from the garden."

"And what about the boot?"

"It supports my version that he was killed when he was taking off his boots before going to bed. He took off one boot, but the other one, I mean the one in the garden, had only been partially removed. Then it fell off his foot while they dragged the body across the garden."

"You are smart, I can see that," Rusty smiled. "You are very clever! And when are you going to stop talking? Instead of talking so much, you should take a sample of the blood-stained grass for analysis."

After they made a sketch of the garden, the detective went to the estate manager to write a report and to have breakfast. There, they continued their conversation.

"The watch and the money—everything is intact," Rusty began. "He was apparently not killed for money."

"And he was killed by an intelligent man too," inserted Dukovsky.

"How did you come to this conclusion?"

"I have a Swedish match as proof of this. Local farmers don't use these matches. They are used by the local landlords, and even then, not by everyone. And there was not just one killer, but at least three of them. Two people held him, and the third strangled him. Mr. Banks was a strong man, and the killers should have known this."

"How could he use his force, if, for example, he was asleep?"

"The killers got him when he was taking off his boots. This means that he was not asleep."

"Don't imagine things! Eat your breakfast!"

"It is my understanding," said the gardener Efrem, when he put the big teapot on the table, "that this dirty deed was done by Nicholas, and none else."

"It is quite possible," said Post. "And who is Nicholas?"

"He is the landlord's butler, your honor," said Efrem. "Who else but he could do this? He looks like a real robber, your honor! He is so drunk and dissipated that all are disgusted! He always supplied the landlord with vodka, and put him to bed. Who else? And one day, he even boasted in the pub that he could kill his landlord, your honor. This all happened because of the woman named Annie. Her husband is away all the time, making money, and she was the butler's girlfriend for a while. The landlord noticed her, he liked her, and he paid attention to her. So, Nicholas was very mad about all this. Now he is completely drunk, lying on the kitchen floor. He was crying, lying about how sorry he was that the landlord was dead."

"And really, this woman Annie can drive everyone mad," Post said. "She is just a farmer's wife, a country woman, but once you've seen her, you will at once—Even Mark Ivanovich used to call her 'babe.' There is something magnetic about her, something . . ."

"I saw her, I know," said the detective, blowing his nose into a red handkerchief.

Dukovsky blushed and looked down. The police chief nervously tapped at the saucer with his finger. The police officer coughed and started shuffling papers in his case. It seemed that only the doctor was impervious to the news about Annie.

The detective ordered them to bring in Nicholas. He was a tall young man; his nose was covered with smallpox scars, his chest was thin and fallen; he was dressed in an old coat given to him by the landlord. He came into Post's room, bowed very low, and stood silently in front of the detective. His face looked sleepy, and his eyes were red from crying. He was so drunk that he could hardly keep his balance.

"Where is the landlord?" Rusty asked him.

"He was killed, your honor." After saying this, Nicholas blinked, and started to cry.

"We know that he was killed. But where is he now? Where is his body?"

"People say that they pushed his body through the window and buried it in the garden."

"Really? Hmm. The results of this investigation have already leaked to the servants."

"This is bad. Please, tell us, my dear, where were you on the night the landlord was killed, that is, on Saturday night?"

Nicholas lifted his head, stretched his neck and thought for a while.

"I don't know sir. I was drunk and I don't remember anything.

"Alibi," Dukovsky whispered, smiled and rubbed his hands.

"Well, all right. And why is there blood under the landlord's window?"

Nicholas looked up and thought again.

"Think faster," the police officer said to him.

"Wait a minute! That blood came from nothing, just from a chicken, your honor. I had to kill a chicken for the kitchen. I cut its neck, as I always do, but then the chicken got away from me, and ran across the garden. That's where the blood came from."

Efrem testified that Nicholas really did slaughter chickens for the kitchen, in different places every time, but no one thought that a chicken with its throat half cut could run across the garden. On the other hand, no one could deny it either.

"Alibi," smiled Dukovsky. "And what a stupid alibi."

"Were you close to Annie?"

"Yes, I sinned with her."

"And did the landlord take her away from you?"

"Not exactly. Right after me, it was Mr. Post, then Ivan Mikhailovich, and then it was milord himself. That's how I was."

Post looked embarrassed and scratched his left eye. Dukovsky stared at him closely, read the embarrassment on his face, and trembled. He noticed dark blue pants which the manager wore, a detail to which he had previously paid no attention. The pants reminded him of the blue thread he had found on the bush.

Rusty, in his turn, looked suspiciously at Post.

"You can go," he said to Nicolas.

"And now, may I ask you a question, Mr. Post. You were definitely here on Saturday night, weren't you?"

"Yes, at ten p.m. I had a dinner with Mark Ivanovich."

"And what happened then?"

Post became embarrassed, and stood up from the table.

"Then—then—I don't remember," he mumbled. "I drank a lot that day. I don't even recall where I fell asleep. Why are you all looking at me this way? Do you think that I killed him?"

"Where did you get up the next morning?"

"In the servants' room, in a small bed next to the oven. Anyone can testify to that. I don't remember how I got there though."

"Please don't get excited. Do you know Annie?"

"There was nothing special about her."

"Did you pass her on to Banks?"

"Yes. Hey, Efrem, bring us some more mushrooms. Do you want any more tea, Egraf Kuzmich?"

After these words, there was a heavy, horrifying silence which lasted for about five minutes. Dukovsky remained silent and stared at Post's pale face, as if he wanted to hypnotize it with his sharp eyes. The detective broke the silence,

"We should go to the big house, and talk to Maria Ivanovna. I wonder whether she might be helpful to us."

Rusty and his assistant thanked Post for the breakfast and went to the manor house. There, they found Maria Ivanovna, a forty-five-year-old spinster who was Banks's sister, in the family room. She grew pale when she saw the large leather bags in the guests' hands, and the badges on their uniform caps.

"First of all, dear lady, I must beg your forgiveness for interrupting your, so to speak, special mood," started the old detective in a very gallant and courteous manner. "We have come to you to ask just a few questions. You must have heard about what has happened. We think that your brother was, so to speak, killed. Well, no one can escape from death, neither kings, nor peasants. Can you please help us with any advice, or explanation?"

"Oh, don't ask me," said Maria Ivanovna, growing ever more pale and covering her face with her palms. "I can't tell you anything. Anything. Please, I beg you. I can't. What can I do? Oh, no. Not a word about my brother! No, even if I have to die, I won't tell you!"

Maria Ivanovna burst out crying, and ran into another room. The detectives exchanged glances, shrugged their shoulders, and prepared to leave.

"Damned woman," swore Dukovsky as they were leaving the mansion.

"She probably knows something, but she won't tell us about it! Oh, have you noticed it? The maid had a very strange expression on her face, as if she knew something too. Just wait, you fools! We will discover everything!"

In the evening, Rusty and his assistant were going home along the pale moonlit road. They sat in the carriage and thought over the results achieved during the day. They were both tired and silent. Rusty did not like to talk on the way, as a rule, and the talkative Dukovsky kept silence to please the old man. At the end of the road, however, the assistant detective could not bear the silence, and broke it.

"Nicholas is involved in the case," he said, "and this fact cannot be disputed. Just look at his face! I also have no doubt that, however, he is not the organizer of the crime. He is a stupid tool, and he was hired to kill. Do you follow me? The humble Post plays a role in this case as well: the blue pants, the embarrassment, lying on the bed, scared after the murder, no alibi, and then there's Annie."

"You can talk as much as you want; this is all just an empty chatter. So, you think that the killer must be among those who knew Annie? This conclusion is too hasty. You are too young for your job. You are a sucker. You should be sucking milk, and not investigating crimes. You were also among those who tried to flirt with Annie—does that mean anything? Annie—she lived at your house as your cook for a month, but I'm not leaping to any conclusions. On Saturday night, I played cards with you. I saw you on that night, with my own eyes; otherwise I would have suspected you as well."

"The problem is not just this woman, it's all the mean, nasty feelings that we have. A humble young man is angry about his disappointment in love. His ego suffers. He wants revenge. Next point. His thick lips indicate his strong sensitivity. Remember how he smacked his lips, when he spoke about Annie? I have no doubt that this scoundrel is dying from hidden passion. We can see here his hurt pride and unsatisfied lust. This is reason enough to commit murder. We have two persons on our hands. Who is the third one? Nicholas and Post held him. But who actually strangled him? Post is a humble man who is afraid of everything. And people like Nicholas simply do not know how to strangle with a pillow. If they kill, they kill with an axe. There must be someone else, the third person who strangled him, but who is it?"

Dukovsky moved his hat over his eyes and became lost in his thoughts. He kept silence until the moment the carriage arrived at the detective's house.

"I have it now!" he cried out, as they came into the house and he took off his coat. "I've got it. I am surprised that it never struck me before! Do you know who the third person was?'

"Stop it, please! Here, supper is ready. Take a seat at the table, and let's eat!"

The detective and Dukovsky sat down to have supper. Dukovsky poured a shot of vodka for himself, stood up, stretched himself and said, with his eyes shining,

"You must know the name of the third person who acted with the scoundrel Post. You should know that this was a woman! I am talking about the landlord's sister, Maria Ivanovna."

Rusty coughed, as he drank his vodka, and started at Dukovsky,

"Are you mad? How is your head? You don't have a headache, do you?"

"I'm fine, just fine. All right, maybe I am going too far, maybe I have gone mad, but how can you explain her embarrassment when she saw us come in? How can you explain her unwillingness to testify? Let's admit that this is not the most important thing. All right. But then, remember about their relationship. She hated her brother! She has strict morals, and he is a very dissipated man. Here is where the hatred abides! People say that he convinced her that he was Satan's angel. And he even practiced Spiritualism in her presence."

"And so what?"

"Don't you understand? She killed him because she was a fanatic! She didn't just kill a bad and dissipated man, but she also relieved the world of a bad man. And she thinks that this was her merit, her virtuous and heroic deed. Oh, you simply don't know these old spinsters, these fanatics! Read Dostoevsky! Read Leskov! It was her, I am certain that it was her, and you call kill me if I am wrong. His sister strangled him. Oh, nasty woman! She attempted to deceive us. She thought, 'Let me stay here and pray, and they will think that I am only a quiet, pious woman, and they won't have any interest in me.' This is the way all amateur criminals behave! My dear friend, Nikolai Ermolaeveich! Give this case to me! Let me personally complete the investigation and close the case. Dear sir! I have started it, and I want to finish it."

The detective shook his head and frowned.

"I know for myself how to deal with complicated cases like this one!" he said. "And it is none of your business to interfere, unless I have asked you for your opinion. You should write down what I dictate to you—this is the duty for which you are paid. That is all."

Dukovsky snorted and left the room, closing the door with a bang behind him.

"A clever young man, yes he is," said Rusty looking toward the door. "However, he is too hot and unbalanced sometimes. I should buy him a gift at the next fair, a cigarette case or something."

On the next day, a young man from the local village was brought to the detective. He had a big head and a harelip, and identified himself as the local shepherd Daniel. He gave a very interesting testimony.

"I was drunk a few days ago," he said. "I visited my girlfriend and stayed there until midnight. On the way home, I was drunk and decided to take a swim in the pond. While I was swimming, I saw two men bring something heavy, wrapped in a black sack. I watched them climb onto the dam.

"Hey you, what's up?" I called out to them. They got scared and ran away from me as fast as they could, in the direction of the Makarevo's garden. I am pretty sure that the sack contained the landlord's body."

On the same day, in the late afternoon, both Mr. Post and Nicholas were arrested and brought under police guard to town. There, they were put in the local county jail.

Part Two

Twelve days passed.

In the morning, the detective, Nikolai Ermolaevich, was sitting at his desk in the office shuffling through the case file. Dukovsky, as impatiently as a wolf in a cage, was pacing the room from one corner to another.

"If you are positive that Nicholas and Post are guilty," he said, nervously fingering his small beard, "then why can't you be sure that Maria Ivanovna is guilty as well? Don't you have enough evidence?"

"I didn't say that I am not convinced in this. I am convinced, but I still cannot believe the obvious. We don't have enough material evidence, only philosophy—nothing more than the woman's fanaticism."

"Do you need an axe and blood-stained sheets? You lawyers! I will have to prove it to you! You should never discount human psychology. Maria Ivanovna will end up in Siberian prisons, I will prove it to you. And if you don't think that philosophy is enough, I have something material. You will tell me yourself that my philosophy is right. I just need to go and make a few trips."

"What are you talking about?"

"I am talking about the Swedish match. You forgot, but I have not forgotten it! I know who burned the match in the murdered man's room. It was neither Nicholas nor Post—they both had no matches on them when we searched them. It was the third person, that is, Maria Ivanovna, and I will prove it to you. Let me just trace the match along the county, and make some inquiries."

"All right, all right, but for now, you'd better have a seat at your desk. We will be starting the interrogations soon."

Dukovsky sat at his desk, and buried his nose in the papers.

"Let Nicholas Tetekov be brought in for interrogation," said the detective.

Nicholas was brought in by a guard. He was pale and very thin, almost skeletal. He was trembling.

"Mr. Tetekov," Tchuhikov started. "Five years ago, in the town of M., you were placed under probation by the judge of the first district for stealing, and you received a prison sentence. Three years ago, you were convicted of theft for the second time, and imprisoned."

They saw the expression of surprise clearly displayed on Nicholas's face. He was amazed that the detectives knew everything about him. But soon his amazement changed into uncontrollable grief. He started crying, and was asked to go wash his face and calm down. He was taken away.

"Bring Mr. Post in," ordered the detective. They brought Post. The young man had changed a lot during the last few days.

He had lost a lot of weight, and his skin had become pale and papery. Apathy and depression were obvious in his eyes.

"Take a seat, Post," said Rusty.

"I hope that this time you will be more considerate and won't lie to us, as you have on previous occasions. For days, you have denied your participation in the murder of Mr. Banks, in spite of the numerous pieces of material evidence which speak against you. This is not logical. If you make a full deposition, your sentence will be reduced. I am requesting your cooperation for the last time. If you don't accept your guilt by tomorrow, it will be too late. So, start telling us the truth."

"I don't know anything. I don't know any of your material evidence," said Post.

"You are wrong. Let me tell you how the events developed during the night of the crime. On Saturday night, you sat in Banks' bedroom, drinking vodka and beer with him."

At this moment, Dukovsky cast a piercing glance at Post, and did not avert it during the whole monologue.

"Nicholas served you. At some point after midnight, Mark Ivanovich told you that he wanted to go to bed. He always went to sleep at one o'clock. When he was taking off his boots, and giving you orders for the morrow, you and Nicholas, at a particular special sign, jumped at your drunk master, caught him by his hands, and pressed him against the bed. One of you sat on his legs; the other one sat on his head. At that moment, a woman whom you know very well, in a dark-colored dress, came from the entrance hall. You had agreed with her earlier about her participation in this criminal case. She snatched a pillow, and started strangling the poor man with it. During the fight, the candle went down. The woman took out a box of Swedish matches, and lit the candle. It is so? I see from your face that I am telling the truth. Listen further. When you had strangled him, and made certain that he was no longer breathing, you and Nicholas pushed him through the window, and put him under the thistle bush. You were afraid that he might come back to life, so you hit him with something sharp. Then you dragged him to the lilac tree. You were thinking about how to dispose of the body. You dragged him further, across the fence and along the road. Then, you brought him to the dam at the pond. There, you were scared by a peasant. What happened to you?"

Post's face had lost all its color. He looked like a corpse. He stood up and swayed, almost fell, losing his balance.

"I can't breathe. All right, all right. Let it be as you want, but let me breathe. Please." The guard removed Post from the room.

"Finally, he has accepted his guilt," said Rusty, making a sweet yawn. "He finally gave himself up. I did it in a very clever manner. I gave him all these facts."

"He did not even deny the woman in black," inserted Dukovsky. "But I can't forget about this Swedish match. I can't stand it any more. Good-bye. I have to go."

Dukovsky put on his hat and left.

Rusty started interrogating Annie. She said that she did not know anything.

"I only slept with you, and no one else," she said.

At six o'clock that evening, Dukovsky came back. He was more excited than he had ever been. His fingers were trembling to such an extent that he was not able to undo his coat. His cheeks were burning. It was clear that he brought very important news. "We are done with the case," he said, arriving in the Rusty's office and dropping into the armchair.

"I can swear on my word of honor that I am a genius."

"Listen, you damned devil! Listen to me carefully, and you will he surprised, my dear friend. It is both funny and sad. We already have three people involved in this case, and I have found the fourth person; to be exact, the fourth woman, because she is a woman. And what a woman! I would have given away ten years of my life, just to touch her shoulders, she is so beautiful. But listen. I went to Banks's estate and started making circles around it. I went to all the country stores, drug stores, pubs, and restaurants, asking for Swedish matches everywhere. Everyone said no. I searched all day, until night came. I lost hope at least twenty times, and twenty times I had it again, entering the next place. So, I spent the whole day like this, and finally, about an hour ago, I found what I was looking for. The place is not far from here, maybe three miles or so. They gave me a package with ten boxes of matches, one box was missing. So I asked the owner who had bought the box. He told me about this woman, and named her. He said, 'She liked them, so she burned them one after another.' My dear friend, Nikolai Ermolaevich. Look at me, and you will see what kind of a man a school dropout can become! You won't believe it! Today, I have found my self-respect. Well, well, let's go now!"

"Where are we going?"

"We have to go to the fourth member of the gang. We have to hurry. Otherwise, I will burn with impatience. Do you know who she is? You'll never guess, never! She is the young wife of our doctor, the old man. Her name is Olga Petrovna, that's who she is. She bought this box of matches."

"My friend, you are completely crazy."

"Listen to me. First of all, she smokes. Secondly, she was completely, madly in love with Banks. He rejected her love for this peasant woman, Annie. It was her revenge. Now I remember that once I saw them hiding behind the kitchen curtain. She swore that she loved him, and he took a drag from her cigarette and blew the smoke in her face. But it is getting dark, my friend, let's go faster."

"Have I become so foolish that I would allow an idiot like

you to bother a noble and honest woman in the middle of the night?"

"Do you think that she is noble and honest? Then you are a spineless wimp and not a detective! I have never scolded you before, but now I have to speak my mind. You are a coward with no willpower! My dear, Nikolai Ermolaevich."

The detective motioned him away and spat on the floor.

"Please, let's go! I am not asking this for my own benefit, but in the interest of the law. I am begging you. Please, do me this favor, just once in your life! Look, I can kneel in front of you! Dear Nikolai Ermolaevich, please be so kind, please. You can call me stupid, if I am wrong about this woman. But this is such an outstanding case. You will be famous all over the country. They will make you a special investigator for the most important cases. You must believe me, old man."

The old detective frowned, and slowly and reluctantly moved his hand to his hat.

"Damn it! I will have to go with you," he said.

It was dark when the detective's carriage arrived at the entrance of the doctor's house.

"We are swine," said Rusty, ringing the doorbell. "We should not be troubling people at this time."

"This is nothing. Don't be afraid. Tell her that your carriage is broken."

A tall, plump woman, about twenty-three years old, opened the door for Rusty and Dukovsky. She was a lush brunette, with shining hair and full red lips. It was Olga Petrovna herself.

"Oh, this is so pleasant," she said. "You have come just in time for dinner. My husband is away on business. But we can have dinner without him. Have a seat, please. Did you come from your investigation?"

"Yes, you see, my carriage has broken next to your house," said Rusty, entering the living room and taking a seat in an armchair.

"Tell her at once. Scare her!" Dukovsky hissed. "Scare her! Do it now!"

"The carriage, yes. We just decided to drop in."

"Scare her at once!" Dukovsky whispered again. "Otherwise, if you procrastinate, she will guess that we know."

"Leave me alone," Rusty murmured, standing up and going to the window, "I can't do it! You started this, so you will have to finish it."

"Yes, the carriage," said Dukovsky, coming to the woman and wrinkling his long nose. "But we haven't come to have dinner, or see your husband. We came here to ask you, dear lady, where is Mark Ivanovich, whom you killed?"

"What? Which Mark Ivanovich?" mumbled the woman, blushing all over. "I don't remember anything."

"I am asking you in the name of the law. Where is Mr. Banks? We know everything."

"From whom?" asked the woman, unable to stand Dukovsky's piercing glance.

"You must show us where he is."

"But how did you find me? Who told you?"

"We know everything. I insist, in the name of the law!"

The detective, encouraged by the woman's embarrassment, came to her and said,

"Lead us to his body, and then we will leave. Otherwise, we will have to take legal measures."

"Why do you want him?"

"Why? Are you asking us questions, dear lady? We should be asking you the questions. You are trembling, and you are embarrassed. Yes, he was murdered, and he was killed by you. You are one of the participants, and the other gang members have given your name to us."

The doctor's wife became pale.

"Let's go," she said in a quiet voice, clasping her hands.

"I hid him in the bathhouse at the end of our property. But please, I implore you, don't say anything to my husband. He won't be able to stand this news."

The woman took a big key from the nail on the wall, and brought her guests through the back entrance, first to the kitchen and then to the backyard. It was dark outside. A light rain was drizzling. The woman went forward. Rusty and Dukovsky followed her, stepping through the tall grass, smelling the damp scent of the wild weeds and some food scraps which crunched under their feet. It was a big backyard. Soon the garbage ended, and their feet felt the freshly ploughed soil. They saw the figures of the tall trees in the dark, behind the trees they saw a small house with a slanted chimney.

"This is the bathhouse," the woman said. "But please don't tell anyone, I implore you."

As they came to the bathhouse, Rusty and Dukovsky saw a huge lock hanging on the door.

"Prepare your matches," said the detective to his assistant. The woman opened the lock and led the two guests into the bathhouse. Dukovsky lit his match and the light fell into the bathhouse. There was a small table in the middle. Next to it, there was a small, heavy teapot, a bowl of cold soup, and a few other plates with the remains of some sauce.

They went into the second room, the sauna itself. In the middle, there was another table. On the table, there was a big plate with ham, a bottle of vodka, some plates, knives, and forks.

"Where is the body? Where is he?" asked the detective.

"He is on the upper shelf," whispered the woman, pale and trembling all over.

Dukovsky took a piece of candle from the table, lit it, and climbed to the upper shelf. There he saw a man's body lying quietly on a goose down mattress. The body produced a quiet snoring.

"We've been deceived! Look at this! This isn't him. This is some man who is alive."

"Hey, you! Who are you, damn it!"

The body moved a little, and made a loud whistle. Dukovsky nudged him with his elbow. The body lifted up a hand, stretched and tried to stand up.

"Who is out there?" said the hoarse and heavy bass. "What do you want? What?"

Dukovsky lifted the piece of candle to the face of the unknown man and cried from amazement.

In the red face, in the untidy and uncombed hair, in the very black mustache, one end of which was nicely curved up toward the ceiling, he saw Mr. Banks himself.

"Mark Ivanovich! Is it you? I can't believe my eyes!"

The detective looked up and froze in amazement.

"Yes, it's me. And this is you, Dukovsky. What the hell are you doing here? And there, below, who's that dirty devil down there? Oh my god! It's the detective himself. What are you doing here, my old buddy?"

Banks jumped down and embraced Rusty. Olga Petrovna vanished.

"How did you get here? Let's have a drink, damn it. Let's drink! Who brought you here, my friends? How did you find out that I was here? However, no matter. Let's have a drink!"

Banks lit the lamp, and poured three shots of vodka.

"Well, I can't quite understand. Is it you, or not?" asked the detective.

"Cut it out, will you? Are you going to read me a moral on how to behave? Stop it. Cut it out. And you, young man Dukovsky, have a shot as well. Let us talk about life, my friends, let us talk. Why are you staring at me? Drink!"

"I cannot understand," said the detective, drinking his vodka automatically. "What are you doing here?"

"Why not here, if here is a good place for me to be?" Banks had a drink, and took a big piece of ham.

"As you can see, I live with the doctor's wife. I live here, in a very quiet and desolate place, like a spirit of the house. Drink, brother! You see, I decided to take pity on her, and to stay here in this remote and forgotten bathhouse. I live here like a hermit. I eat good food. Next week, I am going to leave her. I am bored by this life."

"I cannot understand," said Dukovsky.

"What cannot you understand?"

"I cannot understand how one of your boots ended up in the garden."

"Which boot?"

"We found one of your boots in the bedroom, and the other one in the garden."

"Why do you want to know about that? This is none of your business. Have another shot, damn it! If you woke me up, then you should have another shot."

They had another shot and Banks continued,

"This is an interesting story, brothers, with this boot. You know, I didn't want to go to Olga. First of all, I was feeling ill, and then I was a little bit drunk. So she came under my window and started scolding me. All women are the same. So I took a boot and threw it at her. Ha-ha-ha, I said, 'Stop scolding me.' So she climbed up to the window, lit a lamp, and gave me a good beating when I was drunk. She gave me a good beating, brought me in here, and locked me in. Now I enjoy good cooking here. Love, vodka, and good food. And what about you? Rusty, where are you going?"

The disappointed detective spat on the floor and left the bath house. Dukovsky, his head down, followed him. Without saying a word to each other, they sat in the carriage and went home. It was the longest and the dullest trip they had ever made together. They were both silent. Rusty was trembling uneasily all the way. Dukovsky was hiding his face in the collar of his coat, as if he was afraid that the darkness and the drizzling rain could read the feeling of shame on his face.

When they arrived home, the detective found the old Dr. Tutuev in their house. The doctor was sitting at the desk, making deep sighs and shuffling a newspaper.

"What sort of a world are we living in?" He met the detective with a sad smile. "Again Austria presses its demands. And Mr. Gladstone, the British prime minister, I am worried for him."

Rusty threw his hat in the corner of the room, shaking with all his body.

"Hey you, damned skeleton, don't even approach me! I have told you a thousand times not to talk to me about politics. I have other things to do besides politics. You'd better go home. And you," he threatened to Dukovsky with his fist, "I will never forgive these things."

"But it was the Swedish match. How could I know?"

"I wish you would choke on your Swedish match. Get out of here, out of my sight, otherwise I will beat you black and blue. I don't want to see you for another second."

Dukovsky made a deep sigh, took his hat, and left.

"I will go and have a good drink," he said walking out of the gates and going slowly to the pub.

--- ❦ ---

When the doctor's wife came in from the bathhouse, she met her husband in the living room.

"Why did the detectives come?" her husband asked her.

"They came to tell you that they have found Banks. And, can you imagine, they found him with somebody else's wife."

"Oh, Mark Ivanovich, Mark Ivanovich," said the doctor, lifting his eyes to the ceiling. "I told you that dissipation is no good. I told you this, and you did not listen to me."

A NIGHT OF HORROR

⊷ ◄◆═ ⊶

Dedicated to my friend N. N., gravedigger

J im Undertaker grew pale as he turned down the lights a little, and began to tell his story in a very excited voice:
"It was dark, a completely dark, chilly and spooky night. I was covered with fog as I walked home after visiting my sick friend. You know who I mean, for he died just recently. On that night, of course, he was still alive, and the whole company had visited him, as we held a spiritualistic séance at his house. Afterward, I crept along the narrow, unlit streets, trying to make my way through the fog. At that time, I lived in the heart of Moscow, next to Old Graves Street. I rented an apartment in the house of Mr. Deadman. It was situated in one of the remotest and darkest lanes, next to the downtown Arbat Street. I felt anxious and depressed while I walked along those dark and gloomy streets.

" 'Your life will be over soon. The time has come to repent!' This was the message told to me by Spinoza, the ancient

35

philosopher, whose spirit we had managed to contact and engage in conversation. I asked him to repeat this to me once again, and to explain what it meant, but the spirit just added a few words, 'It will happen this night.'

"Now, I do not believe in spirits and spiritualism, but thoughts about my death, even any hints about it, always upset and depressed me.

"Dear ladies and gentlemen! We all know that death in inevitable, for it is a part of our life, but at the same time it is unpleasant to contemplate your own demise.

"And so, on that night I was completely surrounded by the dark, cold fog. The wind howled above my head. I met no one as I walked along, and an unexplainable fear soon filled my soul. I am a man without prejudice, but that night I was walking fast, looking only straight ahead. I dared not glance beside or behind, for I feared that I would see Death itself, walking behind me as a ghost."

At this point, Mr. Undertaker made a deep sigh, drank some water, and continued:

"My feelings of dread and horror did not leave me when I reached the fourth floor of Mr. Deadman's house, opened the door, and entered my modest apartment. It was completely dark. A sudden wind arose outside, beginning to howl and cry in the chimneys of my fireplace, as if trying to come inside.

"If I believed Spinoza, then this night I would die, accompanied by this howling. I was scared.

"I lit a match in the pitch darkness. A powerful gust of wind tore at the roof of the house, creating a violent roar. Outside, the window shutter was slamming against the wall, and the small gray door of my fireplace was squeaking, as if asking for help.

" 'This is a terrible night for homeless people,' I thought.

"This thought was quickly snatched away when the sulfur match lit my room, and I cast a brief glance around. What I saw was unexpected and completely horrifying. I regretted that the drafts of wind had not extinguished my match at once, for then I could not have seen this dreadful sight and my hair would not have started to bristle. I cried out, stepping backward toward the door, and closed my eyes because I was overwhelmed by my feelings of horror, desperation and excitement.

"Right before me, in the middle of my room, stood a coffin.

"The dim blue light of my match had briefly lit my room, just long enough to see its design and detailing. Its glazed pink cover shone and sparkled.

"Dear ladies and gentlemen! There are moments in your life that forever remain ingrained in your memory, even if you experience them only for a brief moment. I saw this coffin for only a fraction of a second, but I remember it down to its smallest detail. It was a coffin made for a person of average height and, judging by its pink color, had been designed for a young lady. It was finely made, with carved legs beneath it, and bronze handles on its sides. It was obviously intended for someone well-to-do.

"After taking this all in, I finally rushed out of my room into the dark corridor as fast as I could, filled with inexpressible horror, and ran down the stairs to the first floor. It was completely dark there. My legs were trembling and catching in the tails of my coat. It still remains a great mystery how I did not fall down on that length of stairs and did not break my neck. When I finally reached the fresh air of the street, I leaned against a wet lantern, standing and trying to calm myself down. My heart was pounding, and I felt short of breath."

At this point in the story, a young lady, who had been

listening very attentively, turned up the lights. She moved closer to Mr. Undertaker as he continued,

"I would not have been more surprised if I had a fire in my room, or had run into a thief or a crazed dog. I would not have been surprised if the ceiling had fallen on my head, or the floorboards had cracked open, or the walls had fallen down. . . . These are all natural things and can be easily explained. But how had this coffin come to be in my room? Where had it come from? How had this very expensive coffin, designed for a rich young lady, come to be in the tiny apartment of a poor office worker like me?

"As I leaned against the lantern, my thoughts were racing. Perhaps the coffin was empty. Perhaps there was a dead body inside it. Perhaps it was the body of a mysterious young lady whose life had ended tragically. And yet, who had arranged for her to visit my house? This remained a terrible mystery for me.

" 'If this is not a mystery, then this is definitely a crime,' was my first thought.

"I gave myself over to my thoughts. During my absences, the door to my apartment was locked. The place where I hide my key was known to only a few of my closest friends. Would any of my friends have placed the coffin in my room? Of course not! Then was it possible that an undertaker had brought the coffin to me by mistake? He could have brought it to the wrong floor in the building, or to the wrong door, or to the wrong address entirely. However, everyone knows that undertakers do not leave until they receive payment, or at least a handsome tip.

Perhaps the spirits who had predicted my death tonight had brought the coffin into my room. I do not believe and I never believed in spirits, but all of these questions could throw even a philosophical mind into a very mystical and depressive state. In the end, I cowardly swept the mystery aside, with simple logic. I thought, 'That was an optical illusion, and nothing else!' I felt so gloomy and frightened when walking home, that it was perfectly understandable that my upset nerves had created the coffin. Certainly it had been an optical illusion! What else could it have been?

"Rain was now pouring down my face, and the wind was playing with the tails of my coat, teasing away my hat. . . . I was cold and wet to the bones. I had to go somewhere—but where? I needed shelter, but my logic abandoned me at the prospect of returning to my apartment. I did not want to run the risk of seeing the coffin again, for that would be more than I could bear. There was not a single human being in sight. Not a single human noise. I was in complete solitude. No, I did not want to be alone, in my apartment, just me and a coffin, and perhaps a dead body inside. I could go crazy up there. At the same time, it was impossible for me to stay outside in this terrible, cold rain.

"I decided to go spend the night with my friend, Mr. Graveyard, who, as you all know, later shot himself. He lived on Dark Tomb Street, in the house of the entrepreneur Mr. Scully."

"At this point, Mr. Undertaker wiped away the cold sweat that had formed on his face, sighed deeply again, and continued.

"My friend Mr. Graveyard did not answer at my knock at his door, and I feared he was not at home. I then decided to have a closer look, and picked up his key hanging on a nail in the corridor. I opened the door and entered his room. My friend was definitely not at home; still, I gratefully took off my wet coat, felt for the sofa in the darkness, and rested on it. It was completely dark. I listened to the wind howl outside, punctuated by the monotonous noise of a cricket in the fireplace. A huge tower clock started beating its early-morning hours. I took a box of Swedish matches from my pocket and lit one, but the light did not help my mood. On the contrary, the sight before me filled me with unbearable horror. I cried out and, losing control, ran out of his apartment.

"In the middle of my friend's room, I saw another coffin.

"It was almost twice as large as the one in my quarters, with a dour, dark brown velvet cover. How had it come to be there? My optical illusion theory was shattered, for I had no doubts about this vision; the coffin I had just seen was real. It was impossible to have a coffin in each of the apartments. And if these coffins were not optical illusions, then perhaps I was suffering from a nervous illness, or hallucinating like a madman. Everywhere I went I would see a coffin, a terrible hole where death abates. Therefore, if I was going insane, then I had developed some kind of mania, so to speak, 'coffin-mania.'

"For a moment I remembered the séance, and the words spoken to me by philosopher Spinoza.

"'I am going insane!' I thought in horror, clutching my head with my hands. 'Oh God, what should I do?'

"I now had a terrible headache, and my feet were weak and trembling. The rain was pouring; the wind was howling and piercing my shirt, for I had neither my coat nor my hat on. It was impossible for me to go back inside my friend's apartment to pick them up; I simply did not have the energy or the courage to do this. I was completely immersed in horror. . . . My hair rose on the back of my head. My face was covered with cold sweat. I thought it was just a hallucination."

"What could I do in that situation?" continued Mr. Undertaker. "I felt I was going insane, and at the same time I was running the risk of getting a terrible cold. Luckily, I remembered that another good friend of mine, Mr. Gravedigger, lived nearby. He was a doctor who had only recently graduated, and he lived not far from Dark Tomb Street. He had been present at the spiritualist séance earlier that night. Much later, of course, after all these events, he married the daughter of a rich salesman. But at that time he rented a tiny upper room in the house of the general, Mr. Veil.

"When I came to Mr. Gravedigger's place, my shattered nerves were tried yet again. I was climbing up the stairs to the fifth floor, when I heard strange, loud noises from above. A door was violently slammed and someone rushed down the stairs toward me.

"'Help! Anybody!' 'Help!' I heard a piercing scream. 'Come to me! Help me, please, anybody, please come here and help me!'

"In the next second I met a figure on the stairs, dressed in a warm winter coat and with an untidy hat on.

"'Mr. Gravedigger, is that you? What a surprise!' I exclaimed, as I saw my friend. 'What's happened with you?'

"He came closer to me and seized my hand. His face was very pale. He was out of breath, and his body was trembling. His eyes were senselessly moving in all directions.

"'Well, well . . . Hello, Mr. Undertaker,' he said in a rushed voice. 'Nice to see you here. Is it really you? You are as pale as if you had just come from grave. Are you a hallucination? Are you real? Oh my goodness! You look so terrible!'

"'Better that you tell me what has happened to you! I barely recognize you. You look completely crazy.'

"'Oh, my dear friend, wait a second. I am out of breath. I am so glad that I ran into you . . . if it's really you, and not an illusion. That séance was terrible! It shattered my nerves.

Do you know what I saw when I entered my room? I saw a coffin!'

"I could not believe what I had heard. I asked him to repeat it.

"'A coffin, a real coffin!' said the doctor, as he sat down on the stairs. 'I am not a coward, but the devil himself would be scared, if he stumbled upon a coffin in the darkness in his house.'

"Mumbling and frequently pausing, I told the doctor the story of the coffins I had seen.

"For a moment, we just looked at each other without saying a word, our eyes bulging. Then, in order to make sure that we were not hallucinating, that it was not simply a bad dream, we lightly punched each other.

"'We both felt pain,' the doctor said. 'Therefore, we are experiencing reality. And the coffins which we saw were not illusions, but really exist. What can we do now, dear friend?'

"We talked for almost an hour on the dark stairs, discussing what we should do. Then it became too cold to stay there, so we determined to overcome our shameful fear, and to go up to the doctor's room. We turned on the light as soon as we entered the apartment.

"In the center of the room stood a coffin covered in a luxurious golden velvet cloth. Dr. Gravedigger, a religious man, whispered a prayer.

"'Let us find out,' said the doctor, trembling all over from fear, 'whether this coffin is empty, or there is someone inside.'

"After a rather lengthy hesitation, the doctor bent down, pressed his lips tightly together, and resolutely snatched the cover from the coffin. I came closer, and we both saw that the coffin was empty; there was no dead body inside.

"Instead, we found a letter, which read as follows:

"My dear friend, Dr. Gravedigger,

"You are well aware of the fact that my father-in-law owns a business. Now he is completely in debt, and the time has come for him to give it up.

"Tomorrow, or at the latest, the day after tomorrow, people from the bank will come here to assess his estate. This will completely destroy his and my family; and my financial state will be in ruins. This will also destroy the good name of our family, which is most precious to me.

" 'Yesterday,' we held a family council and decided to hide the most precious and expensive family valuables. As you know, my father-in-law's major financial assets are his coffins. As the owner of a funeral home, he is well-known for making the best-quality coffins in this town. Therefore, we have decided to hide the most expensive models. I ask you, as a friend, to help us save our money and honor! I hope you will help me in saving my estate, and I am sending you one coffin, which I ask you to hide in your house for some time until we ask it back. We could be completely ruined without the help of our good friends. I hope you will not refuse me, and I promise you that this coffin will not remain in your apartment for more than one week. I have also sent coffins to several others whom I consider to be my real and closest friends. I hope that you all possess a great and noble nature.

"Sincerely yours,

"Jack Blackman.'

"After the events of that day, I spent three months in the care of psychiatrists, recovering from a serious nervous breakdown. But my friend, the coffin-maker, managed to save both his honor and his financial assets. Now he has his own business, a funeral home.

"He also has a second business, selling granite monuments and bronze markers. Actually, this business is not doing so well. Every evening, when I return to my apartment, I expect to find a white marble monument, a cemetery plaque, or a tombstone in my humble apartment."

WILLOW

<hr />

Have you ever traveled from B to C along the highway? If you have, you should remember the Andreevka mill that stands on the Kozavka River. It's a small mill with only two millstones. It was built over a hundred years ago. It has not been operational for a long time, and reminds one of an old woman with a hunchback, who is going to fall over at any moment. This woman would have fallen to the ground a long time ago, except that an old willow tree supports her.

The willow is so old and so wide that it takes two people to embrace it. Its shining leaves fall onto the roof and the bridge, and the lower branches fall onto the water and the ground. The willow is so old that it looks like a hunchback as well. The trunk of the tree is distorted by a huge dark hole. You can put your hand into the hole, and there you will find dark, wild honey. Wild bees start flying around your head, stinging you.

How old is this tree? Arkhip, my friend, told me that the tree was already old when he was working as "a French servant" for the local landlord. After that, he served as "a black servant" for the old landlady. That means it was a very long time ago.

The willow tree supports another old creature. That is the old man, Arkhip, who sits at its trunk, fishing all day. He is old, and he also has a hunchback, like the tree. And, like the willow tree, his mouth has no teeth and looks like the hole. He fishes during the day, and at night he sits next to the tree, lost in dreams. Both of these creatures, Arkhip and the old willow, whisper day and night. They have lived for a long time, and they know many things. Just listen to them.

Thirty years ago, on a Sunday morning the old man was sitting under the tree, looking at the water and fishing. It was quiet, as usual. You could hear only the whisper of the willow tree and the jumping of the fish, splashing in the water. He fished until noon. At noon he started cooking fish soup under the tree. When the shadow from the willow left the bank of the river, it was midday. Arkhip also measured time by postal delivery. Exactly at noon, a postal carriage would cross the bridge.

On that Sunday, Arkhip heard the bells ringing. He put his fishing rod aside and looked at the bridge. The troika moved up the hill, then down, and then slowly went up to the bridge. The postman was asleep. When the troika came to the bridge, it stopped for no obvious reason. Arkhip was never surprised, but he was surprised this time. Something odd happened. The groom looked around, took the kerchief from the postman's face and hit him with a stick. The postman did not move. There was a red spot on his blond head. The driver jumped from the cart and struck another blow. In a moment, Arkhip heard somebody's footsteps. The driver was coming directly toward him, down to the river. His sunburned face was pale, and his eyes were glassy. He was trembling all over, and, without noticing Arkhip, he put the mailbag into the hole in the tree. Then he ran up the hill, jumped into the cart, and did something that to Arkhip seemed very strange. He hit himself on the temple; then, his face covered with blood, he whipped the horses.

"Help, robbers!" His words echoed across the valley for a long time.

About six days later, police inspectors came to the bridge. They made a plan of the mill, a plan of the bridge; they measured the depth of the river for some unknown reason, then they had dinner under the willow and left.

All this time, Arkhip was sitting under the wheel of his mill trembling and looking at the bag. There, in the bag, he saw several envelopes with five seals each. He looked at the seals and checked them day and night. Looking at the willow tree, he thought that it was quiet by day and cried by night. "You willow, you are a stupid old woman," said Arkhip to himself, listening to her cries. A week later, Arkhip went to the nearest town, with a bag on his shoulder.

"Where is the police station around here?" he asked the first officers he met in the street.

They showed him a big yellow building with a guard at the door. He went inside, and in the corridor he saw a man in a uniform with bright buttons. The man was smoking a pipe and scolding a guard who had done something wrong. Arkhip came up to the man and, trembling all over, told him about the episode by the old willow tree. The official took the bag in his hands, opened it, blanched, and then blushed.

"Wait," he said, and went into another room. Suddenly, other officials surrounded him They were running around, making noises, and whispering. Ten minutes later, the official brought the bag to Arkhip and said,

"You have come to the wrong place, brother. You have to go to the Lower Street. This is the government accounting building. You have to go to the police."

Arkhip took the bag and left.

"The bag is much lighter now," he thought. "It's only about half the weight."

At the Lower Street, they told him to go to another yellow house. Arkhip came in. There was no entrance hall, just the office room, with many desks. He came to one of the desks, and told his story.

They tore the bag from his hands and called the senior official. A fat man with a mustache came. He interrogated Arkhip briefly, took the bag, and locked himself in his office.

"Where is the money?" he heard from behind the door. "The bag is empty! Tell the old man he can go. No, tell him to stay. Let him in. Take him to Ivan Markovich. No, better let him go."

The old man bowed, said good-bye, and left.

The next day, he went fishing, his gray beard reflected in the river. He caught perches and snappers.

Soon it was fall. The old man was sitting with his fishing rod. His face was as grim as the yellow willow tree. He did not like fall. His face became even darker after he saw the driver. The driver, without noticing the old man, came to the willow and put his hand into the hole in the trunk. The wet, lazy bees climbed up his sleeve. He moved his hand here and there, and some time later he was sitting at the bank of the river, looking listlessly into the water.

"Where is it?" he asked Arkhip.

At first, Arkhip was silent. He looked gloomy and pretended not to notice the killer. But then he took pity on him.

"I brought it to the officers," he said. "But don't be afraid, fool. I told them that I found it next to the willow tree, by accident."

The driver jumped to his feet, howled, and started beating Arkhip. He beat the old man for a long time. He struck him in the face, and after the old man fell to the ground, he kicked him. After he finished the beating, he did not go away, but stayed. And they lived at the mill together, Arkhip and the driver.

During the day, the driver slept and was silent, and at night he walked on the bridge. The shadow of the postman also walked on the bridge, and he spoke to the shadow.

Spring came, and the driver was still silent during the day and still walked on the bridge at night. One night, the old man came to him.

"Stop walking about and loitering, you fool! Get a life! Get out of here!" he said to the driver, looking at the shadow of the postman, who was standing nearby.

The postman said the same, and the willow whispered the same.

"I can't do that," said the driver. "I would like to go away, but my soul is in pain and my feet are shaking; they are too weak."

Then the old man took the driver by the hand and brought him to the city. When he brought the driver to the same building at the Lower Street, where he had returned the bag, the driver knelt in front of the chief and confessed his sin. Then the man with the mustache looked at him in surprise and said,

"Why are you accusing yourself of this? You fool! Are you

drunk? Do you want me to lock you in? You are a fool, making things up. We could not find the murderer, and that's that. What do you want? Get out of here! Get lost!"

When the old man reminded them of the bag, the mustached men started laughing, and all the other officers sitting in the room expressed their surprise. They had conveniently forgotten about the bag.

The driver could not confess his sins at the police station on Lower Street, so he had to go back to the willow.

He was tortured by his conscience, and therefore he jumped from the bridge into the water, exactly where Arkhip used to fish. The driver drowned himself. Now, at night the old man and the willow can see two shadows walking across the bridge. Do they whisper anything to each other?

A THIEF

The clock struck twelve. Fyodor Stepanovich put his fur coat onto his shoulders, and went outside. He felt the damp night air; a cold wind was blowing. It was drizzling. Fyodor Stepanovich stepped above the remains of a fence and went quietly along the street. It was a wide street, almost as wide as a square. He saw few streets so wide in the European part of Russia. There were no lights and no sidewalks, no signs of such luxuries.

Next to the fences and the walls he saw the dark figures of people in a hurry to get to the church. Fyodor Stepanovich saw two of these figures in front of him, walking in the mud. In the first figure, he recognized the old doctor—a short man with a curved back, the only educated man in town. The old doctor was very friendly to him, and every time he met Fyodor Stepanovich, he sighed deeply. This time the old man was wearing a triangular uniform hat, which looked like two duck heads glued together. The end of his sword could be seen from under his long coat. Next to him was a tall thin man with the same kind of triangular hat.

"Happy Easter, Gury Ivanovich," Fyodor Stepanovich said to the doctor.

The doctor shook his hand in silence and revealed the medal that hung from the front of his jacket, beneath his fur coat.

"Doctor, I would like to talk to you later today," Fyodor Stepanovich said. "I would like to share a holiday dinner with you; we always had dinner in my family. And it will give me some good memories."

"It isn't convenient. You know I have a wife and family. But I am not prejudiced, so if you want to come—hmm. Sorry, I am coughing, I have a sore throat."

"What about Barabaev?" Fyodor Stepanovich added with a sour grin on his face. "Barabaev was sentenced with me, but he has dinner with you every day and drinks tea. He stole more money, that's why."

Fyodor Stepanovich stopped and pressed himself against the wet picket fence. Very far away he saw small lights. They were flickering in the darkness and moving in one direction.

"This is the holiday procession, with the lights," thought the exile. "It looks exactly the same as in the place I used to live."

There were sounds of distant bells and voices: the tenors were barely audible, and the singers seemed to be in a hurry.

"This is my first Easter in this cold, and it is not the last one," Fyodor Stepanovich thought. "It is so bad here. And, at home, it is probably completely different." He tried to imagine how life looked there, in his hometown. "They do not have dark dirty snow and sleet underfoot in the streets, and in the pools of water. Instead, there are fresh green leaves on the trees. Instead of this sharp wet wind, there is a breath of spring. The sky is different there. It is darker, and there are more stars, with a white stripe across the sky in the east. There is a green picket fence instead of this shabby, dirty fence, in front of my little cozy house with its three windows. And there are warm, well-lit rooms behind those windows. In one of these rooms, there is a table covered with a nice, white, clean tablecloth with bread, appetizers, and vodka.

It would be nice to have some vodka from home. The local vodka is terrible; you can't drink it.

In the morning you feel refreshed after a good night's sleep, then you visit your friends and then you can have some more to drink.

And he remembered his wife Olya, her catlike face that looked as if she were about to cry. She is probably asleep now, not dreaming about him. This sort of woman forgets things quickly. If there had been no Olya, he would not be here. It was she who gave him an idea to steal. She had wanted the money. She had wanted it terribly; she had wanted to spend it on fashionable clothes. She could neither live nor love without money; she would suffer without it.

"And if they send me to Siberia, will you follow me there?" he asked her one day.

"Of course! I will go with you to the ends of the earth!"

When he stole the money, he was caught, and was sent to Siberia. Olya did not go with him; she felt too weak. Now her silly head is lying on a clean, white lace pillow, and his feet are shuffling through this dirty snow and sleet.

"She came into the courtroom in a fashionable dress, and she did not even look at me," he thought. "She laughed when the lawyer made jokes during his speech. I think I'm ready to kill her."

All these memories made Fyodor Stepanovich tired. He felt sick and weary, as if he were thinking with his whole body. His feet became weak, and he had no energy to walk. He went home and, without removing his fur coat or heavy boots, simply fell onto his bed.

A cage with a songbird was affixed above his bed. Both cage and bird belonged to the landlord. The bird was very thin, strange, with a long beak, and he did not know its name. Her wings were clipped, and her head had lost its feathers. The owner fed her some disgusting sour stuff, which filled the room with a terrible smell. The bird was moving around the cage kicking her water-dish, and singing different songs, like a blackbird.

"I can't sleep because of this bird," Fyodor Stepanovich thought. "Damn it!"

He stood up and shook the cage with his hand. The bird fell silent. The exile lay down and took off his boots. After a moment, the bird started making noise again. A piece of the sour food fell on his head and became tangled in his hair.

"Can't you stop singing? Can't you sleep in silence? Shut up!"

Fyodor Stepanovich jumped on his feet, picked up the cage in a fit of rage, and threw it into a corner of the room. The bird fell silent.

Ten minutes later, it seemed to the exile, the bird appeared from the corner of the room, and flew at him with its long beak, and then started picking up something from the floor. To him, there was only a long endless beak and flapping wings, and then it seemed to him that he was lying on the floor, and the bird was flapping her wing at his temples. Then the bird's beak was broken, and a bunch of feathers was all that remained of the bird. The exile fell asleep.

"Why did you kill the animal, you filthy criminal!" He heard moaning.

Fyodor Stepanovich opened his eyes and saw the face of the landlord, an unpleasant-looking old man.

The landlord was trembling with rage, and tears were flowing down his face.

"Why did you kill my bird, you villain? Why did you kill my singer, you devil? Why? You wretch, get out of my house! You dirty dog! Get out of my sight! This instant! Get out!"

Fyodor Stepanovich put on his coat and went out into the street. It was a gray and windy morning. The sky was overcast. He saw the solid gray sky and could not believe there was a sun somewhere above the clouds. The rain was drizzling.

"Hello! Happy holiday, my dear fellow!" The man heard a familiar voice as he stepped into the street.

Barabaev, with whom he used to live in the same hometown, was passing him by in a carriage. He wore a top hat, and held an umbrella.

"He is paying visits," Fyodor Stepanovich thought. "Even here he has a comfortable life. He has friends. I should have stolen more money."

Coming near the church, Fyodor Stepanovich heard another voice. It was a woman's voice. He saw a postal carriage packed with travelers' suitcases and bags. There was a woman's face peering from behind all the bags.

"Where is . . . Oh my dear, Fyodor Stepanovich, it's you!" the little face was calling.

Fyodor Stepanovich ran to the carriage, looked intently at the woman's face, and held her hand.

"What is this? Am I dreaming? Have you come back to me? How did you come to this decision, dear Olya?"

"Where does Barabaev live?"

"Why do you want to see Barabaev?"

"Because he invited me here. He sent me two thousand rubles, and promised three hundred rubles per month in addition. Are there any theaters around here?"

Until late that night, the exile walked around the town looking for a place to live. It rained the whole day, and there was not a moment of sunshine.

"How can these animals live without sunshine?" he thought, trudging through the deep slush. "How can they be happy without sunshine? They're probably used to it."

THE ONLY WAY OUT

(*From the* History of the St. Petersburg Mutual Fund)

There was a time when accountants ripped off our company. It is terrible, thinking about those times! Not only did they embezzle, they drained the accounts. The inside of our safe was covered with green velvet, and one morning even the green velvet had been stolen. One man was in so deep that, when he took the money, he took the lock and the lid with him, too. We've had nine accountants in the last five years, and now, during the holiday season, we get postcards from all of them, from Krasnoiarsk, Siberia. All of them went to prison.

"This is terrible, but what can we do?" we said to each other, disappointed, when the police arrested the ninth accountant. "It is terrible, disgusting, shameful. All nine of them were scoundrels," we said to each other, trying to think who the new accountant could be.

Who would be the best man for the job? And then we chose Ivan Petrovich, a junior accountant. He is a quiet man; he

57

believes in God; he does not live a cushy or extravagant life, and he does not overspend. So we chose him, we prayed, and we trusted him. But not for long.

On the second day, Ivan Petrovich came to work wearing a beautiful new tie. On the third day, he came in a cab, which he had never done before.

"Have you noticed?" we were whispering a week later. "He has a new tie and new glasses, and today he invited all of us to come to his birthday party. He prays more often also; he probably has some sins to confess."

We reported our doubts and concerns to the director.

"You think the tenth man could be a scoundrel as well?" The bank director sighed deeply. "He is a such an honest, quiet man. All right, let's go talk to him!"

We all went up to Ivan Petrovich and crowded around his desk.

"Excuse me, Ivan Petrovich," said the director imploringly. "Of course, we trust you. We really do! But please, let us search your desk. Please, let us do this!"

"Very well, go ahead,' the accountant said at once.

We started counting. When we had counted out the bills, we found that four thousand rubles were missing. That was very bad. First of all, if he had stolen that much money in one week, then how would he steal in a year? Or two years? We were numb with horror and despair.

"What shall we do? Should we take him to court? We tried that before, and it didn't work. Next, the eleventh and then twelfth accountant will steal also. You can't take all of them to court. Should we beat him up? He will be offended. Should we sack him, and hire a new one? But the new one will steal as well. That's not the way out. What shall we do?" Our faces were pale.

The red-faced director was looking straight into Ivan

Petrovich's eyes, leaning over the yellow counter. We all suffered, trying to think what to do with him. He was sitting in his chair, with his back straight, making calculations. We were quiet for a ling time.

"Where have you spent the money?" the director finally asked him in a trembling voice, with tears in his eyes.

"I have some personal needs, your honor."

"Ha! Very good! You have some needs, ha! Shut up! I am going to punish you!" The director paced the room and then continued, "What shall we do? How will we stop ourselves from repeating this mistake? Gentlemen, silence, please! What shall we do?" The director thought for a while and decided,

"We can't beat him up! Ivan Petrovich, listen, we will put the money back ourselves, and we won't make a fuss. The hell with you! But tell us all, tell us everything plainly. Do you like women?"

Ivan Petrovich responded with a confused smile.

"Yes, I see," said the director. "I understand. Everyone needs love, as some philosopher said. I see. Look, if you like women, then listen to me. I will give you a letter of introduction to someone. She is a wonderful woman. And I will pay for your expenses. Do you want another one? I will give you a letter of introduction to another one. A third one? I will give you a third letter as well! All three women are nice, well-grown, and attractive. Do you like wine?"

"There are different wines, your honor. For example, Lisbon Port: I cannot stand its taste. Everything has its purpose in this world, as the saying goes."

"Don't talk so much. I will send you a dozen bottles of champagne regularly, every single week. Listen, you will have all this, but please, do not embezzle our money. I am not ordering, but imploring you! Do you like the theater?"

And so on, and so on. In the end we decided that we would triple his salary and would provide him with a season ticket to the theater, a couple of good horses, and a brief vacation out of town every week, all at company expense. We also agreed to pay for his tailor, his cigars, his photographs, his flowers to be sent to actresses, his furniture, and his lodging. He could do whatever he wanted, as long as he did not embezzle. He must not steal!

The result? A year has gone by. Ivan Petrovich is still sitting in his chair, working at his desk. And we are delighted; we could not find a better man for the job! Everything is open, honest, and wonderful. He does not steal. Every week though, we review all our transactions, and we find a hundred or so rubles missing.

But there isn't serious theft, it's nothing. And besides, he said he had his accountant's instinct still alive, so we have to make sacrifices. Let him take a little money, at least he will not dip into the thousands!

Now, our company is flourishing, and our cash desk is filled with money all the time. We pay an awful lot for our accountant, but he is only a tenth as expensive as his nine predecessors were. I guarantee you, there is hardly any other bank, company, or mutual fund that spends so little on its accountant. We are the leaders; therefore, all you managers, you are all making a big mistake if you aren't following our example.

AN EXPENSIVE DOG

Sergeant Oaks, an elderly officer, and his friend, the post office worker Mr. Knapps, were sharing a bottle of wine in the Oaks house.

"A great dog!" said Mr. Oaks, showing his dog Darling to Mr. Knapps. "A wonderful dog! Just look closely at its face!! A dog with a face like this costs a lot. A true dog lover would pay at least two thousand rubles for this face. Don't you think so? Don't you believe me? Then, you don't understand anything about dogs."

"Well, I only know a little about dogs."

"Just look here; this is a setter, a British purebred. It can smell game from a great distance. Do you know that I paid one thousand rubles for a puppy? What a great dog! Darling! Look at me, Darling, come to me, my little doggy!"

Mr. Oaks brought his Darling doggy closer and kissed her between her ears. Tears of admiration appeared in his eyes.

"I will never give you away, my special dog! I know you love me, Darling, don't you? Hey, get away; you put your dirty paws on my uniform jacket. Now, Mr. Knapps, listen, I paid fifteen hundred rubles for a puppy. It was worth it! But it's a pity that I don't have time for hunting. This dog's instincts are wasted without hunting practice, and its rare talent is slowly being lost. So, I would like to sell it. Buy this dog, Knapps, you will be grateful to me forever. . . . If you don't have enough money, I'll cut the price. Take it for five hundred, and rob me as you do it."

"No, my dear friend." Mr. Knapps sighed. "If your Darling were male, maybe then I would have bought it."

"Darling is not a male?" The sergeant looked puzzled. "Knapps, you are joking! Darling is not male? Humph! Why do you think he is a female? Look at him! Ha-ha! My understanding is that you cannot see the difference between a male and a female."

Knapps looked offended, "Surely, this is a female. You talk to me as if I were a blind man or a little baby."

"And maybe you are going to tell me that I am a woman, too? My dear Mr. Knapps! And you have graduated from a technical school! No, my dear, this is a real purebred male dog! Even more—he will give ten points ahead to any other male. And you say that he is not a male dog! Ha-ha-ha."

"Excuse me, Michael, my friend, but do you take me for a complete idiot?"

"All right, if you don't want it, you do not have to buy it. I can't make you. Maybe soon you are going to tell me that this is not a tail but a leg! I was just trying to do you a favor. Hey, Vakromev, bring us some more brandy."

The butler brought another bottle of brandy. Both friends poured a glass each. They were lost in their own thoughts. Half an hour passed in silence.

"Even if this is a female," the sergeant interrupted the silence, looking gloomily at the bottle of brandy, "it is even better for you. She will give you puppies, and every puppy could be sold at least for two hundred fifty rubles each. Everyone would come to you to buy her puppies. I don't know why you don't like females! They are a thousand times better than males. Females are more grateful and more attached. If you are so afraid of females, all right, take it for two-fifty."

"No, my friend, I won't give you a single penny. First of all, I do not need the dog, and second, I do not have money at the moment."

"You should have told me about this earlier. Hey, Darling, get out of here. Vakromev, bring us something to eat!"

The butler served scrambled eggs. Both friends started eating, and cleared their plates in silence.

"You are a great guy. You're an honest, straightforward man," said Mr. Oaks, as he was wiping his lips. "But I don't see why you should be going away empty-handed. You know what? Take this dog for free!"

"Where can I keep it?" Knapps asked, sighing. "Who will take care of it?"

"All right, all right. If you don't want it, then you don't need it. What the hell? Where are you going? Sit down, everything is fine. Sit down." Knapps stood up and stretched.

"It is time for me to go," Knapps said after a deep yawn.

"Wait a second! I will see you off," said Mr. Oaks.

Mr. Knapps and Mr. Oaks got their coats on and went out into the street. They walked the first hundred steps in silence.

"Do you know where I can give my dog away?" the sergeant inquired, breaking the silence. "Do you know anyone? The dog is nice, it is purebred, but I really do not need it."

"I don't know, my friend, really. I don't have any other friends around here."

The rest of the way to Mr. Knapps's house, not a single word passed between them. In front of the Knapps house, as they shook hands in front of his gates, Sergeant Oaks suddenly cleared his throat and undecidedly asked,

"Do you know where the local animal shelter is? Maybe they accept dogs now."

"I think they do. But I cannot tell you for sure."

"I will send my butler to bring the dog to them. What the hell! It's a terrible, disgusting dog! As if it is not bad enough for it to go to the washroom in my living room, but—even more—yesterday, it ate all the meat in my kitchen. Dirty dog! And if only it were a nice breed—but no, it is has no breeding at all, just a cross between stray dog and pig. Good night!"

"See you later," said Mr. Knapps, and closed the gate that led to the street.

CURVED MIRROR

›‹ ‹›

I went into the living room, accompanied by my wife. It smelled of moss and darkness. Swarms of rats and mice jumped to each side as light penetrated a darkness that had been there for a hundred years. As I closed the door behind us, a gust of wind ruffled sheets of paper, scattered in piles across the floor. As some dim light fell on the paper we saw ancient script and medieval illuminations.

The walls were covered with green slime and were decorated with portraits of ancestors. They looked very strict and haughty, as if they would say,

"You need a good beating, brother."

The sounds of our steps could be heard all over the house. The same echo, which answered my ancestors, resounded all over the house.

The wind was howling and blowing outside. It sounded as if someone were crying and howling in the chimney, and I felt a quiet desperation in this cry. Huge drops of rain were striking the dark, dim windows, giving additional poignancy to the scene.

"My dear ancestors," I said, heaving a deep sigh, "if I were a writer, then after looking at your portraits I would write a long novel. Because each of these old men was young once, and probably had a love story behind him—probably, an exciting story. Just look at this old woman, my great-grandmother. She is not beautiful; perhaps she was even ugly, but she could tell an exciting story.

"Do you see that mirror hanging there in the corner?" I said to my wife, and I pointed at a large mirror in the corner, framed in black bronze, hanging next to the portrait of my great-grandmother.

"That mirror has magical powers. It destroyed that woman, my great-grandmother. She paid a lot of money for it, and she couldn't go away from the mirror until she died.

"She looked into the mirror day and night without ceasing; she looked even when she ate and drank. When she went to bed, she took the mirror with her, and when she was dying, she asked to have the mirror put into her coffin. Her wishes weren't followed, though, because there wasn't enough room for the mirror in the casket."

"Was she very much interested in men?"

"Probably. But don't you think she could have had other mirrors? And why did she like this particular mirror? You think she had no better ones? No, dear, there is a terrible mystery hidden here; I am sure of it. Legend says that a devil was living in the mirror, and that my great-grandmother had a weakness for the devil. Of course that's nonsense, but there's definitely some mysterious force hidden within this bronze frame."

I swept the dust off the mirror, looked at it, and started

laughing. The sound of my laughter resounded in echoes. The mirror was curved, and my face was distorted in various directions. My nose was on my left cheek, and my chin became doubled and moved to the side.

"My great-grandmother had strange tastes," I said.

My wife also came closer to the mirror and looked at it, and then something terrible happened. She blanched, trembled all over, and screamed. The candlestick fell from her hands and rolled onto the floor, and the candle was snuffed out. We were in total darkness. I heard some heavy object fall onto the floor. It was my wife, who had fainted.

The wind blew louder, more rats scampered about, and mice made a terrible shuffling noise amid the papers scattered on the floor. The hair on my head stood up and started tingling when a window shutter fell outward, into the street. I saw moonlight through the window.

I clutched the body of my wife, and brought her out of my ancestors' old house. She came to her senses only the next evening.

"The mirror! Where is it? Give me the mirror!" she said, as soon as she came to her senses.

For several days she neither drank nor slept, and kept shouting that she needed the mirror. She was nightmarish and fevered in her bed, and when the doctors said that she might die of exhaustion, and that her state was perilous for her health, I went down to the basement, and brought my great-grandmother's mirror to her. When she saw the mirror, she started laughing with happiness and pierced the mirror with her gaze.

Ten years have passed, and she has been looking at the mirror all the while, without diverting her glance for a second.

"Is it me?" she whispers, then her face flushes, and an expression of joy and happiness appears on her face.

"Yes, it's me! Everything lies except for this mirror! People lie to me; my husband lies! If only I could have seen myself like this earlier. If only I had known how beautiful I am, I would have never married this man! The most beautiful and noble men would lie at my feet."

One day, as I was standing behind my wife, I cast a sidelong glance into the mirror, and the terrible mystery was revealed to me. In the mirror, I saw a woman of striking beauty, a woman so beautiful that I had never seen such a fine-looking person in my life. It was a mystery, nature's own harmony of beauty, perfection, and love.

But what had happened? What had actually happened? How did my ill-favored, vile, awkward wife seem so beautiful in the mirror? This phenomenon happened because the curved mirror changed her features, moving them to different sides.

From all these deformations her face suddenly became beautiful in the mirror. A negative times a negative equals a positive.

And now both I and my wife sit in front of the mirror, and without averting our gazes for a second, we look into it. My nose has moved to my left cheek; my chin has became doubled and moved to one side, but my wife's face is amazing. Then, I become filled with her terrible, mad passion.

"Ha, ha, ha!" I cry wildly.

And my wife whispers, "I am so beautiful!"

A COURT CASE

A case took place in N. Town Court, during one of the last jury sessions. Mr. Sidor [Translator's Note: Russian for nasty], a man of about thirty years, with a lively gypsy's face and lying eyes, a citizen of N., was sitting in the dock.

He was accused of burglary, fraud, and violating passport regulations. The last charge was compounded by his impersonations of a nobleman.

The assistant prosecutor was pressing the charges. The name of the prosecutor is legion. This was a man lacking any of those special features or outstanding qualities that bring big salaries. He was like many others of his kind: he spoke nasally, could not pronounce the letter "k," and blew his nose constantly.

The defense attorney was one of the most famous and popular men in his profession. Everyone had heard of this lawyer. People still quote his speeches and remember his name with respect.

This kind of lawyer plays a key role in those cheap novels that end in a guilty verdict for the protagonist, and the applause of the public. The names of such lawyers in these novels are often associated with thunder, lightning, and other natural wonders.

When the assistant prosecutor had proved to everyone that Mr. Sidor was guilty and should be convicted, and when he had wrapped it all up by saying, "The prosecution rests," the defense lawyer stood up. Everyone listened carefully. There was total silence in the hall. The lawyer started talking—and the nerves of the people of the Town of N. were shattered. The lawyer stretched out his sunburned neck, moved his head from side to side, flashed his eyes, lifted his hand, and poured his sweet, magical speech into the listeners' eager ears.

His tongue played on the people's nerves as if on the strings of a balalaika. After the first two or three phrases, someone in the gallery heaved a deep sigh; then an unconscious lad was carried out of the courtroom. Three minutes later, the judge had to reach for the bell and ring it three times. The bailiff, a man with a small red nose, began shifting nervously in his chair and looking threateningly at the gallery. All eyes were open wide; all faces grew pale; everyone expected something unusual from the lawyer. And what happened in the people's hearts?

"We are all human beings, members of the jury, so let us make this a human courtroom," the lawyer said, among other things. "Before facing you this day, this man suffered six months of prison time, during the investigation. For six straight months, his wife has been separated from her most beloved husband. His children's eyes haven't dried for a moment as they thought that they didn't have their beloved father with them. Oh, if only you could see the children! They're hungry because there's no one to feed them, and they're in tears because they're miserable. Just look at them! They're stretching their hands out to you, imploring you to give them back their father. They're not here, but you can imagine the picture. (A pause.) Prison? Him? He was put into a cell with thieves, and with murderers. Him! (A pause.) You can imagine his moral suffering in that cell, when he was separated from his wife and children, just in order to—what else can I say?"

Sobs were heard in the audience. A young woman wearing a large brooch on her bosom started to wail. Her neighbor, a little old lady, joined her.

The defense lawyer went on with his speech. He omitted the facts and emphasized the psychology.

"To study this man's soul means to study a rare and protected world, full of subtleties. And I have studied this world. And I must tell you truly that in studying it, I came to know a human being. I genuinely understood this human being. Each movement of his soul tells me that, in my client, I have an ideal man."

The bailiff stopped looking threatening and pulled a handkerchief from his pocket. Two more women were carried out of the hall. The judge did not touch the bell anymore, but put on his eyeglasses, so that no one could see the tear in his right eye. Everyone pulled out handkerchiefs. The prosecutor himself, the man of stone and ice, the insensitive beast, was shifting nervously in his chair. He reddened and looked at the floor. His ears were glowing beneath his eyeglasses.

"I shouldn't have taken this case at all; I should drop the charges right now," he thought. "I'm going to be utterly defeated. What next?"

"Just look into his eyes," the defense lawyer continued. His chin trembled; his voice trembled also, and his suffering was clear in his eyes. "Do you think those tender, humble eyes could look upon a crime in cold blood, without any feelings? No, those eyes can cry; they can shed tears. A very sensitive disposition is hidden underneath that rough, rugged, square-jawed face. A tender heart, not a criminal's, but a human being's, beats beneath that rough, crippled chest. And you would dare call him guilty?"

At this point, the accused could stand it all no longer. He burst into tears. He blinked, cried aloud, and shifted in his place.

"I am guilty!" he said, interrupting the defense attorney. "I am guilty! I accept my guilt completely. I stole, and I defrauded, and I lied.

"I took the money from the chest, and I brought the stolen fur coat to my sister-in-law, and I asked her to hide it. I confess. I'm guilty."

He told the court everything. And so he was convicted and sentenced.

THE BROTHER: A SLICE OF LIFE

⋯━◆━⋯

A young woman was standing in front of the window, lost in thought, looking at the dirty sidewalk. A young man dressed in the official uniform of a civil servant was standing behind her. He was touching his mustache and speaking in a trembling voice.

"My dear sister, do me this favor! It is not too late yet! You have to say no to this fat merchant, this wealthy pig. Please do me a favor and bid good-bye to this fat man. Please do me a favor!"

"I cannot, brother. I gave him my promise."

"I ask you, listen, and be good to our family! You belong to nobility; you are a well-educated, noble lady, but who is he? He is rude and illiterate, you understand? He sells old, smelly fish and kvass in the market. He cheats people. Yesterday you gave him your consent to marry him, and this morning he stole five kopecks from our servant. He robs people! And what about

73

your old dreams? Oh, my God! Listen, I know that you love Michael from our department, and that he loves you, too."

The sister blushed. Her chin was trembling; her eyes were filled with tears. It was obvious that the brother had hit a sore spot.

"Sister, do you wish to destroy both of you, Michael as well? He has started drinking! Sister, all you ever want is money and jewelry. All you ever do is calculate how to make a profit from your marriage. But this is appalling. How can you marry an illiterate? He cannot even sign his name. Look, Ne-ko-lan instead of Nikolai. He is old, he is revolting, and he looks very clumsy. Please do me this favor!"

The brother's voice started trembling. He cleared his throat and wiped the tears from his eyes.

"But I gave him my word of honor, brother. And besides, I hate our poverty."

"I will tell you everything," said the brother, "if you want to hear it. I did not want to tell you this before, but now I will. I would rather lower myself in your eyes than lose my sister completely. I know a secret about your merchant. Listen, Cathie, if you find out his secret, you will say no at once. . . . I saw him in a terrible place. Do you want to know which place? Do you?"

"Where was it? Where?"

The brother opened his mouth to answer, but he was stopped. At that moment, a man came in. He wore a vest and dirty boots, and carried a large paper bag. He crossed himself and stood in the door.

"Dmitry Terentievich said to say hello to you, and he wanted to give you a small gift because today is Sunday: And he asked me to deliver this and to put it directly into your hands."

The brother took the paper bag, looked at it, and smirked in disgust. "What is in it? Hmm, some stupid thing! A head of sugar."

The brother took the sugar in his hands and tapped it with his fingernail. "I wonder what kind of sugar this is? Ha! Bobrinsky—not bad for tea. What's this in the bag? Some garbage or other: sardines, raisins and cheese. He—he wants to bribe me! No, my friend, you cannot do a thing! Why did he put coffee in here? I cannot drink coffee—it shatters my nerves! All right, go away, go! And say hello to him!"

The delivery man left. The sister ran to the brother and caught him by the hand.

The brother had moved her with his words. One more word, and the merchant would be ruined.

"Tell me, brother, where did you see him? Tell me!"

"Nowhere, I was just kidding. You can do whatever you want," said the brother, and tapped the head of sugar with his fingernail once again.

A CONFESSION

I t was a clear, frosty, sunny day. I felt as euphoric as a cabman who just received a ten-ruble tip instead of a quarter. I wanted to cry with happiness, to smile, and to pray. I was in seventh heaven. Me, an ordinary man, to be a cashier! I was delighted because now I could steal as much money as I wanted. I'm not a thief, and I would kill anyone who called me one. But I was happy about my promotion because I had made another tiny step in my career and a small addition to my wages. That's all.

I was happy for a few other reasons, too. When I became a cashier, I seemed to see the world through rose-colored glasses. It seemed that people had changed. It's true, take my word of honor! It seemed to me that everyone suddenly became better. Ugly people became beautiful; proud people became humble; evil people became good; greedy people became generous. I seemed to see the world around me in a much better light. I could find good qualities in people whom I had never imagined had any.

"Strange," I said to myself, looking at people and rubbing my eyes. "Either something has happened to all these people, or I was dull before and could not notice their qualities. What wonderful people they are!"

Mr. Kazusov, a director of our company, had also changed. He was a proud man and had previously taken no notice of lower employees like myself. I don't know what happened to him, but he came over to talk to me. He smiled kindly at me and slapped me on the back, saying,

"You're too self-conscious; it doesn't suit your young years. Why don't you drop into my office for a chat from time to time? Don't be shy, my friend. I often invite young people like you into my home, and they have a good time there.

My daughters were just asking,

"Father, why don't you invite Gregory Kuzmich? He is such a nice fellow."

I said to them,

"How can I bring him into my house?"

"But you know, I promised them that one day I would invite you over. So don't hesitate, my friend; come visit me."

It's so strange. What happened to him? Perhaps he has gone mad. He used to be a terrible man who hated everyone, but look at him now

When I got home, I was amazed again. At dinner, my mother gave me four helpings instead of the usual two. In the evening she served me jam, fresh rolls, and cookies. It was the same the next day: four servings and jam for tea. We had guests, and we ate chocolate. On the third day, the same thing.

"Mother, what's happened to you?" I asked her. "Why are

you spending so much? My salary hasn't doubled. I've only had a tiny increase."

My mother looked at me with surprise and said,

"How are you going to spend all this money? Are you going to save it? Invest in your bank account or what?"

What was going on? My father bought an expensive fur coat and hat; he started drinking those pricey mineral waters and eating grapes in the middle of the winter! Five days later, I received a letter from my brother. Before, my brother could not stand me. I had said good-bye to him because of differences in temperament. He thought that I was an egoist, a ne'er-do-well; that I could not make sacrifices; and he hated me for it. In his letter, I read the following:

"Dear brother, I love you very much. You cannot imagine how much I suffered after our last quarrel. Let us be reconciled, let us extend the hand of friendship; and let there be peace between us, I implore you. I await your answer. Love and kisses, Evlampy."

Oh, my dear brother. I replied that I loved him, too, and that I was very joyful. A week later, I received a telegram from him, saying,

"Thank you, I am so happy. Please send me a hundred rubles. I need them very much. Embracing you, Ivan (Evlampy)." I sent him a hundred rubles.

Even she changed. She never used to love me. When I hinted to her that something had happened to my heart, she told me that I was rude, that I was too bold; and she slapped my face. A week later, after the promotion, she invited me to see her; she smiled sweetly, making dimples in her cheeks, and looked surprised.

"What's happened to you?" she asked, looking at me. "You

look so nice today. How did you manage to change so fast? How come you've become so handsome? Let's go out dancing together."

Oh, dear! A week later, her mother became my mother-in-law: I became a better person for all of them. I badly needed three hundred rubles in cash, so I quietly took it from the company. Why shouldn't I take it? I know that I will put it back as soon as payday comes around. So, I took the money, and I also took a hundred rubles for Mr. Kazusov. He had asked me for a loan. I could not refuse him. He is an important person in the company, and he could have me fired. ["This is where the editor found the story too long, and crossed out 73 lines, thus cutting down on the author's royalties."—Chekhov's comment.]

A week before I was arrested, I threw a party for them at their request. Let them eat as much as they want, let them fill their fat bellies, what the hell! I did not count the people at the party, but I remember that all nine of my rooms were packed. Big and small, young and old—there were even some dignitaries before whom Mr. Kazusov bowed to the ground.

His daughters, the eldest of whom was my love, blinded us with their gowns. I had paid a thousand rubles just for the flowers for them. It was delightful. The music was loud, the lights were bright, the champagne flowed like water. People made long speeches and short toasts. A local journalist dedicated an ode to me, and another wrote a ballad in my name.

"Here in Russia, we do not appreciate kind people like Ivan Kuzmich," Mr. Kazusov cried during dinner. "And what a pity! What a pity for Russia!"

All of them who were smiling, yelling, kissing me—they were whispering behind my back, and pointing at me whenever I looked away. But I saw all of their secret vicious smiles and fingers.

"He stole all this money, what a naughty boy!" they whispered to each other, smiling evilly.

But neither their fingers nor their smiles interfered with their abilities to eat and drink, and enjoy their dinner.

Not even wolves and diabetics eat as much as they ate. My wife, who was shining with gold and diamonds, came over to me and whispered,

"They say you stole all this. If it's true, be warned: I cannot live with a thief. I'll leave you!"

She said this while adjusting her five-thousand-ruble dress. Well, who knows about women! Later that evening, Kazusov borrowed another five thousand from me. My brother Evlampy borrowed again.

"If what they say is true," my honest brother whispered, pocketing the money, "then beware. I cannot be the brother of a thief."

After the party was over, I hailed several luxurious cabs and troikas and took them all out of town for a ride.

It was six in the morning when we finished. We were exhausted with wine and women, and we decided that it was time to go home.

When the sleigh started moving away, they shouted after me, "Tomorrow we will begin the audit. Thank you, merci!"

Ladies and gentlemen, I was caught. To be exact, yesterday I was an honest and decent man. Today I am a scoundrel, a thief, and a con artist. Now you can yell at me, gossip about me. You can be shocked, you can take me to court, send me to prison, write editorials, throw stones, but please, not all together! Not all at once!

IN THE DARKNESS OF THE NIGHT

———◆———

There are neither moon nor stars in the sky. Not a shadow; nor a single spot of light. Everything is immersed in impenetrable darkness. You look and look into it, but you see nothing, as if you were blind. The rain is pouring down, and the roads are covered with mud.

A pair of horses goes slowly along the village road. Three people are sitting in the carriage: a man dressed as a railway engineer and his wife, both completely soaked, and a driver who is as drunk as a fish. The first horse trembles and goes very slowly. The second horse is stumbling and continually tries to jump to the side. The road is terrible. At every step, there is a pothole, or a hump, or a small bridge that has been washed away. To the left, a wolf is howling, and to the right there is a ravine.

"It's a terrible road—I'm pretty sure that we're lost," the engineer's wife sighs deeply. "Yes, it's so easy to go off the road and get lost. Don't go into the ditch."

"Why should I go into the ditch? Hey, you rotten horse, go, go! Go on, love!"

"He seems to have completely lost his way," said the engineer. "Where are you taking us, you villain? Can't you see? Is this the road?"

"Yes, that means that it's the road."

"It can't be the road! It's like driving in a field! Turn right, you drunk. Now, turn left. Where is your whip?"

"I lost it, your highness."

"I will kill you if you lead us wrong. Hey, where are you going? Isn't the road this way?"

The horses stop abruptly. The engineer hangs on to the driver's back and shoulders and pulls the right rein. The first horse splashes in the mud, turns sharply, and convulses oddly.

The driver falls from the carriage and vanishes into the darkness. The second horse stumbles at the cliff, and the engineer feels the carriage is falling somewhere into the abyss.

The ravine is not very deep. The engineer gets to his feet, picks up his wife, and climbs up the hill. At the top of the ravine, he sees the driver sitting on the edge of the rock, moaning. The engineer rushes over to him. He shakes his fist in the air, ready to smash the driver 's face.

"I will kill you, you wretch, you scoundrel!" he yells.

The fist has already moved backward, then forward, and it is halfway to the driver's face. One second, and it will happen.

"Michael, remember Siberia and the prisons!" the engineer's wife says.

Michael trembles, and his terrible fist stops halfway to the driver's face. The driver is saved.

THE INTENTIONAL DECEPTION

·—·≡◆≡·—·

Zakhar Kuzmich Diadechkin was having a New Year's party. The idea was to celebrate both New Year's Eve and the birthday of Malania Tikhonovna, his wife and the mistress of the house.

Many people were there. All of them were serious, respectful and sober; not one scoundrel among them. All wore pleasant expressions and held respect for their own dignity. Some were sitting in the living room, on a long sofa covered with cheap vinyl. The landowner, Gusev, and the owner of the nearest grocery store, Razmakhalov, were there. They spoke about bribery and drink.

"It's so hard to find a man," said Gusev, "who doesn't drink nowadays, a serious man. It's hard to find a man like that."

"And the most important thing, Alexei Vasilievich, is law and order."

"There must be law and order. Right here at home, so many

bad things are happening. How can you establish law and order?"

Three old women were sitting in a half circle around them, looking at the men's mouths with amazement. They looked, astonished and awed, at the two men talking about such clever things. Gury Markovich, their in-law, was sitting in the corner of the room, looking at icons. Suddenly, a soft noise came from the lady's bedroom. There, some younger boys and a girl were playing bingo. The bet was one kopeck. Kolya, a first-year high school student, was standing next to the table, crying. He wanted to play bingo, but the other children would not let him. Why should a young boy play if he did not have a kopeck?

"Don't cry, fool! Why are you crying? I think your mother should beat you."

"I have beaten him enough," sounded the mother's voice from the kitchen, "you bad boy. Varvara Gurievna, pull him by the ear."

Two young girls in pink sat on the mistress's bed, which was covered with a cotton blanket that had lost its original color. A man, twenty-three years old, sat in front of them, a clerk from the insurance company. His name was Kopalsky, and his face reminded one of a cat. He was flirting with them.

"I am never going to marry," he said, looking dashing and adjusting the tightly fixed collar on his shirt. "A woman is a wonderful thing for a man, but at the same time she can ruin him!"

"But what about men? Men can't fall in love. They can only . . ."

"You are so naive! I don't want to be cynical, but I happen to know that men stand much higher than women when it comes to love."

Mr. Diadechkin and his elder son Grisha were pacing from one corner of the room to another, looking like two wolves in a cage. They were burning with impatience. They had already had a couple of drinks at dinner before, and now, they wanted another. Diadechkin went to the kitchen. There, the mistress of the house was covering a pie with powdered sugar.

"Malania, the guests would like some more snacks to be served," said Diadechkin.

"They'll have to wait. If you eat and drink everything now, what am I going to serve at midnight? You can wait. Get out of the kitchen and don't get in my way."

"Can I have just one small shot, Malasha? You won't even notice it."

"What a man! Out of the kitchen! Out! Go talk to our guests! You're not wanted here, in the kitchen."

Diadechkin went out and looked at the clock. It showed only eight minutes after eleven. There were fifty-two minutes before the long-awaited moment. The waiting was terrible! Waiting for a drink is one of the worst things. It is better to wait for a train for five hours outside in the snow than it is to wait for a drink for five minutes. Diadechkin looked angrily at the clock, took a few steps across the room, and moved the big hand five minutes ahead. And what about Grisha? Grisha was thinking that if he did not get a drink then he would have to go to the pub and drink by himself. He was not ready for that.

"Mother," he said, "the guests are upset that you're not serving them any treats. This is no good. You want to starve them to death? Give them a shot."

"Wait for it! It's coming soon! Don't hang around in the kitchen!"

Grisha slammed the kitchen door noisily and went to look at

the clock for the hundredth time. The big arm was merciless; it was almost at the same spot.

"This clock is slow," Grisha said to himself, and moved the big hand seven minutes forward.

Later, Kolya was running past the clock. He looked at it and started to calculate the time. He was waiting for the moment when they would start crying "Hurray," but the hand of the clock seemed to be motionless. He got very upset; he climbed the chair, looked around furtively and stole five more minutes from eternity.

"Do you want to see what time it is now? I am dying with impatience," said one of the young ladies to Kopalsky. "The New Year is approaching, and it brings us new hopes and new happiness."

Kopalsky made a bow and ran to the clock.

"Oh my goodness," he murmured, standing by the clock. "It is such a long wait, and I am so hungry. I can't wait to kiss Katya, as soon as they cry 'Hurray!' "

Kopalsky came back, then returned to the clock and shortened the old year by ten minutes. Diadechkin drank two glasses of water, but the burning inside did not stop. He paced around all the rooms. Every time he went into the kitchen, his wife pushed him out. The bottles standing on the window were tearing his soul apart. What should he do? He had no power to resist. He jumped at his last chance.

He went into the children's room to the clock, but he saw a scene that disturbed his heart. Grisha was standing in front of the clock moving the minute hand.

"What are you doing? You fool! Why are you touching the clock?" Diadechkin wrinkled his forehead and cleared his throat. "What are you doing? Nothing? Then get out." He pushed his son away from the clock and moved the big hand a little forward.

"There, now there are eleven minutes until the New Year." Grisha and his father went to the hall and started setting the table.

"Malania, the New Year is coming!" Diadechkin cried to his wife.

Malania Tikhonovna came out from the kitchen to check the time. She looked carefully at the clock. Her husband had not lied to her. "What am I going to do?" she whispered. "The peas for the ham are still sitting in the oven raw. What am I going to do? How can I serve it?"

Then, after a short pause, Malania Tikhonovna moved the clock backward with a trembling hand. The old year received another twenty minutes back.

"They can wait," said the woman, and returned to the kitchen.

ON THE SEA: A SAILOR'S STORY

—◦—✦—◦—

I could see only the dim lights of the harbor we had just left, and the black sky above us, darker than pitch. We felt a cold wind that was blowing in the dark sky above; it was about to rain. We felt suffocated, despite the wind and the cold. By "we" I mean we sailors who stood in the hold, making bets. I could hear some noisy laughter; somebody was cracking jokes, and somebody else was crowing like a rooster to entertain the others.

I was trembling all over, from the crown of my head to the soles of my feet; it was as if I had a hole in the back of my head, from which cold sweat was pouring down my naked spine. I was trembling from the cold, and from other things I don't want to tell you about.

I think man is a vile creature, and a sailor worse than any other, worse than an animal; but sometimes there is a faithfulness that tells me I may be mistaken. Maybe I don't understand life, but it seems to me sometimes that a sailor has more reason to hate and blame himself than any other man. A man who is prepared to fall from the mast into the sea, to be covered forever by the waves; a man who could be drowned at any moment, going headfirst into the abyss: such a man need not fear or regret anything. We drink lots of vodka, and we are dissipated because we don't know whether we need virtue in the open sea.

But I should continue my story.

We were making bets. There were twenty-two of us, idle hands after hours. Only two men out of the whole crowd could see the spectacle. The thing is, our ship has a special cabin for newlyweds, and that night it had occupants, but the walls of the cabin had only two holes we could use.

I made the first hole myself using a little saw, first making a small hole plugged with a cork, and my friend made the second hole with a knife. The two of us worked for more than a week.

"One hole is for you," they shouted to me.

"What about the other one?"

"The other one's for your father."

My father, an old sailor with a big crooked nose and a face like a baked wrinkled apple, came to me and slapped me on the shoulder.

"My boy, tonight will be a happy one. You hear me, boy? There is some enjoyment for you and me both tonight, and that's what important." He asked impatiently, "What time is it?"

It was about eleven.

I went out of the cabin onto the desk, smoked my pipe, and looked at the sea. It was dark but seemed to reflect my own soul's working. I seemed to see some dark images, and I felt something was lacking in my young life.

At midnight, I passed the passengers' lounge and looked through the door. The newlyweds were there. A young pastor with beautiful blond hair was sitting at the table, a New Testament in his hand. He was explaining something to a tall, thin Englishwoman. The new bride, a slender and very beautiful woman, was sitting next to her husband and did not move the gaze of her blue eyes from his blond head. A large, fat, old Englishman with a foul, fat face and red hair, a banker, was pacing the room from one corner to the other. He was the husband of the tall woman whom the newlywed pastor was addressing.

"Pastors have a habit of running off at the mouth. I suppose he won't be finished until morning," I thought.

At one in the morning, my father came to me, pulled me by the sleeve, and said, "It's time. They just left the passengers' lounge."

I sprinted down the long, steep steps and ran up to the wall I knew so well. Between this wall and the cabin's wall was an empty space filled with water, dirt, and rats. Soon, I heard my father's heavy tread. He stumbled over some bags, wastepaper, gasoline drums, and boxes. He swore. I felt my hole and removed the little square wooden plug I had spent so much time cutting. I saw a thin translucent veil, through which I saw some dim pink light. Along with the light I had found some sort of unpleasant, smothering odor. It was probably the smell of an aristocrat's bedroom. To see into the room, I had to move aside the veil, which I did.

I saw some bronze, velvet, and lace. Everything was bathed in pink light. About two meters from my face, I saw a bed.

"Let me see through your hole," father said to me, impatiently shoving in behind me. "I can see better through yours."

I was silent.

"Look, boy, your eyes can see better than mine; it's the same to you looking from close up or farther away."

"Shut up! Let's keep quiet; they can hear us."

The newlywed woman was sitting at the edge of the bed, with her small feet on the fur carpet. She was looking at the floor. Her husband, the young pastor, was standing before her. He was talking to her, saying something, but I could not hear what. The noise of the engines muffled his speech and kept me from hearing him. The pastor was speaking passionately, gesticulating, flashing his eyes. His wife was disagreeing with him, shaking her head in refusal.

"Damn it, I've been bitten by a rat," my father groused.

I pressed my chest against the wall, as if I feared that my heart would jump out of it. My head was on fire.

The newlyweds talked for a long time. Finally, the pastor kneeled in front of her and started imploring her about something. She shook her head in refusal. Then he jumped up and started pacing the room in agitation, almost at a run. I looked at his face, and from its expression I understood that he was threatening her somehow.

His young wife stood up, slowly came to the wall, right at the place where I was hiding, and stood in front of the hole. She stood, considering something, and I devoured her face with my eyes. She seemed to be hesitating from some kind of suffering, and her face expressed some kind of hatred.

For about five minutes we stood like this, face to face. Then she turned, moved to the middle of the room, and nodded, saying that she agreed to his demand.

He joyfully smiled, kissed her hand, and left the cabin.

About three minutes later, her door opened, and the pastor entered the room. Behind him was the tall red-headed

Englishman I mentioned before. The Englishman came to the bed and asked the nice-looking woman something. She sat with pale face, without looking at him; she nodded.

The English banker pulled something from his pocket, a bunch of papers, maybe a bunch of bills, and gave them to the pastor. The pastor looked at them, counted them and left with a bow. The Englishman closed the door behind him.

I jumped away from the wall as if a snake had bitten me. I was terrified. It seemed to me that the wind was tearing our ship into pieces so that we would drown. My old, drunken, debauched father, took me by the hand and said, "Let's get out of here. You needn't see this. You're still just a boy."

He could hardly stand. I carried him up the steep winding steps, up onto the desk. It was raining, and it was autumn.

IVAN THE CABMAN

I t was almost two o'clock in the morning.

Commerce Councilor Ivan Vasilievich Kotlov left the restaurant "Slavic Bazaar" and walked along Nikolsky Street toward the Kremlin. It was a beautiful, starry night. The stars peeked from behind small clouds as they merrily twinkled, as if it were a pleasant task to gaze upon the earth. The air was clear, and all was quiet.

"The taxi drivers near the restaurant district are so expensive," Kotlov thought, "I have to keep on walking until they become cheaper. Besides, I could use the walk, as I did overeat and I am drunk."

Near the Kremlin, he hailed the night cab driver, "Ivan." This is the nickname given to any Moscow taxi driver.

"Take me to Yakimovka Street!" he told the cab driver.

This particular Ivan, a young man about twenty-five years old, smacked his lips and lazily drew his reins. The short horse left its resting spot as it moved slowly until it reached a slow, steady trot. Kotlov saw that he had a real, typical Ivan-the-cabman. It was enough to catch a glimpse of his sleepy, rough face, covered with pimples, and one could tell that he was a cabman.

They headed through the Kremlin.

"What time is it now?" asked Ivan.

"Two o'clock," answered the Commerce Councilor.

"Yes, it is becoming warmer. It was cold for a few days, and now it is warming up again. Hey you, lame one! What kind of a lazy horse are you?"

The groom stood up in his seat and whipped his horse on its back.

"I don't like winter," he continued, sitting more comfortably and turning back toward his customer. "It is too cold for me during the winter. When I stay in the frost, I freeze and start shaking all over. As soon as the temperature drops, my face explodes and swells. I am not accustomed to the cold!"

"You must get used to it. You are in a profession that requires it, so you must."

"A man can get used to anything, which is true, yes sir!

"But before you get used to it, you'll most likely freeze at least twenty times. I am a tender and spoiled man, your honor. I was spoiled by my parents. They did not think I would end up being a groom. They treated me with such tenderness, God bless them. They put me as a baby next to the warm oven in our country house, and I slept there until I was ten. I stayed there eating pies like a stupid pig. I was their beloved son. They dressed me in the best clothes, taught me how to read and to write for my future happy life. When I wanted to run barefoot, they warned me: 'You will get a cold, boy,' as if I were not a peasant but a landlord or man of prominence.

"When my father beat me, my mother cried. When my mother yelled at me, my father took my side. Every time I went to the forest to accompany my father to collect firewood, my mother put three fur coats on me, as if I were off to Moscow or something."

"Were you rich as far as farming goes?"

"We were neither rich, nor poor, just like all farmers. We thanked God for every day. We were not rich, but we did not starve or feel hunger, thank God. We lived as family, sir, that is, like a family. My grandfather was still alive then, and his two sons lived with him. One son, that is my father, was married; the second son was single. I was the only child. And so they spoiled me, even my grandfather. You know, he was very good at making money, and he thought that I was too smart for a farmer.

"I will buy you a general store, Petruska, when you grow up," he said. So I was raised well and spoiled, until something terrible happened that changed everything.

"My uncle stole the old man's money, about twenty thousand rubles. After he stole the money, we became bankrupt. We had to sell our horses and cows, and my father and grandfather had to become hired workers. You know how we peasants live. As for me—I became a hired shepherd."

"And what happened to your uncle?"

"Nothing. Everything happened for him just like he wanted. He rented a pub along the major road and did quite well. About five years later, he married a rich woman from the town of Serpukov. She had around eight thousand rubles for her dowry. Soon after they married, the pub burned down. Why shouldn't it burn down, as it was insured? After the fire, they moved to Moscow, and rented a hardware store there. People say that he became so rich that you could not approach him. Some men from my village saw him then and passed all this information on about him. I have not seen him since he ran off with the money. His name is Kotlov; his first name is Ivan Vasilievich. Have you heard of him?"

"No, but please, go on."

"We were abused terribly by Ivan Vasilievich, very much so. He forced us into poverty, for we even lost our house. If it were not for him, do you think I would be out here in the freezing cold with my complexion and weakness? Huh! No. I would stay in my hometown."

"Oh, these are the chimes of morning vespers! That reminds me. I want to pray to God that my uncle will pay for what he has done to us. No, let God forgive him! I will endure this!"

"To the side entrance."

"Yes, as you say. We have arrived. And for my story you can pay five kopecks."

Kotlov took a coin from his pocket and gave it to Ivan.

"Can you spare more?"

"No, that's enough."

The Commerce Councilor rang the bell and after a moment disappeared behind the thick carved wooden door into the building.

The cabman jumped back into place and slowly turned his carriage. A cold wind blew. Ivan wrinkled his face, tucking his cold hands into his worn-out sleeves. The cabdriver had not gotten used to the weather conditions, nor was he likely to, as he had been too spoiled as a child.

PERPETUAL MOBILE

———※———

The court detective Grishutkin, an old man who started his career a very long time ago, and Dr. Svintsitsky, a melancholy gentleman, headed off together to perform an autopsy.

It was autumn. They took a carriage along the country roads. It was pitch dark, and pouring rain.

"What kind of nasty place are we in?" mumbled the detective. "It is not civilized, nor does it have a good climate around here. What kind of country is this! Do you think we can call this part of the world Europe? Look at it this way—it is really bad. Hey, you, man," he cried to the groom. "Go faster, or I'm going to beat you."

"It is very strange, Agei Alexeevich," said the doctor with a sigh, pressing deeper into his fur coat. "But I do not notice this weather. I am obsessed by a strange premonition. I feel like misfortune is going to come to me in the near future. As

I believe in omens, I know that anything can happen . . . an infection during an autopsy from a dead body, a death of a beloved creature—anything of this sort."

"You should be ashamed to talk about the premonitions in the groom's presence. You're behaving like a grumpy old woman. Do you actually think that life can get worse than it is now? Look at this rain—can it be worse than this? You know what? I cannot travel like this, in this weather. You can kill me if you like, but sorry, I can't go any farther. We should spend the night somewhere. Do you know anyone who lives around here?" the detective inquired of the groom.

"Ivan Ivanovich Ezhov," said Mishka the groom. "Right there, on the other side of that forest. All we have to do is to cross this small bridge."

"Ezhov? Let's pay him a visit. I have not seen him for a long time, that old dog."

They crossed the forest and the bridge, turned to the left and then to the right, and entered the large yard belonging to retired Major-General Ezhov.

"He is at home," said Grishutkin, getting out of the carriage, and looking toward the lit windows. "It is good that he's at home. We will have something to eat, to drink, and a good sleep. He is not a very nice man, but he is hospitable, I must admit."

Mr. Ezhov met them in the entrance hall. He was a small wrinkled man with a face gathered in a small ball of wrinkled flesh.

"You came just in time, just in time, gentlemen!" he said. "We just sat down to supper and have only just finished the ham. I have a guest, you know, a prosecutor's assistant. Thank him for coming. He is such a nice guy. Tomorrow, we will have a conference, thirty-three at once."

Grishutkin and the doctor entered the living room with a big table covered with meals and drinks. Nadezhda Ivanovna, the owner's daughter, dressed in black due to mourning for her deceased husband, sat at one of the table settings. Next to her sat Mr. Tulpansky, the prosecutor's assistant, a young man with whiskers and many small blue veins on his face.

"Do you know each other?" asked Ezhov, indicating each of them with his finger. "This is the prosecutor, and this is my daughter."

The brunette closed her eyes for a second and then stretched her hand to the guests for a handshake.

"Now, let us have a drink," said Ezhov, pouring three shots. "To our guests! You are God's people, and I will drink to keep you company. Thirty-three at once. To your health."

They had a drink. Grishutkin chose a pickle and started eating ham. The doctor drank, and sighed. Mr. Tulpansky smoked a cigar, after first asking for permission from the lady, and when he smiled, everyone saw that he had all thirty-three teeth in his mouth.

"Now what, gentlemen? Your shots are empty, and we cannot wait. Doctor, let's have a drink to medicine. I love medicine. And in general, I love you people, thirty-three at once. No matter what you say, the young generation still walks in front of the others. To your health!"

They began a conversation. All were talking at once, except for the prosecutor, who sat in silence, blowing the cigar smoke through his nostrils. It was obvious he considered himself a nobleman, and despised both the doctor and the detective.

After the supper, Grishutkin, the host, and the prosecutor sat down to play cards. The doctor and Nadezhda Ivanovna sat near the grand piano and continued talking.

"Are you going to perform an autopsy?" the young, pretty widow said. "An autopsy on a dead body? Wow. What will power that would require! An iron will. To take a knife, and without a hesitation, to stab it into the body of a breathless man. You know, I adore doctors. They are very special people, I think doctors are saints. But doctor, why do you look so sad?" she asked.

"I have a premonition, a bad feeling, like I am going to lose a member of my family, or a close relative."

"Are you married, doctor? Do you have a family?"

"Not a single soul. I am single, and I don't even have friends. Tell me lady, do you believe in premonitions?"

"Oh yes, I believe . . ."

While the doctor and the lady talked about the premonitions, Grishutkin and the prosecutor were playing cards, returning to the table with food and having another drink from time to time.

At 2 a.m. Ezhov, who was losing money in the game, suddenly remembering the conference he had to attend later that day, slapped his forehead, and said, "Oh my God, what are we doing up so late? We are violating the law. Tomorrow, we should be leaving for this early conference, and we are still up playing cards. So let's all go to bed. Thirty-three at once! Nadezhda, please go to bed. I pronounce our meeting over."

"You are lucky, doctor, that you can fall asleep at night," whispered Nadezhda Ivanovna when she said good-bye to the doctor. "I cannot sleep when the rain is hitting the window and my pine trees rustle outside. I will head to my room, and I will be bored reading a book. I cannot fall asleep now. And in general, if a lamp in front of my door in the corridor is lit, it means that I cannot sleep and that I am very bored."

The doctor and Mr. Grishutkin found two huge beds in their rooms, made from mattresses put on the floor. The doctor undressed and lay down on his mattress, covering himself completely with a blanket, even his head. The detective also undressed and lay down, but then he jumped back up and started pacing the room, from one corner to another. He was an easily excited man.

"I am thinking about the landlord's daughter, the young widow. Such a beautiful, refined young woman. I would have given anything to have had a woman such as her—her eyes, her shoulders, and her feet in those purple stockings. This woman has set me on fire. And she would belong to God knows whom—to a judicial civil servant, a prosecutor! He is a fool and he looks like an Englishman! I hate those legal people. When you spoke to her about premonition, she blushed, and he almost burst into pieces from jealousy. What can I say—a luxuriously beautiful woman. A wonderful woman! One of nature's wonders."

"Yes, she is a nice, respected lady," said the doctor, talking from under the blanket. "She is sensitive, nervous, responsive, and a very easily excited person. We can fall asleep in an instant, but she cannot. Her nerves cannot stand this stormy night. She told me that all night—through the whole night—she would be bored, and would be reading a book. Poor woman, I pity her. Probably her lamp is on right now."

"What lamp?"

"She told me that if the lamp in front of her door is on, it means that she is not asleep."

"Did she tell you this?"

"Yes, she did."

"Then, I don't understand you. If she told you this, then you are the happiest of men—what a man. Congratulations. I am jealous of you, of course, but anyway—congratulations! I am happy not only for you, but I am happy to see that scoundrel, that legal young man to be defeated. I am happy that you would lock horns with him. Now get dressed and go."

Grishutkin, when drunk, becomes too relaxed at times. "You are joking, of course. God only knows what you are telling me," said the doctor, embarrassed.

"Now, don't talk, doctor. Get dressed, and go to her. Now, as they sing in the opera, 'A Life for the King.' 'We should pick up the flowers of love every day.' Get dressed, brother. Faster, faster."

"But . . ."

"Faster, you animal."

"Excuse me, but I don't understand you."

"What is there to understand? It's quite clear. Is this astronomy or what? Just get dressed and go to the lamp."

"I am surprised that you have such a low opinion about that person and me."

"Stop your stupidity!!!" Grishutkin began to get angry. "How can you behave like this, so cynical?"

He tried for a long time to convince the doctor to go. He kneeled in front of him, and finished his plea by shouting, and swearing with filthy language, even jumping on his bed. He went to lie down, but fifteen minutes later, he jumped up and woke the doctor up.

"Listen," he said, "do you refuse to see her? Are you positive?" he asked in a strict tone of voice. "Yes, why should you go? You are so easily excited. It is so hard to go to autopsies with you. I am no worse than that lawyer, the womanizer, or you womanish doctor. I will go by myself."

He got dressed very quickly and headed for the door. The doctor looked at him with surprise, stood up, and walked over to lock the door.

"I think you are joking, sir," the doctor said.

"I don't have time to talk to you right now. Let me out."

"No, I will not let you go. Go back to bed. You are drunk."

"What right do you have not to let me go, doctor?"

"I have the right to do it, as a noble and honest man, who wants to defend an honest woman. Think about your actions. You are sixty-four."

"You say that I am a nobleman. Who is that scoundrel who told you that I am old?"

"Agei Alexeevich, you are drunk and excited. Don't forget, you are a human being, not an animal. An animal would act as you are trying to, guided by instinct. But you—you are a human being, the king over nature."

The detective stuck his hands in his pockets. "I am asking you for the last time, will you let me go out or not," he cried in a very piercing voice, as if outdoors. When he finally realized that the answer was no, he yelled, "You scoundrel!"

But then he backed away from the door. He was drunk, but he nevertheless understood that his piercing cry had probably woken everyone up in the house.

After a brief period of silence, the doctor came to him and touched him on the shoulder. The doctor's eyes were red, and his cheeks were burning.

"Agei Alexeevich," he said in a trembling voice. "After all those rude words, after you forgot about respect and called me a scoundrel, you should agree that we cannot stay together under the same roof. You treated me terribly. Let's assume that I am guilty, but what exactly am I guilty of? She is an honest and noble lady, but all of a sudden you allow yourself these words. Excuse me, but we cannot be friends anymore."

"All right, I don't need such a friend."

"I am leaving this instant. I will not stay here with you any longer. I hope that we will not meet again."

"How are you leaving?"

"I will take my horses."

"And then how will I leave? What did you think? Why are you being so mean? You brought me here with your horses, and you must take me with you when you go."

"I will bring you, but I am leaving now. I am sorry, but I will not stay here any longer."

The doctor and Grishutkin got dressed in silence and went out into the backyard. They awoke the groom, climbed into the carriage, and left.

"You are so comical," the detective mumbled all the way. "If you don't know how to treat an honest woman, you should not visit a house where a woman lives." It was hard to know whether he was addressing himself or the doctor.

When the carriage pulled in at the front of his apartment building, the doctor jumped from the carriage and said, before he closed the door behind him, "I don't want to know you any longer, or have anything in common with you."

Three days passed.

One day, the doctor had finished his visits and was relaxing on his couch, killing time by looking through "The Doctor's Calendar." He read the list of family names of the doctors in Moscow and St. Petersburg. He tried to find a beautiful and nice-sounding name. He had a very good, pleasant feeling in his soul, as if he looked into the sky, with a lark in the middle. He had this nice feeling, as he seen a fire in his dream the night before, which meant happiness. Suddenly he heard the noise of an approaching sleigh, as snow had recently fallen.

Grishutkin knocked at his door and entered. The doctor stood up, and looked at the visitor with a mix of emotions and fear.

Grishutkin lowered his eyes, and slowly moved in the direction of the sofa. "I came to ask you for your forgiveness, Ilia Vasilievich. It was not nice and polite of me, and it seems that I said some unpleasant words to you. You should understand my excitement, and the amount of alcohol that we drank with that scoundrel, and I am here to apologize for what I did."

The doctor jumped up from his place, with tears in his eyes, and stretched out his hand to the one reaching for his.

"Hey, please forgive me, too."

"Mary," he called out to his servant. "Bring me tea, please."

"No, I don't want tea. I am too busy. Instead of tea, I would prefer kvass. Let me drink the kvass and go to the autopsy of the next dead body."

"What dead body?"

"The same dead body of the sergeant that we were going to perform together, but did not."

Grishutkin and the doctor dressed in their outerwear and left to perform the autopsy.

"Certainly, I will have to apologize," repeated the detective on the way. "And it's a pity that you do not intend to lock horns with that prosecutor, that scoundrel."

When they were going through the Alimonovo estate, they saw the Ezhovs' troika.

"Look, Ezhov is here," said Grishutkin. "Look, those are his horses. Let's go in and say hello. We will drink soda water, and just look at this woman, she is so beautiful, this lady. One of nature's wonders."

The travelers got out of the sleigh and entered the tavern. They saw Mr. Ezhov and Mr. Tulpansky sitting at a table drinking herbal tea.

"Where are you off to?" Ezhov addressed them with surprise.

"We are heading to the autopsy. A dead body has been found at the crime scene. But we cannot seem to get there. It appears we are in a magic circle, and we cannot get out. Where are you going?"

"To a conference."

"Why so often? You went there three days ago."

"Yes, we did, however, the prosecutor had a toothache, and I also did not feel well those days. Have a drink? Take a seat, thirty-three at once. What kind of beer would you like? Hey, waitress, please bring us each both vodka and a beer. What a nice woman!"

"Yes, a pretty woman, this waitress!" the detective agreed. "A wonderful, nice-looking woman. Well."

Two hours later, the groom left the tavern and told the general's groom to unharness the horses. The men began a card game, and the landlord waved his hand in the air to let them know that the chief of police was coming

"Now, we will wait here until tomorrow. Look, the chief is coming," the detective explained.

The police chief's carriage arrived at the tavern. He recognized the Ezhovs' horses, smiled to himself, and ran up the stairs.

EVILDOER

——— ✦ ———

A short and very thin farmer, dressed in a bright-colored shirt and torn pants, stands before the court investigator. The farmer has a pock-marked and excessively hairy face. His eyes can hardly be seen from under his thick eyebrows, which give him an evil and morose look. His huge pile of messy and tangled hair completes his gloomy, spiderlike appearance.

"Your name is Dennis Grigoriev," the interrogator begins. "Please step closer to me and answer my questions. On July seventh of this year, you were observed by the railway security guard, Mr. Ivan Akintov, while walking along the seventy-sixth kilometer of the railway to be unscrewing the nuts that fix the rails to the railway ties. Here is his deposition. He caught you while you were holding this iron nut in your hands. Is this true?"

"What did you say?"

"Did it happen in the way Mr. Akintov explained it?"

"Sure, it is true."

"Well then, why did you unscrew this nut?"

"What? What's up?"

"Stop asking questions. Tell me why and how you unscrewed this iron nut from the railway tracks."

"If I did not need it, I would not have done it," Dennis answers in a very hoarse voice, looking up at a spot somewhere high up on the ceiling.

"Then why did you take this nut?"

"Why did I take the nut? With these nuts, we make plummets for the fishing rods."

"What do you mean by 'we'?"

"'We'—means common people, the folks from the Klimov village, that's who I mean.

"Listen to me, man. Do not pretend to be an idiot. Tell me straight, why are you telling me these lies about fishing rods and plummets?"

"I have never lied in my whole life, and now you say that I am lying?" Denis winks with his eye. "Your honor, do you think that I can go fishing without a plummet? If I go fishing with live bait, how can it get to the bottom of the river without a plummet? You think I am lying." Dennis gave a short subdued laugh. "What would happen to the live bait if it flowed on the surface of the water? All the big fish worth catching, whether perch or pike, always live near the bottom. And if the bait only floats on the surface, then only small fish are caught, like baby perch or trout. But we do not have trout, for it likes big spaces."

"Why do you tell me stories about the lake trout?"

"Because all of the gentlemen who come to our river all fish in the same way; even the youngest boys never go fishing without a plummet. Only people who do not know anything about fishing can go without it. You can always find a stupid guy who does this."

"Let me see if I understand you correctly. Are you telling me that you unscrewed this nut for the sole purpose of making a plummet?"

"Yes, what else? I was not going to play knuckle-bones."

"But you can get lead for the plummet, using a bullet or a big nail of some kind."

"You cannot just find a piece of lead on the road, you have to buy it, and the nail won't do the trick. You cannot find anything better than the nut from the railway track, for it is heavy and already has a hole."

"It seems to me that you are pretending to be a fool—as if you were born yesterday, or you just fell from the sky. Do not you understand what could have happened as a result of unscrewing those nuts? If the railway guard had not noticed you, then the train could have gone off its rails, causing an accident where people could have been killed. You could have killed many!"

"God save me from this, your honor. Why would I kill? Do you think that we do not believe in God, or that we are some sort of criminals? Thank God, I have lived a long life and have never killed anyone, but I never even had thoughts about doing so. Help us, holy mother; what are you talking about, dear sir?"

"Why do you think that train accidents happen on the railway? After you unscrew a couple of nuts, the rail won't hold in its place, and an accident can occur."

Dennis smiles as he squints his eyes at the interrogator in disbelief. "Don't tell me this! All the guys in our village have been unscrewing nuts for years. Only now has anyone mentioned train accidents and people being killed. You would unscrew a whole section, carry the rail away, or cut a tree and put a huge log across the railway—then maybe the train would have an accident, but in this case—this is nothing, it's just a trifle, just a nut!"

"Do you not understand that these nuts are attaching the rails to the railway ties?

"We understand this, for we do not unscrew all the nuts. We take just some, here and there, and we try to calculate how we do it, logically. We do understand."

"About a year ago, a train fell off its rails at this location," the interrogator comments. " Now I understand why it happened."

"What did you say, sir?" asks Dennis.

"Now I understand why that train had its accident."

"You are an educated person, and so you understand everything, your honor. God gave you this understanding. But we know that the security guard is one of us, just a peasant, but he showed me no respect. He grabbed me roughly by my shirt collar and dragged me before the police. First you should talk to people, and then take action. Yes, he is a peasant with a peasant mind. You should make note, sir, that he hit me right on my jaw, and then my chest."

"When they were searching your house, they found another nut. Where did you unscrew it from and when did you do it?"

"Are you talking about the nut that was lying under my little red chest?"

"I don't know exactly in what part of your house it was hidden, but they found it. When did you unscrew this nut?"

"I did not unscrew it. It was John, the son of the lame Sam, who gave it to me."

"I am talking about the second nut, the one we found in the front yard in the carriage, that we have linked to Dimitry."

"What nut are you talking about? Who's Dimitry? The only other place anyone can get nuts from is Mat Petrov. He makes fishing nets and sells them to the landlords. He gets lots of nuts like this every year. For each fishing net, he needs at least ten of them."

"Listen to me. Paragraph 1081 of the criminal code says that for any damage done with malicious intent to the railway, which endangers the railway train while moving on its particular railway track, which leads to the possibility of a train accident, should be punished. You should have known about the possibility of an accident, and the punishment is that this person is to be sentenced to prison."

"You know better, your honor. We are uneducated people. I cannot even read. How can I understand what you are talking about?"

"You understand everything. You are lying to me, you pretender."

"How can I pretend or lie? Ask anyone in the village if you do not believe me. Without the plummet, you can go fishing only for the perch or small trout, which are worse than gudgeon, and even then you cannot catch it with the fishing rod without a plummet."

"Then tell me more about the trout."

"They cannot have much trout there. Sometimes we go fishing with fishing rods using butterfly as bait, then you can catch some salmon. But this rarely happens."

Several moments of silence follow this conversation. Dennis shifts his weight from one foot to the other. He squints at the interrogator, who is quickly writing something down.

"Can I go now?" Dennis asks after a period of silence.

"No, I have to take you into custody and send you to prison."

Dennis lifts his glance to the investigator, and says, "What do you mean you are sending me to prison? Your honor! I do not have time. I have to go to the market. I have to pay three rubles to George for the meat he took from the butcher."

"Keep silent! Do not interfere with my work."

"How can you take me to prison? If only I did something bad, but—for this, over nothing? I did not steal anything, and I did not beat anyone. If it's about my not paying my debts, your honor, please do not listen to the city hall clerk. He does not know what he is talking about.

"Keep quiet."

"I am keeping quiet."

"Stop talking."

Dennis mumbles under his breath, "The city hall clerk was lying in his report. There are three brothers in the family— Koozma, then George, and then me, Dennis."

"You are interfering with my work!! Officer," the interrogator cries out on the hall. "Take him into custody right away and deliver him to his cell."

"There are three brothers, three of us," Dennis mumbles as two big strong officers take him by the arm and bring his to a cell. "A brother should not be responsible for his brother's actions. If he does not pay taxes, why should I be responsible for his actions? Hey, judge, too bad the general has died; he was a great man who would have told you how to deal with this properly. You can flog me, or beat me up, at least that way I get what I deserve for what I have done."

DEATH OF AN OFFICE WORKER

━━◦❈◦━━

One wonderful evening, an office gofer, Mr. Ivan Dmitrievich Worm, sat in the second row of a theater, watching the play *Bells of Cornville*. He watched the play and felt himself at the height of bliss. But suddenly . . .

Many stories have that phrase, "but suddenly." Authors are right: life is filled with unexpected turns of events.

But suddenly, he scowled, rolled his eyes upward, stopped breathing for a while, averted his gaze from his binoculars, bent his body and, and then, "Achoo!" he sneezed, as you see.

Everyone is allowed to sneeze. All kind of people sneeze: peasants, police chiefs; even secret councilors do it sometimes. Anyone can sneeze.

Mr. Worm was not confounded; he wiped his forehead with a handkerchief and, being a polite man, looked around to make sure he had not disturbed anyone with his sneezing. At this point he did become confounded. He saw an old man sitting right in front of him, in the first row, diligently wiping his bald head with a glove and mumbling to himself. Mr. Worm instantly realized that the old man was the state general Whining, who served at the Ministry of Railways.

"I sneezed on him; I spewed my saliva all over his head!" Mr. Worm thought. "He is somebody else's boss, not mine; but I do feel rather uncomfortable. I must apologize."

Mr. Worm cleared his throat, leaned his body forward, and whispered in the general's ear:

"Excuse me, Your Honor, for sneezing on you; I did not mean it."

"Quite all right; think nothing of it."

"Please do forgive me, for heaven's sake. I did not—I did not intend to do it."

"Please, do be quiet. I want to hear the play."

Mr. Worm became even more confused, forced a stupid smile, and turned his gaze to the stage. He watched the play but got no more pleasure from it. He felt anxious.

During the intermission, he approached Mr. Whining, cornered him, and then, fighting his shyness, mumbled, "I spit at you, Your Honor. I did not mean it. So please forgive me, dear sir."

"Please stop this. I have already forgotten it, and you still remember? Please let it go," the general said, impatiently twitching his lower lip.

"He's forgotten, but he has this evil look in his eyes," thought Mr. Worm, looking suspiciously at the general. "He doesn't even want to talk to me. I must explain to him that I didn't intend to do it; it's the law of nature. Otherwise he might think I did it on purpose. He won't think about it right now, but he might later on."

When Mr. Worm came home, he told his wife the story of

his ignorance. It seemed to him that his wife paid too little attention to the event; at first she was alarmed, but then, after she found that the general was from another ministry, she calmed down.

"But, anyway, you ought to go ask for forgiveness," she said. "Otherwise he might think you don't know how to behave in public."

"That's it; that's exactly how I feel. I apologized to the general, but he behaved somewhat strangely. He said nothing definite. And besides, we didn't have enough time to talk then."

The next day, Mr. Worm put on his new uniform coat, cut his hair, and went to Whining to explain and apologize. When he entered the general's waiting room he saw many visitors, and then the general himself, surrounded by the crowd. After the general had spoken to a few people, he lifted his eyes to Mr. Worm.

"Your Honor, you might remember me. Yesterday, at the Arcadia Theater," the executor reported, "I sneezed, and then, quite by chance, I dropped it on you."

"What a trifle, for heaven's sake! What are you going on about? How can I help you?" the general addressed the next visitor.

"He doesn't even want to talk to me," thought Mr. Worm, turning pale. "He must be angry with me. No, I can't leave this in such a state. I will explain everything to him in a moment."

When the general finished talking to the last visitor and turned to go into the back room, Mr. Worm stepped up to him and mumbled, "Your Honor! If I dare impose on your time, sir, it is only due to the feelings of remorse I am experiencing at the moment. I did not do it on purpose, sir."

The general made a sour face and waved his hand in the air.

"You mock me, sir!" he said, taking cover behind the door.

"What mockery?" thought Mr. Worm. "It's nothing of the

kind. The general just didn't get it! I won't apologize to him anymore, the freak. Forget that. I'll write him a letter, but I'm not going to go to see him in person again."

Mr. Worm thought about it all the way home. He did not write a letter to the general. He thought about the text of the letter, but could not make up his mind what to write. So, he had to go see the general in person the next day.

"Yesterday I dared disturb Your Honor," he started mumbling when the general lifted his inquiring eyes to him. "But I did not do so with the purpose of mocking you, as Your Honor informed me. I was merely apologizing for sneezing and dropping my sneeze upon you; I did not at all plan to mock you. How could I dare mock you?

"If we simple people should start mocking important persons, then there would be no respect for such persons, and then, you know—"

"Get out of here! Get out!" yelled the general at the top of his voice, his face turning blue and his body trembling.

"What did you say, sir?" asked Mr. Worm in a whisper, frozen with terror.

"Get out!" repeated the general, and stomped his foot with rage.

Suddenly something broke in Mr. Worm's heart. Hearing and seeing nothing, he backed out to the door, went out into the street, and dragged himself home. He got home mechanically, and, without taking off his official uniform coat, lay down on the sofa and died.

75 GRAND

‹‹ ⊨‡⊨ ››

L ate at night, about midnight, two friends were walking along Tverskoy Boulevard. The first man was tall and handsome, with brown hair. He was wearing an old bear fur coat and a brown top hat. The second man was a short redhead who wore a dark red coat with polished ebony buttons. Both were silent as they went. The first whistled a tune, and the second looked gloomily under his feet as they walked, and spat to the side from time to time.

"Would you like to sit for a while?" the brown-haired man suggested as they were passing the dark monument of Pushkin and the dimly lit entrance of the Strastnoi Monastery. The redhead consented, and the two friends sat down on a park bench.

"I have a small personal favor to ask you, Nikolai Borisovich," said the dark-haired man after some silence between them. "Dear friend, can you lend me ten or fifteen rubles? I will give the money back to you in a week." The redhead said nothing.

"I would never have asked you if not for extreme necessity. Fate has played a lousy joke on me. My wife gave me her bracelet earlier today to pawn. She has to pay for her sister's tuition.

"So I pawned it, then played cards and lost the money."

The red-haired man moved on his seat and cleared his throat.

"You are not a serious man, Vasily Ivanych," he said with an evil smile.

"Not a serious man at all. You had no right to sit down and play those cards. How could you gamble if you knew that it was not your money you were betting?"

He continued, "Wait, don't interrupt me, let me tell you once and for all. Why do you need all these new clothes, this pin on your tie? You are a poor man, why do you want to look fashionable? Why are you wearing this stupid hat? You live at your wife's expense and then go and pay one hundred fifty rubles for that hat on your head." Vasily touched the hat he was wearing on his head.

"You could have a nice fur hat that only costs three rubles, and neither fashion nor beauty would suffer. Why do you always boast about your important friends, if you don't know these people? You said that you personally know Ivanov, Plevako, and other publishers. I was burning with shame at your name-dropping nonsense. You lied without even blushing! And when you played cards and lost your wife's money to those women tonight, you were wearing such a stupid grin, I would be ashamed to have anything to do with you. I don't even want to slap your face."

"Stop it. You're in a rotten mood today. Enough!"

"All right, I can admit that you act like an idiot because you are too young. But Vasily, I can't understand it. How can you play cards and cheat? I saw you pull the ace of spades from the bottom of the pack!"

Vasily Ivanovich blushed like a high school student and tried to apologize. The accusations of the red-haired man continued. They had a long, loud dispute. Finally, they calmed down and became silent.

"Yes, it is true, I have done wrong," said the brown-haired man after a long silence. "It is true. I spent too much money. And now I am in debt. I spent my wife's money and I can't find the way out. Have you ever felt like you are itchy all over, and there is no cure? This is how I feel now. I feel terrible about myself. I'm in it up to my neck. I am ashamed of myself, and of the human race in general. I make mistakes, I do bad things, I have low motives, and I cannot stop, I am too bad!" He scratched his chin. "If I were to receive an inheritance or win the lottery, then I think I would be able to give up my bad habits and start all over again. And you, Nikolai Borisovich, please don't blame me. Don't throw stones at me. Remember Mr. Clumsy."

"I remember him very well," said the red-haired man. "I remember him. He spent somebody else's money at a restaurant to show off in front of his girlfriend, and he wound up crying on her shoulder, although he wasn't crying before he did it.

"It's shameful to even speak of that scoundrel. If he didn't have good manners or such nice looks, the girl would never have fallen in love with him and he would never have repented. Bad people are good-looking as a rule. Like you, for example.

"You're all womanizers. Women don't love you; they only want to have an affair with you. It's strange. You're very lucky with women." The redhead stood up and started pacing around the bench.

"Your wife, for example. She is an honest and noble woman. Why did she fall in love with you? And today, for example, that pretty blonde never moved her glance from you for a second when you lied and played the fool. Women fall in love with men like you. It is completely different with me. I have worked hard all my life. I am an honest man, and I deserve at least one moment of happiness. And then, do you remember, I was engaged to Olga Alekseevna, your wife, a long time ago, before she knew you, and I had a little bit of happiness, and then you came along and I was totally ruined."

"You're jealous!" The dark-haired man smiled. "I didn't know that!"

Anger and disgust appeared on the face of Nikolai Borisovich for a moment. Without understanding what was doing, he stretched his hand forward and waved it. The sound of a slap broke the silence of the night. The brown top hat fell and rolled over the hard-packed snow. The red-haired man became ashamed. He stood up and pushed his nose into the collar of his shabby coat and walked along the boulevard. When he came to the Pushkin monument, he looked back at the brown-haired man, stood for a moment quietly and then, as if afraid of something, started running along Tverskoy Boulevard.

Vasily Ivanych sat in silence, motionless, for a long time. A woman passed him and, laughing, gave him his hat. He mechanically thanked her, stood up, and walked away.

"Now she's going to scold me," he thought, climbing the stairwell to the apartment. "She'll be scolding me the whole night through. Damn her! I'll tell her that I lost her stupid money!"

When he came to his door, he timidly rang the doorbell. The maid let him in.

"Congratulations!" she said, smiling broadly.

"What for?"

"See for yourself! Finally God has had some pity on you!"

Vasily Ivanovich shrugged his shoulders and entered the bedroom. There his wife, Olga Alekseevna, a short blonde with curlers in her hair, sat at the desk. Several finished, sealed letters were in front of her on the desk. The moment she saw her husband, she jumped to her feet and hung around his neck.

"You have come, finally!" she said. "I am so happy! You can't believe how happy I am! I was hysterical for a while after this pleasant surprise. Here, read this!"

She jumped to the table and brought the newspaper to her husband's face.

"Read this! My ticket won seventy-five thousand. Yes, I had a ticket. I give you my word on it. I hid it from you and kept it secret, because you would have pawned it.

"Nikolai Borisovich gave it to me as a gift when he was my fiancée, and then he did not want to take it back. That Nikolai Borisovich is such a nice man! Now we are very rich! You will change for the better now, you can change your life! I understand that you drank and lied to me because of our poverty, I know this. I understand you. I know that you are a clever and honest man."

Olga Alekseevna walked across the room and laughed.

"What a surprise! I was waiting for you, pacing the room. I scolded and hated you for your dissipation, and then I got bored and sat down to read a newspaper. And then I saw it! I have already written letters to all my sisters, my mother. They will be so happy for me! Where are you going?"

Vasily Ivanovich looked at the newspaper. He stood speechless for a while, thinking about something, then replaced his hat and left the room, went out of the house and into the street.

"To Great Dmitovka Street, the furnished apartment N.N.," he told the cabman.

He did not find the woman he was looking for there. The room was locked.

'She's probably at the theater. And after the theater she'll go have supper. I'll wait for a while.'

He waited. He waited for half an hour, then for an hour. He went along the corridor and spoke to a sleepy concierge. He heard the old clock downstairs strike three. Finally, out of patience, he started back down the stairs, but his luck returned.

At the entrance of the building, he bumped into her, a thin, tall brunette wearing a long boa. A man in dark blue sunglasses and a cheap fur hat followed her.

"Excuse me," Vasily Ivanovich addressed the woman. "Can I talk to you for a moment?"

The man and woman frowned.

"Wait a second," the woman said to her companion and went to the nearest lamp post with Vasily Ivanovich.

"What do you want?"

"I want to talk to you—well, let's talk business, Nadine," started Vasily Ivanovich, stumbling. "It's a pity you have this man with you, otherwise I would have told you everything."

"What do you want? I don't have time for this."

"Oh, so you have new admirers and you're in a hurry! Look at you! Do you remember some time ago, before Christmas, when you threw me out? You did not want to live with me because— because I did not make enough money for your lifestyle. But you were wrong. Yes. Do you remember the lottery ticket I gave you as a birthday gift? There, look here! Read! That ticket won seventy-five thousand!"

The woman took the newspaper into her hands and scanned it with eager, almost frightened eyes. And she found what she wanted.

At the same time another pair of eyes, reddened by tears and dumb from woe, looked in the jewelry box for the ticket. These eyes searched for the ticket the whole night through, and could not find it.

The ticket was gone, and Olga Alekseevna knew that her husband had stolen it.

On the same night, the red-haired Nikolai Borisovich turned restlessly in his bed and could not fall asleep until the morning. He was ashamed of that slap on the cheek.

AT THE CEMETERY

⸻

"Where are his jokes, his cases, and his tricks?"
—Hamlet

"Dear gentlemen, it is cold, and dark, shall we head home?"

The gust of wind touched the yellow leaves of old birch trees.

The leaves drenched us all with many droplets of water. One of us slid on the claylike soil and had to grab at a big gray cross in order to stop his slide downhill. Its inscription read,

'A general, a secret councilor, decorated with orders and medals, George Black, is lying here.'

"I knew this man. He loved his wife, had medals of honor, and never read anything in his life. His stomach was working properly. He died from an accident. Truly, but if not for that accident he would have kept on living. He died as a victim of his own observations. One day, he was eavesdropping behind a door, which swung to hit him so hard he was given a severe concussion from the blow, dying shortly after. Now, look at this monument. This man hated poetry all his life, see his headstone there? Do you see the irony? His entire tombstone is completely covered with poetry; what an ironic twist of fate! Look, someone is headed our way."

A man in a shabby old overcoat and a reddish complexion with a blue aftershave hue on his face was coming over to us. He had a bottle of vodka under his arm and a ham sandwich sticking out of his pocket.

"Do you know by any chance where I can find the grave of the actor Bugsy?" he inquired of us in a hoarse voice.

We led him over to the grave of that actor, who had passed away about two years ago.

"Are you an office worker?" we asked him.

"No, I am an actor. These days, it is hard to see a difference between an office worker and an actor, which we actors do not find very flattering."

So, we finally found Bugsy's grave. It had partially fallen down in the earth, and was covered with weeds, and did not look like a grave at all. There was small cheap cross on it, lying crooked to one side, covered with moss, looking worn out, as if it were ill. The inscription said, ". . . forgettable friend Mr. Bugsy."

Time and the elements had worn out the prefix "un" from the word "unforgettable" and revealed the human lie.

The actor bowed in front of his friend's grave, almost touching the grass, as he mentioned how his fellow actors and journalists had raised money for a great monument, then drank most of it away.

"How did you know they drank the funds away?" we asked.

"It's very simple, they took an ad out in the local paper

asking people to contribute to his monument, then spent it all getting drunk. To your health,"—he turned to us—"and to his eternal memory."

"Our health will not get any better, and eternal memory is a very sad thing."

"You are right! He was a famous artist, Mr. Bugsy. They brought lots of flowers and several wreaths for his funeral, but now he is completely forgotten! Those he had been kind to have forgotten him, and those he treated badly will never forget him. For example, I will never forget him because he only acted with evil toward me. He's a dead man now, God save his soul!"

"What bad things did he do to you?"

"He caused a huge misfortune for me, a terrible blow." He sighed again, and an angry expression appeared on his face. "He was a bad man for me, God save his soul. When I was but a young man, I saw him perform, and decided to choose acting as my profession. He lured me from my parents' home, brought me into the artistic life and gave me only tears and failure. The life of an actor is truly tragic! I lost both my youth and my sobriety. I do not remotely look now as if I was created in the image of God. I am completely broke, the heels on my shoes are worn out, my pants have turned into laces at the bottom and look like a chessboard covered with numerous dirty spots. And my face—it looks like a dog has been chewing on my face for a long time! I had liberal ideas, and free thought. He took away even my faith! If only I could have the talent of a great actor—but no, I just wasted my entire life.

"It's getting cold, dear gentlemen. Would you like a drink? There's enough for all of us. Ha-ha-ha! Let us drink for the peace of his soul. Even if he is dead, I do not like him; he was the only person in this world left to me, and now I am all alone.

I am seeing him for the last time. The doctors have told me that I will soon die from alcoholism. So I came to say good-bye. We have to forgive our enemies."

We left, and the actor kept on talking to the dead Mr. Bugsy as the cold drizzle started again. We returned to the major alley, where we met another funeral procession. Four porters dressed in white belts, wearing dirty high boots plastered with leaves were passing as they carried a brown coffin. It was getting dark, and they were in a hurry. The coffin swayed as they hurried along on their way.

"We have been here for only two hours, and we have just seen our third funeral procession, dear gentlemen. Should we not go home now?"

THE CONVERSATION OF
A MAN WITH A DOG

t happened one winter, on a frosty night, with the sky lit by a full moon.

Alexander Ivanovich Singer plucked a little green devil from his sleeve, carefully opened the wicket-fence gate and entered his front yard.

"The man, as a human being," he was philosophizing while trying to balance in mud and not to fall in a heap of garbage, "man is a bunch of dust, a hallucination, and ashes. For example, let us take my overseer Pavel Nikolayevich. He is the governor, so he is ashes as well, but his greatness is just a dream, a fog, an illusion—the wind will blow at it and it will disappear."

"Grr-rrr-rrr!! Woof, woof!" The sounds of a dog interrupted the philosopher's line of thought.

Mr. Singer looked to his side and saw a huge gray sheepdog, the size of a large wolf. It was sitting near the little house of the security guard, clinking with a chain. Mr. Singer thought about something, and his face took on a surprising expression. Then he shrugged his shoulders and smiled sadly.

"Grr-rrr-rrr! Woof!" the dog repeated.

"I do not understand." Singer waved his hands at his sides. "You growl at a human being. I am here for the first time in my life. Don't you understand that man is the crown of creation? Look at me, I am talking to you. Look! Am I human or not?"

"Grr-rrr! Woof!"

"Are you trying to make a point? Give me your paw." Mr. Singer stretched his hand out towards the dog.

"You don't want it? Then I will slap you, just lightly. I do this with affection!"

"Woof, woof! Grr-rrr!" The dog's fur was raised as he snarled at the man.

"Aha, now I see your point. You want to bite me. I will take notice of this. So, you do not respect me, as a man, the crowning achievement of creation? This means that you can bite even Pavel Nikolayevich, doesn't it? Do you really mean it? Everyone respects him, and you—you do not show any respect to him. Do I correctly understand your meaning? Does it mean that you are a socialist? Listen, you should tell me the truth— are you a socialist?"

"Grr-rrr! Woof! Woof!"

"What I was talking about? Do not bite! Wait! Yes, the ashes. The wind will blow, and the ashes will disappear. Puh! And what is the purpose of our existence, may I ask you kindly? We were born to our mothers, and then we eat, drink, and study science. Why? Why do we do this? This is all ashes. A man's life does not cost anything! You are a dog and you cannot understand me, but if you could get into human . . . human psychology! If only you could understand me!"

Mr. Singer turned his head and spat on the ground.

"Dirt is on my lips! You think that I, Mr. Singer, an office worker, am the crown of creation and the king of all animals? You are mistaken! I am an idler, a bribe-taker, and a hypocrite. I am a bad man."

Mr. Singer hit himself on the chest and began to weep.

"I am a gossiper as well. And I whisper in other people's ears. Right now, I am reporting to the overseer on other people. Do you think that George Korney was fired without my help, hmm? Hmm? And what do you think—who was it, if not me, who stole the two thousand from the charity money and them blamed it all on Mr. Staples? Was it not me? Yes, I am a hypocrite, a Judas, a liar, a yes-man, an extortionist, and usurper. I really am a nasty, bad man."

Mr. Singer wiped tears from his face with his sleeve, crying in earnest.

"Bite me! Eat me! Tear me to pieces! No one has said one sincere and kind word to me my entire life. They all say behind my back I am a mean person. When they talk to me and look me in the face, they smile and praise me. I really would prefer to be slapped across my face and scolded for all that I've done!

"Eat me, dog! Bite me! Tear me to pieces!"

Mr. Singer waved his hands in the air, trying to keep his balance, and then fell on top of the dog, "Yes, exactly like this, tear my face! I do not care. It is painful, but feel free to bite me, and my hands, too! Aha! Look, I am bleeding, this is what I deserve. Thank you, Buddy!

"You can tear my expensive fur coat as well. I received it as a bribe. I ratted on my neighbor, and for the money from that deal I bought this coat. And my hat as well, I do not care. What can I tell you? Time for me to go! Good-bye, dear dog! Good-bye, my friend!"

"Grr-rrr! Woof!"

Mr. Singer petted the dog one more time, let it bite his calf again, then covered himself with his torn overcoat and, wobbling heavily from side to side as a drunk man might, headed to his door.

When he woke up around midday the next day, Mr. Singer saw something very unusual. He noticed his head, his hands, and his legs were covered with bandages. Next to his bed, he spotted his wife, her face covered with tears, and the doctor with a concerned expression on his face.

THE WALLET

❧

Three traveling actors—Mr. Popov, Mr. Smirnov, and Mr. Drummer (Balabaikin in Russian), were walking along the railway tracks one beautiful morning, when they found a wallet. Upon opening it, to their great surprise and pleasure, they were shocked to find twenty bank notes, six winning lottery tickets, and a check for three thousand rubles inside.

Elated with this fortunate and unexpected turn of events, they cried "Hurray, hurray!" They then sat down beside the railway tracks and began to talk about what they could do with this money.

"How much did we find in total?" Mr. Smirnov asked out loud, as he counted the money. "Oh my, we have about fifteen thousand four hundred fifty rubles cash plus lottery tickets. I would die for such money!"

"Not only am I happy for myself," said Drummer, "but for you both as well, my dear friends. Now none of us will go hungry, or have to walk barefoot ever again. I am also happy about art, and what this will do for our profession, as we are all actors. First of all, brothers, I'm going to head straight for Moscow, to meet with the best clothes designer, Mr. Aiat. I will have him custom design me a real French costume. I do not want to take the farmers and secondary roles anymore. I will only take lead roles of playboys, from now on. I will also buy a beautiful hat and a classy suit."

"First, I suggest we have something nice to eat and drink," decided Popov, the young romantic lead actor. "For the past three days, we've only been eating junk food. What do you think?"

"Yes, my dear friend," Smirnov agreed. "We have lots of money and we have nothing to eat at the moment. You know what, Popov, you are the youngest here and you are the fastest walker. Here, take some money—here is ten from the wallet—and fetch us some food. My dear, see that small village over there? There, right behind that hill, see the top of the church? That looks like a nice little town, with a tavern; you should be able to find all we need. Buy a bottle of vodka, a pound of sausage, two loaves of bread, and some fish. We will wait for you here, my talented friend."

Popov took the money and turned toward town. Mr. Smirnov, with tears in his eyes, hugged him three times, and called him his dearest friend, his angel, and his inspiration. Mr. Drummer also embraced him, with tears in his eyes, and the three pledged to their eternal friendship.

After all this, Popov walked along the tracks, heading for the village. He began to talk to himself. "What happiness is this? Between us, we did not have a single penny, and now we are rich. We've really made it big. As for me, I am going to return to my small home town, Kostroma, hire some staff and build a really nice theater. However, with only five thousand you cannot buy even a decent barn. If only the whole wallet were mine! That would make all the difference. Then I could build a huge theater! There you go! My compliments!" he pretended to direct people into his theater. "Truthfully, those two friends of mine—Smirnov and Drummer—are terrible actors. They have no talent. They are complete buffoons. They would waste this money on nothing important, but me, I would bring some happiness to our country and become famous. I know what I will do—I will poison the vodka. Unfortunately, they will die, but there will be a theater in the town of Kostroma, a huge and magnificent theater the likes of which this country has never seen. I seem to recall the British prime minister, McMahon, saying that any actions can be justified if they serve the proper purpose. And he was a great person."

As he was walking and pondering his choices, his companions, Smirnov and Drummer were having the following discussion.

"Our friend Popov is a nice man," Mr. Smirnov said with tears on his eyes. "I love him and I recognize his great talent. But do you know what I think? This money will destroy him. He will either waste it entirely on vodka, or he will start up one of his schemes, another faulty business enterprise, lose it all, and destroy himself. He is way too young to have such a large amount of money at his age, my dear friend. Don't you agree, Drummer?"

"Yes," Mr. Drummer agreed, as he clasped Smirnov around the shoulders in a brotherly manner.

"He still behaves like a child. What purpose will this money serve him? We are so different from him. We are family-oriented, positive people. For us, some extra money means so much more than just money." There was a pause.

"You know what, brother, there is nothing more to say. Let

us kill him later today, and get it over with. Then, we will both have eight thousand each. When we head back to Moscow, we will say that he was killed by a passing train. I love him dearly, as you well know, but I think in the interest of great acting, above all, and it is the right course of action to take. Besides, he has no real talent and he is as emotional as a piece of wood."

"What did you say?" Smirnov inquired nervously. "He is such a nice, honest boy. But, on the other hand, to tell you the truth, he is a smart-ass, a nosy little bugger. We'll kill him now, and he would even be grateful to us for sending him to a better place, I truly believe. Oh, my dear friend! He should not be sad, because when we get back to Moscow, we will write the most touching obituary for the newspapers. That's what true friends would do!"

They did just as they had said. When Popov returned from the village with the food, his friends, Smirnov and Drummer, welcomed him back warmly, hugged him, and spoke to him for some time trying to convince him that he was a great actor, before killing him. Then, they put him on the railway tracks, to hide the evidence.

After dividing the money that they had found, Smirnov and Drummer, emotionally uplifted, sat down for a drink and a bite to eat, being completely sure that their crime would go unpunished.

But goodness always wins in the end, and evildoers are always punished. The poison Popov had put in the vodka was a very strong one. After their first shot, they were both lying breathless on the railway track.

An hour later, the crows were flying over them, crowing.

This story teaches us that no matter how an actor praises you, calls you his best friend and very talented, never forget that by trade he is, after all, an actor.

A DEAD BODY

———❦———

I t was a quiet, still night in August. The fog slowly lifted from over the field and covered everything as far as could be seen. In the full moon, it looked like either a quiet limitless sea or a huge white wall. The air was damp and cold. Dawn was still a long way off.

A few steps away from the edge of a huge forest, a small, flickering light could be glimpsed. Under a young oak lay a dead body, swathed from head to toe in clean white linen. A small amulet lay on its chest. Next to the dead body, there were two guards on duty, two local farmers who were doing one of the most unpleasant and disrespected duties in the neighborhood. One had a barely visible mustache and thick, dark eyebrows. He was sitting on the wet grass in a torn overcoat and peasant boots, stretching his legs, trying to pass the time with a little work. He made a loud noise as he drew his breath, carving a spoon from a piece of wood.

The second, elderly man was short, his face covered with smallpox scars, with a thin mustache and a small goatee. He sat with his hands clasped around his bent knees, motionless on the ground, looking at the fire. Right between them was a little bonfire, flickering slightly and almost dying, lighting their faces with a red glow. It was quiet: only the wood being scraped by the cutting knife and the firewood crackling as it burned could be heard.

"And you, Sam, do not fall asleep," the young man said.

"I am not sleeping," the man with the goatee said. "It is too scary for just one person to sit here alone."

"You are a strange man, Sam! Others would laugh, tell stories, but you—well, you just sit here staring at the fire, like a scarecrow, with your eyes wide open. You cannot even say a word properly. You speak as if you are afraid of something. You've already passed fifty, and you have less intelligence than a child. Are you disappointed that you are a half-wit?"

"Yes, I am," the goateed man replied gloomily.

"Then, what do you think, is it pleasant for the rest of us to be around your stupidity? You are a kind man, you don't drink, but with this misfortune, you simply don't have any brains. Since God took the ability to think away from you, then you should at least make the effort to try to think by yourself. Just try, Sam. When you hear people say something clever, you would do well to listen and think it over. Think! If you do not understand something, make an effort, try to understand the meaning of the word. Do you know what I am talking about? Make an effort! For if you do not, you will live out the rest of your life like this, and die a half-wit."

Suddenly, there was a sharp, loud noise that came from the forest, from not too far off. It seemed that something fell from the top of a tree, making a shuffling noise as it fell to the ground. The night echo repeated the sound. The younger man trembled, looking at his friend with a questioning face.

"It's an owl, it is out hunting little birds," Sam stated gloomily.

"Sam, the birds should have flown south by now."

"Yes, the time has come."

"The nights are growing colder."

"Yes, they are."

"Herons are very tender and sensitive birds. A cold like this would be the death of them. I am getting cold, too. Can you put more wood on the fire?"

Sam stood up and disappeared into the dark forest.

While Sam was busy breaking up the dry branches, his friend closed his eyes, startled by every sharp sound. Sam brought a bunch of firewood from the bush and placed it on top of the bonfire. The fire lazily licked the black branches with its fiery tongue. Suddenly, as if given an order, the fire embraced the branches, illuminating the road, the contours of the bush, the dead body, and the faces of two men with a red glow.

The guardmen kept silent. The younger man bent his neck even lower as he nervously returned to his work. The man with the goatee sat motionless as before, without averting his gaze from the fire.

"Those who hate Zion will be ashamed by God," they suddenly heard a male voice recite in the dark. Then they heard quiet steps and glimpsed a dark figure appear, lit by the crimson light of the bonfire. He was dressed in a long black overcoat and a white hat, wearing a dark knapsack on his back.

"God has his will for everything. Oh, my Lord," the man spoke in a very high-pitched voice. "I saw light in the darkness, and rejoiced. First I thought you were one of locals bringing their herds to the pastures. But I figured that you could not be cowboys because I could not see your horses. Then I thought that you were robbers, or traveling gypsy musicians. However I thought that whatever happens will happen, and I hurried due to the cold. When I got closer, I realized that you were neither robbers nor traveling gypsies. Peace be to you!"

"Hello. What can we do for you?"

"Hey brothers, can you tell me how to get to the Mackuhin factory?"

"It is close by. Go straight, just keep on walking along this road for about two miles, and you will see the village of Ananovo. That is where we live. From there, my friend, turn right at the riverbank and after a while you will see the Ananovo Factory buildings in the distance, about three miles."

"Thank God! And why are you sitting here?"

"We are on guard duty. Do not you see the dead body?"

"What? Where is the body? Oh my goodness!" The wanderer saw the dead body and trembled so hard his hands jittered.

This unusual situation left a depressing impression on the stranger. He bent over, opened his mouth without saying a word, eyes bulging, and stood motionless for about three minutes, as if he did not believe his eyes. He then started mumbling very quickly, "Oh my God! I was walking without bothering anyone, and here I find this ordeal in the middle of the night. Oh my God!"

"Where are you going? Are you a clergyman?"

"No-no, I was just returning home from a visit to a monastery. Do you know the factory manager, Michael, Michael Polikarpych? I am his nephew. Oh my God! Everything in God's hands. And what are you doing here?"

"We are guarding the body."

"Oh yes, yes," the man in the black overcoat mumbled. "And where did he come from, this dead man?"

"He is just a traveler who died passing through town."

"So brothers, I have to go. I am scared to death! I am afraid of dead bodies over all else, and now look at this. When a person is living, no one cares, but when he is dead and decaying, we are afraid of him. Maybe he was a great general, or another important leader. How was he killed?"

"Who knows? Only God knows. Maybe he was murdered, maybe he died by himself. We have no idea."

"Oh, yes, yes. And you know, brothers, maybe his soul is enjoying the pleasures of paradise."

"His soul is still wandering around his body," said one of the men on duty. "The soul does not go far from the body for three days."

"Yes, so people say. So should I go straight, without turning?"

"Yes, until you get to the village. And then you have to turn right, at the riverbank."

"When I get to the riverbank, I walk along it? All right, I'd better get going. Good-bye, brothers!"

The man in the back overcoat took about five steps along the road and then stopped. "I forgot to leave a penny for his burial. Brothers, can I put a penny here?"

"You should know better, because you have been visiting the monastery. If he died from natural causes, then it will be for his soul; if he killed himself, it's a sin."

"It's true. If he killed himself, then it is better I keep my money, for all men are sinners. . . . Even if you give me ten thousand rubles, I would never stay here overnight. Good-bye, brothers."

The man in the black overcoat walked away a few more steps and again stopped. "I cannot decide what I should do next," he mumbled. "Should I stay here near the bonfire and wait till dawn? That is scary. To walk away into the darkness is scary, too. The whole way, the picture of the dead man will be all I can see. Here is my ordeal. I went for a few hundred miles, and it was all right, but now when I get closer to my house . . . Oh my goodness, I cannot walk anymore."

"It's true, this is scary."

"I am not afraid of wolves, robbers, or darkness, but I am afraid of dead bodies. I'm scared, that's all there is to it. Hey brothers, I am asking you—I beg you, please take me to the village!"

"We are not allowed to leave the body."

"No one will know, brothers. I am telling you, no one will see it. God will reward you for this! Hey you, with the beard, please do me this favor! Hey you! Why are you so quiet?"

"He is our village fool," answered the young man.

"Then you will please see me off, my friend! I will give you fifty kopecks."

"If I could, I would," the man said, rubbing the back of his head, "but it is not allowed. However, if Sam agrees to sit here by himself, I will. Hey Sam, will you stay by yourself?"

"Yes, I will," the local fool replied.

"Then we're agreed."

The young man stood up, and went with the man in the black overcoat. A minute later, their steps and their conversation faded away. Sam closed his eyes, and sat quietly. The fire began to die out, getting darker and darker, until the dead body was covered with a big black shadow.

TOO MUCH TALKING!

(Abridged)

———— ✦ ————

When the land surveyor Ivan Gavrilovich Smirnov came to the railroad station at Rottenville (Gnilushki in Russian) he asked around and found out that he had to go another thirty or forty miles to the plot of land he had been requested to survey. He would have to take a cab to get there.

"Can you please tell me, sir, where can I find a cab?" the land surveyor addressed a policeman on the station platform.

"What, a cab? This is such a remote place that you cannot even find a decent dog for one hundred miles around, not to mention cabs. Where are you going?"

"To Devkino, the estate of General Hohotov."

"I think you should go to the station building over there. Sometimes you can find local farmers, and they can give you a lift. They do this on occasion for the passengers." The policeman yawned.

The land surveyor gave a deep sigh and slowly walked toward the station building.

There, after a lengthy search, many conversations and hesitations, he found a huge peasant, a very gloomy fellow with a pox-bitten face, dressed in a well-worn peasant coat and peasant shoes.

"God only knows what kind of cab this is. I cannot tell which is the front or back seat, it is so dark."

"You sit in this seat here and I will sit in the other seat, which we will call the front seat," said the driver. Finally, the cab began to rock and a little later moved slowly from its place.

"Why are you going so slowly?" inquired the land surveyor as they crept their way along the country road filled with bumps and holes. He was quite surprised by the ability of the cabman to drive with such turtlelike slowness with all the shaking that occurred with each bump.

"We will get there," answered the cabman to calm him down. "The cab will warm up. Then no one will stop it, it will go so fast."

When they left the railroad station, it was getting dark. A completely black, frozen prairie stretched to the right of the land surveyor, seemingly without end. If you drive there you will probably reach the devil's remotest place. At the horizon, where the land disappeared as it merged with the sky, the evening autumn sun was dying. To the left of the road, through the darkening air, you could see some hills, either hay bales or village dwellings. The land surveyor could not see what was happening in front of them due to the huge back of the driver obstructing his view. It was cold and frosty.

"What kind of a remote place is this," the land surveyor thought, trying to keep his nose from getting cold with the collar of his winter coat. "Not a single soul around. Anything can happen here—strangers could attack you and rob you, and no one would know. There must be robbers everywhere in these kinds of places. No one would hear you, even if you screamed as loud as you could. This driver is not safe—look at his huge back. This enormous man could flick you with one finger—and I would be done for. Look at him—he has an animallike, suspicious face, too."

"Hey, my dear man, what is your name?" asked the land surveyor.

"My name is Kleem."

"So, Kleem, is it dangerous around here? Do you have any problems with robbers?"

"No, not at all. Who on earth could you rob out here?"

"That's good. Listen, just in case, I brought three revolvers," the land surveyor lied. "I can deal with ten robbers at a time, yes, I'd take care of them."

It was getting increasingly dark. The car slowed down, made a squeaking, squealing noise and, as if unwillingly, turned to the left.

"Where is he taking me?" the land surveyor thought. "We were going straight, and now we've turned to the left. Maybe he's bringing me to a secluded place or forest to try and rob me. Anything could happen out here."

"So you say that it is not dangerous here. That's a pity, because I like to fight with robbers. It only seems that I am a very thin and sick-looking man, but in fact I am as strong as a lion. One day three robbers attacked me, and what do you think happened? I kicked one with such a force that he died instantly. The other two were sentenced to hard labor in Siberia. I don't know where I get my inner strength from. Really. One day, I fought a strong man like you, kicked him once, and then he fell over dead."

Kleem looked back at the land surveyor, winked with all his face, and sped up a little bit.

"Yes, my good man," the land surveyor continued. "You'd better not even try dealing with me on a narrow road. Not only would the robber be without hands and feet, but he would be punished by the court. I personally know a lot of judges and police offices. I am a government officer, a very important person, and all my bosses know where I am headed. They take great care that no harm comes to me. Everywhere on my way, there are undercover police officers, assigned with keeping me safe. Wait! Where are you going?"

"Can't you tell? We've entered a forest."

"Yes, this is definitely a forest," the land surveyor thought. "I get scared so fast. It won't do for him to notice that I am so scared. Why is he looking back at me so often? What's going through his mind? In the beginning the cab was hardly moving, and now—look at how he is speeding."

"Listen Kleem, why are you going so fast?"

"I am not going fast. We were warming up the cab earlier, and now it is warmed enough to run fast, and I can't just stop it all at once. This is the way it works for it to be able to run fast."

"That's a lie, but I do not recommend that you go that fast. Can you slow down, please? Do you hear me? Slow down!"

"Why should I?"

"Because, because . . . my four friends are following us, and it is important that they be able to catch up with me. They promised to meet up with me by this forest, and it will be much more fun to go on as a group. They are huge guys, very strong, all wearing their guns. Why are you looking back at me? Why are you so nervous? You know, I'm really not that interesting. However, I have my handguns here. Wait a second, I will pull them out and show them to you." The land surveyor pretended to be pulling something out of his pockets, when something unexpected happened, even in his state of being scared.

Suddenly, Kleem stopped the cab, jumped out of it, and ran on all fours into the forest.

"Help," he cried out at the top of his voice, "Help! He is trying to kill me! Help!"

The land surveyor heard his fast footsteps, the cracking of the dry wood in the forest, and then everything grew eerily still. The land surveyor, who had not expected such a turn of events, first made sure that the cab was parked. He then sat back down on his seat and started thinking, "He ran away, scared. I am a complete fool. What should I do now? I cannot keep driving as I don't know where we are headed, and besides, everyone will think I stole the cab. What should I do?"

He cried out, "Kleem, Kleem! Where are you, Kleem?"

The echo replied, "Kleem!"

At the thought of sitting here in this dark cold forest for the whole night, listening to the wild animals and the echoes of his voice, the land surveyor felt shivers run down his spine, as if someone had poured a glass of ice water down his collar.

"Kleem! Hey, buddy!" he cried out loudly. "Where are you, Kleem?"

For two hours, the surveyor kept calling the cab driver. Then, when his voice had gotten hoarse, and he couldn't take another minute of thinking he would be here all night, a light wind brought him someone's moan.

"Kleem, is it you, my friend? Let us go!"

"You are going to kill me!"

"I was only joking, Kleem! Look at me! I do not have any hand guns! I was lying to you because I was so scared. Please, let us go. I am asking you! I am really getting cold. It is freezing cold out here. Please, Kleem!"

Kleem probably understood that a real robber would have long disappeared with the cab by this time. He stepped out of the forest, and warily ventured over to his passenger.

"And why was I so stupid that I got scared of you? You made a joke and I got scared! All right, let's get back in the cab. Well, well," Kleem mumbled sitting down in the cab. "If I knew all this, I would never have brought you with me, even for one thousand rubles. I almost died of fear."

Kleem started the cab. It trembled and shook without starting. Kleem started it again and again it shook, making a strange noise. After the fourth attempt, it started moving, slowly rolling down the road. The land surveyor moved up the collar of his overcoat, covering his ears, and was soon lost deep in his thoughts. The rest of the trip he spent in silence. Both the road and the driver did not seem as dangerous as they had before.

CONVERSATION OF A DRUNKEN MAN WITH A SOBER DEVIL

———— ❦ ————

A retired office worker, Mr. Scruffy (Lakhmatov in Russian) sat at his dinner table, drinking his sixteenth shot of vodka while meditating on equality and liberty. Suddenly, a devil looked out at him from behind a table lamp. Now do not be afraid, dear reader. Do you know what a devil is?

This one was a young, well-dressed man with an ugly face as black as a chimney and red, expressive eyes. Even if he is not married, a devil has a pair of horns on his head. His body is covered with green hair and has a doglike smell. Under his back hangs a tail ending in a pointing arrow head. He has claws instead of fingers and horse's hooves instead of feet. Mr. Scruffy grew a little confused after noticing the devil, but then he remembered that green devils tend to appear to all who are drunk, and so he grew calmer.

"With whom do I have the honor?" he addressed the uninvited guest.

The devil grew confused and lowered his eyes.

"Please, do not be shy," continued Mr. Scruffy. "Come closer, please. I am a man without prejudice. You can speak frankly with me, without holding back. Who are you?"

The devil cautiously walked over to Mr. Scruffy, and tucking his tail under him, bowed with respect. "I am a devil," he introduced himself. "I work as a special envoy under the leadership of His Honor, the director of the Administration of Hell, Mr. Satan."

"I have heard of him. It's a pleasure to meet you. Take a seat. Would you like a shot of vodka? What is your occupation?"

The devil grew even more confused.

"Frankly speaking, I am not employed at the moment," he answered, coughing in embarrassment and wiping his nose. "I did have a job some time ago. We were tempting people, seducing them from the path of goodness. Between us, this occupation is not worth a penny. There is no path of good—it does not exist anymore among humans, and so there is nothing to seduce people away from. Besides, people have now become smarter than we are. How can you possibly seduce a person who graduated from college and has seen so much in this world? How can I teach someone how to steal a penny if he, without my help, has already stolen thousands, or even millions?"

"Yes, I agree with that. However, do you do anything special at all?"

"Yes, I do. My old position is mainly a symbolic one. Yet, we do some work. We tempt female junior school teachers, entice the youth to write poetry, and lure young businessmen to break mirrors and windows in public after their parties. I must share that we have not interfered in politics, literature, or science for a long time. We do not understand anything in those areas anymore. Despite this, many of us are working as journalists, and some guys quit working full time in hell and are undercover as humans. Those are the retired devils with different professions—some are lawyers, some are editors and publishers—all very solid, clever, and well-respected people."

"Can you excuse my very personal question—what kind of salary do you get at present?"

"We receive the same as before. Nothing has changed with our pay arrangements. All our expenses, such as lodging, food, and utilities, are paid by the company. However, we are not paid in cash, as we are considered volunteers. You see, a devil is an honorary position. To tell you the truth, our life is hard, and sometimes I feel as if I am a pauper asking for small change. Thanks to humans, we have learned to take bribes. Otherwise, we would have died out a long time ago. So, we live on our small income—giving some supplies and food to the sinners and earning funds via bribes. You see, Satan is getting older, and often hits the nightclubs to see the exotic dancers, and is not taking the time to do proper bookkeeping."

Mr. Scruffy poured another shot of vodka for the devil. He swiftly drank it and grew more talkative. He shared all the secrets of hell, unburdened his heart, and cried for quite a while. Mr. Scruffy liked him so much that he invited him to spend the night as his guest at his place.

The devil accepted. He slept next to the heater, the whole time talking in his sleep as he experienced nightmares. By dawn, he had disappeared.

PSYCHOPATHS

———❦———

The clerk Semyon Alekseevich Nianin, who served his entire career as an assistant secretary in the local county court, and his son George, an utterly colorless retired sergeant who still lives at home, are having dinner together in one of George's small rooms.

As usual, George drinks one glass of wine after another and talks nonstop. His father is pale, and with an expression of deep worry and faint surprise, he looks timidly into his son's eyes and freezes, caught by an inexplicable feeling that reminds him of fear.

"Bulgaria and Romania—this is just the beginning," says George, picking some food from between his teeth with a fork. "You should read what the papers are saying about Greece and Serbia, and what people are saying about England! Greece and Serbia will be the first to start a conflict, then the Turks will join them, and then England will jump in to defend Turkey."

"And France, too. France would never sit out such a conflict." Mr. Nianin remarks, somewhat indecisively.

"Oh my God, you're talking politics again!" Their tenant, Fyodor Fedorovich, is coughing in the next room, clearing his throat. "Have some compassion for a sick man."

"Yes, and France would not stop at this, it would join the fight," George says to his father, ignoring the tenant's cough and remark. "France never forgot about those five billion they lost. You know, my dear, the French know what they are doing! They are just waiting for their chance to have revenge on the Germans and rub salt in their wounds."

"Yes, true. And if the French join the fight, the Germans won't stay back. 'Kommen sie hier, Ivan Andreevich! Sprechen sie Deutsch?' Ha-ha-ha! And then Austria would join the Germans, and then Spain would make advances. Then, China will march into Mongolia. Here you are! Things will happen, my father, that you would never have dreamed of. Just mark my words! You won't believe your eyes."

Mr. Nianin, the older man, is suspicious of everything; ever frightened and distrustful, he stops eating and becomes even more pale. George also stops eating. The father and the son are both cowards, alike in their fear of everything. They are filled with some undefined, inexplicable fear; it comes to them irregularly from nowhere, from beyond measurable time and space. What will become of them? But what exactly will happen, when and where, neither the son, nor the father knows. The old man usually gets scared sitting quietly, without talking; but George cannot live without constantly chattering and irritating both himself and his father with lengthy, wordy conversations. He cannot calm down until he has worked himself into a state of complete terror.

"You will see it all for yourself," he continues. "You will not have enough time to blink, and the whole of Europe will become a boiling pot. There will be a lot of noise and then a great battle—I am telling you! For you it is all the same, you couldn't care less. But for me—they will say, 'Report for duty, please, come and get yourself enrolled in the army!' But I don't care, I would sign up with pleasure."

After scaring himself with politics, George turns to the cholera epidemic.

"During the plague, my dear, they won't even bother to check whether you are living or dead. They will throw you on the cart for the corpses and carry you out of the city! There you will lie among the dead! No one will have time for you, to see if you are sick or if you have actually died."

"Oh my God." Fyodor Fedorovich, their tenant, is still coughing behind the thin wall. "You have not only let your secondhand smoke go into my room, and mixed it with alcohol fumes, but you also want to kill me with your conversation!"

"Tell me please, dear sir, why don't you like our conversation?" Gregory asks, raising his voice.

"Because I do not like ignorance. I think what you say is disgusting!"

"If it is disgusting to you, then do not listen. So, my dear father, many things will happen, I am telling you. You will shrug your shoulders in disbelief. But it will be too late. And over here, people are stealing money from the banks, from their offices, and from City Hall. Here you can see, someone has stolen a million here, and a hundred thousand there, and at some other place just a thousand. And this happens every day. Yes, every single day there is a bookkeeper or a cashier running down the street in a hurry!"

"So what?" the father asks.

"What do you mean by 'so what?' One day you will look out of the window and will see that there is nothing there—everything has been stolen! You'll look around, and see accountants scurrying all over the city—they are running away with your own money. You'll get alarmed, and try to get dressed—but you won't find your pants, because they have been stolen! Here is what will happen—and you ask me 'so what?'"

In the end, Gregory talks about the famous Mironovich case that has been making headlines in all the newspapers. The murdered body of a teenage girl was found under a bridge, and now several famous lawyers are working on this case.

"Don't even dream about an easy life," George says to his father. "This case won't end for ages. Even if they find the accused guilty, and read out the verdict—my dear, this does not mean anything at all. No matter what the sentence may be—it is all seen 'darkly through a glass.' Imagine that Madam Semenova is guilty—then where would you put the evidence that speaks against Mironovich? Or imagine that Mironovich is guilty—then how can you acquit Semenova and Bezak? Everything is in fog, my dear."

"It is all so mysterious and undefined that even after they read out the sentence, people will be talking about this case for decades! It is like asking—'What is the end of the world?' Does it exist? Yes, it exists. And what will happen after the end of the world? Another end. And what would happen after the second end? Etc. etc. That's what this case is like. They will close the case, then reopen it and then reopen it twenty more times, but they would not find the solution but only add some more fog and mystery. Madam Semenova admitted her guilt, but tomorrow she will deny her deposition and say, 'I do not know anything at all.'

"Then Kabichevsky, the prosecutor, would continue his efforts, he would find another dozen assistants and they would be searching, making circles around the city blocks."

"What do you mean by 'making circles'?"

"I mean they will continue the investigation, and finally they will wind up under the Tuchkov Bridge. And then, Mr. Oshanin, the judge, would write an official letter of inquiry asking, 'Have you found the weights?' and Kabichevsky would answer that they could not find the weights since they do not have good divers and a good submarine. Then they would bring in really good divers from England and a good submarine from New York. And during the search of the river bottom, they would be bugging all kinds of experts, and the experts would be making more circles around the city blocks, talking to people. The chief prosecutor would not agree with Mr. Engard, and Kabichevsky would not agree with Mr. Sorokin, and this will go on and on.

"Then they will invite a world-famous expert, Dr. Charcot, from France. He would come to the scene of the murder and say at once, 'I cannot give you an expert opinion because I did not examine properly the spine marrow of the victim. Open up the grave and examine her, and do another autopsy,' he would say. Then, look at the hair! This hair could not just grow on the floor by itself! They have other people's hair. Then they would ask the expert hairdressers to come in. Then they would find out that it does not look like Mr. Monbanzon's hair. Then things would develop faster and faster. The British divers would find not one weight, but five weights from the City Fitness Club in the Neva River. Then they would find another ten weights. They would start examining the weights, and the first question would be, where did they buy the weights? They bought them at Mr. Skokov's hardware store. Come over and make a deposition from the store owner. They will ask, 'Who bought the weights from you?' He would say, 'I do not remember.' 'Then, give us the list of your customers.' The store owner would start remembering and then it would dawn upon him that one day YOU bought something from him, and he would say 'These and these people bought some stuff from me.' And then, among other things, there was an office worker, Mr. Semen Nianin.

"'Then, take in Mr. Nianin into custody. Invite him for interrogation.' There you are, dear dad, they will come and arrest you—there you are."

The father stands up from the table, completely pale, and starts nervously pacing around the room.

"Well, well," he says, "only God knows what you are talking about."

"Yes, invite Mr. Nianin here, with the full subpoena. You would come there, and then Mr. Kabichevsky would pierce you through with his terrible hypnotic glance. He would pierce you through. He would ask you, 'Where were you during the night, on that particular date?' Then, they would compare your hair with that hair. They would invite Mr. Ivanovsky the expert—and then—there you are, you would be accused of murder!"

"But how can you say this? Everybody knows that I did not kill!"

"Everyone knows! Ha-ha! That makes no difference at all. It does not matter that you did not kill. They will start making circles around you, setting their nets around you, and you will kneel before them and make a complete deposition and say, 'Yes, I have killed!' There you are!

"Well, well, this is just an example, take it easy. As for me, I am not married, so if I want, tomorrow, I can go to America. And then, Mr. Kabichevsky would not find me there. Try and find me there!"

"Oh my God!" Fyodor Fedorovich is moaning from behind the wall. "I wish that they would be quiet. Hey you, devils, can you shut the hell up?"

Nianin and Gregory fall silent. The dinner is over, and they lie down on their beds. They are both scared, and thinking and rethinking about it all. Both go to bed, excited and terrified.

ASSIGNMENT

——✦——

As Pavel Sergeevich recalled his promise to the editor of the weekly magazine to write "a scary Halloween story," he sat at his desk with his eyes focused on the ceiling. Several possible ideas were brewing in his mind. After a few minutes lost in thought, accompanied by frequent forehead rubbing, he finally chose one of his ideas, a story that had happened ten years ago in the city where he was born and went to school. He stared at his desk, inhaled deeply, moved closer, and began to write.

That day, he had a few guests sitting on the couch in the room next to his study—two ladies and a university student.

The writer's wife, Sofia Vasilievna, sat at the grand piano, shuffling musical score papers, and playing a few random chords.

"Ladies, who will accompany me on the piano?" she inquired in a complaining voice. "Nadya, will you please play for me as I sing?"

"Oh my dear, I have not played the piano for three months."

"Oh my God, why are you so picky? If you will not play, then I will not sing! Please play, this is an easy piece!"

After a long dispute, one lady moved to sit at the piano. She hit the keys as Pavel's wife started singing the popular song "Why Don't You Tell Me That You Love Me?"

Pavel wrinkled his forehead and put away his pen. He listened for a while, wrinkled his face again, jumped up from his chair, and strode to his door.

"Sofia," he cried out loud. "You are not singing properly. You hit the wrong note with that high one. And you Nadya," he addressed the lady played the piano, "you are constantly playing as if you are in a hurry, as if someone is pulling you by your fingers. It should be played trum-trum-trum."

Pavel gestured in the air with his hands as he demonstrated how they should be singing and playing the song.

A few minutes later, humming the tune that his wife was singing, he returned to his room and continued with his writing:

"Both men, Mr. Winkle and Mr. Ushakov, were young, close to the same age; they were friends who worked in the same office. Mr. Ushakov was shy and humble. Mr. Winkle was the complete opposite of his friend: he had a reputation for being rude, animallike, with terrible habits, and insatiable when it came to satisfying his own desires. He was so outlandish and selfish at times that some thought he was mentally unstable.

"How two such completely opposite characters, Mr. Winkle and Mr. Ushakov, could be friends was hard to understand. They had only one thing in common: they both were rich.

"Ushakov was the only son of a single rich mother; Winkle was the only heir of a huge estate through his aunt, a general's widow who loved him as her only son. Money can be a good connector factor in a relationship; and it was in this case. They both wasted money on all their whims, such as beautiful women, expensive clothes, cab fare, etc., and lived in such a way that made people jealous. Indeed, it was money that united them.

"The friendship between Mr. Ushakov and Mr. Winkle did not last long. They became bitter enemies one day, when they simultaneously fell in love with an exotic dancer, Ms. Wholly, a very self-absorbed but very attractive woman, famous for her luxurious hair. She managed to become intimate with both men for their money, at almost the same time. This pretty woman was savvy and practical enough to know that the best way to get money out of her lover, or both lovers in this case, was to arouse their jealousy.

"The modest Ushakov simply looked at his rival with disgust, but the rude and wild Winkle gave in to his worst instincts."

At this moment, a voice from the living room called,

"Come here, Pavel."

Pavel jumped up from his chair, and proceeded next door to the ladies.

"Come, sing a duo with Michael. You sing the first voice, and he will sing the second one."

"All right, give me the pitch." Pavel walked to the piano, waved with his pen, which was still wet with ink, stamped his foot a couple of times, made a suffering face, and started singing "Those Crazy Nights" with the university student.

"Bravo! Bravo! We were both great!" He embraced the student. "Do you want me to sing more? No, the hell with singing! I have to get back to my writing."

"Give us a break. Don't be shy! Stay and sing!"

"No-no-no! I promised. My deadline for this short story is today."

Pavel threw both his hands in the air, ran back to his study, and continued writing:

"One night at about 10 p.m., when Mr. Ushakov was on duty in the office, Mr. Winkle sneaked into the office building through the back door, entered the room quietly behind his former friend, and hit him with a little axe, right on the back of his head.

"It was obvious that at the moment of the murder he had been in a terrible fit of rage, as the medical experts found eleven wounds in the head of Mr. Ushakov. He wasn't thinking logically before, during, or after the murder. As soon as he had eliminated his rival, covered with blood, with an axe in his hands, he climbed up to the little attic of the office building, and, then climbed through the little window all the way onto the roof. The security guards heard that someone was walking on the iron roof late that night. From the rooftop, he went down the eaves until he reached the roof of the neighboring house. And so he continued on from one roof to another, until they caught up with him.

"The whole city came to the funeral of Mr. Ushakov, filled with music and flowers.

"The public outcry was against the murderer to such an extent that people came in crowds to look at the prison wall behind which Mr. Winkle was incarcerated. Two or three days after the murder, a small monument appeared on the grave of the murdered man, with the inscription, 'He died at the hand of a murderer.'

"But the person who was the most distressed over his death was his mother. When the poor woman found out about her son's death, she almost went crazy."

Pavel Sergeevich wrote one more page, smoked two cigarettes, had a nap on his couch, then returned to his desk, to continue:

"The old woman, Mrs. Ushakov, was brought into to court and gave her testimony from the witnesses' bench. The listeners reported that her testimony was brief. She turned to the bench of the accused, trembling, and addressed him, shaking both fists at him, and cried,

"'You killed my son, it was you!'

"'I don't deny it,' mumbled Mr. Winkle, addressing the judge.

"'You can't deny it! You killed him!' cried the old woman.

"After her, the old general's widow, Mr. Winkle's aunt, came to courtroom to give her testimony. She looked senselessly around herself for several minutes, and then asked her nephew in a tone of voice that made everyone in the courtroom suddenly tremble,

"'Nicholas, what have you done?'

After that, she was not able to speak.

The appearance of both women in court had a very depressing effect on the public.

When these two old women met outside in the courthouse corridors, they caused such an emotional scene that even the court couriers had tears in their eyes.

The old woman, Mrs. Ushakov, who had become very bitter after all her misfortunes, jumped closer to the general's widow, and started scolding her. Her previous testimony was brief in court; however, in the hall she started talking and shouting at the old widow, using all kinds of swear words. She reproached her, she swore at her; she made all kinds of references to God's punishment, etc.

Mrs. Winkle listened very patiently, without saying a word, until Mrs. Ushakov was finished, and then said,

"'Have mercy, please! We have already been punished!' Then, she could not bear it any more, and began to answer the accusations.

"'If this were not for your son, my Nicholas would not have been sitting here. It was your son who destroyed him, etc.,' she cried.

"They pulled the two old women to opposite sides of the hallway.

"The jury found Mr. Winkle guilty, and sentenced him to ten years of hard labor."

"'You know that Nikonov has a wonderful voice, a very nice-sounding voice indeed, a deep bass. Yes, a very nice-sounding voice,' Pavel overheard his wife telling one of the guests. 'I can't understand my dear, why does he sing in the opera?'

"Pavel made a face, jumped up, and ran into the living room.

"'You said that Nikonov has a good bass?'

"'Yes, he does.'

"'Then my dear, you do not understand anything.' Pavel shrugged his shoulders. 'Nikonov sings like a cow; growls like a dog; and neighs in a horselike voice, as if someone were pulling out his intestines. His voice is wobbly like a cork in an empty bottle. I cannot explain it to you in any plainer terms; your Nikonov has the same musical pitch as these springs in my sofa.'

"'Hmm, they say Nikonov is a singer!' he muttered indignantly, as he came back to his desk five minutes later and sat down to read what he just written. 'Nikonov should be a street singer, not an opera singer.'"

Irritated, he grabbed his pen and continued to write:

"The old general's widow, Mrs. Winkle, went to St. Petersburg, the capital, in an attempt to get his punishment reduced, so that her nephew would not be embarrassed so in public. During her absence, Mr. Winkle managed to escape from prison."

"What wonderful weather we are having!" The student made a deep sigh in the living room.

"They finally caught him at the railroad station," Pavel continued, "under the freight train, and it took a huge effort to pull him out. It seemed that this poor man still wanted to live. The poor man grinned at the guard who brought him back to prison, and cried bitterly."

"Yes, it is nice to be out of town on a day like this, " said Sofia Vasilievna. "Hey, Pavel, stop writing, for God's sake!"

Pavel nervously rubbed his forehead with his hand and continued:

"The efforts of the general's widow were in vain. Her appeal was denied, and her nephew had to serve out his sentence in the city square. He could not bear this humiliation, and just before he was to begin his sentence, Mr. Winkle poisoned himself. He was buried behind the cemetery, in the place where they bury those who commit suicide."

Pavel looked out at the weather through his window, cleared his throat, and went out into the living room.

"Yes, it could be nice to go out of town," he said a few minutes later, sitting in his favorite chair. "The weather is beautiful."

"So, let us go out together! Where shall we go?" The women were talking excitedly.

"I have to finish my short story first. I have hardly written half of it. It would be nice to order a couple of cabs, and get out of town for a nice walk, but I would need to start with a couple of drinks."

"Excellent! Let us go, now!"

"No-no, I cannot go before I finish my short story. Do not even ask me about this!"

"Then go back into your study and finish it faster! In the meantime, Michael will order the wine delivery and by the time the cabs come to pick us up, you will have finished it five times over!"

The ladies surrounded Pavel, asking him questions about the place they should go. He waved at them with his hand in the air, and then finally agreed. The student was sent to fetch the cabs and the wine, and the ladies were kept busy getting ready.

When he ran back to his study, Pavel Sergeevich hastily grabbed his pen, hit his manuscript with his fist, and quickly wrote:

"Every day the old woman, Mrs. Ushakov, went to the cemetery to visit her son's grave. No matter the weather, rain or snow, every morning around ten o'clock, her cab would be in front of the cemetery gate. She could be found sitting in front of the grave, crying, eagerly looking at the inscription, as if she were admiring it: 'He died at the hand of a murderer.'"

When the student returned, Pavel quickly downed a glass of wine in a single gulp, and continued:

"For five years in a row, she went to the cemetery, not missing a single day. The gravesite became a second home to her. The sixth year, she fell ill with a severe lung infection, and she was not able to make it to her son's grave for a month."

"Stop writing! Stop! Let's go! Come over here and have another drink!" He heard the voices calling to him.

"I cannot go yet. Wait a few more minutes, my dear, do not interfere," he replied, and went on writing:

"When she returned to the cemetery after her illness, the old woman, to her horror, found she completely forgot where her son's grave was located. Her illness had removed her memory. She was running across the cemetery, deep in snow up to her waist, imploring the guards to show her the grave. 'Where is the place where my son was buried?' she cried.

"But during her absence, the cross marking the grave had been stolen by lowlife thieves who specialize in stealing and reselling cemetery items.

"'Where is he? Where is my son?' the old woman cried. 'You took him away from me for a second time.'"

"Are you going, or what?" Sofia Vasilievna cried at the study door. "It is not nice of you to make five people wait for you! Quit keeping us waiting!"

"Wait, just one more second," mumbled Pavel as he gulped his second glass of wine. "Just a moment, hold on."

Pavel rubbed his forehead intensely, cast a meaningless glance at everyone waiting and, nervously tapping his shoe against the floor, wrote the following:

"She could not find her son's grave, and pale, bare-headed, tired, with her eyes half closed, she walked unsteadily back to the cemetery entrance, to go home. Before getting into her cab, she had to experience one more problem. She encountered Mrs. Winkle."

One of the lady guests ran through the study, snatching the manuscript from his desk, as she yelled, "Let us go!"

Pavel weakly attempted to protest, threw his hands helplessly into the air, tore his manuscript into small pieces, for no reason swore at the editor, then happily whistled as he ran out into the hall to help the ladies finish getting ready and depart.

FIRE IN THE STEPPE: AN EVIL NIGHT

——— ◄◆► ———

You can hear the dogs barking and howling in an alarming way, as dogs usually do when they sense an enemy but cannot understand who it is or where it is coming from. There are unclear, muffled sounds flying though the dark autumn air, disturbing the silence of the night: muttering of human voices from far off, the busy rush of footsteps, front gates squeaking, the clomping of horseshoes, and noises made by their riders.

Three dark figures stand motionless in the Dadkins' estate garden, right in the middle of its main allée, in an empty flower bed. The first recognizable as the night guard on watch, Sam. A distinct figure in his bell-shaped sheepskin coat, tied with a rope instead of a belt, with pieces of fur hanging from it. A tall, thin-legged man in a jacket, with enormous ears, stands next to him. This is Gabriel the butler. The third is dressed in a vest over a loosely hanging shirt, a strongly built, but rather clumsy man, whose angular form brings to mind a wooden doll. He is also known as Gabriel the groom.

All three men grip the top of a short picket fence tightly and look off in the distance.

"Holy mother, save and protect us from this evil!" mumbles Sam in an excited voice. "Just look at that! God is furious at us. Oh, Holy Mother!"

"This is not far from us," says Gabriel the butler in a bass voice. "Six miles, not more. I believe it is happening at the German farms."

"No, the German farms are further to the left," Gabriel the groom interrupts him. "The German farms should be behind this birch tree. No, it must be the Kreshensky village."

"Yes, it is," agrees Sam.

They hear someone with bare feet running across the terrace, stomping his feet on the floor and closing the door with a crash. The big house is immersed in sleep. The windows are as black as tar and look eerily gloomy, with only one window barely lit from the inside by a pink night lamp. The young landlady, Maria Sergeevna, sleeps in that room. Her husband, Nikolai Alexeevich, went out to play cards, and has not yet returned.

"Anastasia!" they hear someone crying.

"The landlady is awake," says Gabriel the butler.

"Wait, brothers, I want to ask her to give me a few horses, and all the farmhands available on the estate, and we will head to the fire as fast as we can. People in that village are stupid, and they will need someone to tell them what to do."

"Really? Just look at you! You're going to tell them what to do. Look at yourself—your teeth are chattering from fear! There are enough people there without you. Policemen, chiefs, other landlords—they should all be there already."

A glass door leading to the terrace opens with a clinking sound, and the landlady herself comes out.

"What is this? What is the meaning of all this noise?" she asks, as she comes closer to the three figures. "Sam, is it you?"

Before Sam has a chance to answer her, she jumps back, horrified, and clasps her hands. "Oh my God, what a terrible misfortune," she cries. "How long it has been going on? And where is it? Why didn't you wake me up?"

The southern part of the sky is densely filled with a red glow. The sky looks inflamed, irritated, with the evil red color flickering and trembling across it, almost pulsing in its appearance. They can see the hills and the bare trees against this huge crimson background. They hear a convulsive, hurrying noise of the church bells ringing with the fire warning.

"This is terrible, terrible," says the landlady.

"Where is the fire?"

"Not far, in the Kreshensky village."

"Oh my God! Nikolai is not at home, and I don't know what to do. Does the manager know?"

"He already left, with three barrels."

"Those poor people!"

"And most important, madam, they don't have a river. There is only one pond nearby, but it isn't in the village itself."

"Is it possible to put out a fire like this with water?" asks Gabriel the butler. "The most important thing is not to let the fire grow bigger. The people who know how to fight fires should go and take command. Madam, please let me go there."

"You should not go," answers Maria Sergeevna. "You will only interfere."

Gabriel coughs disappointingly, and takes a step back. Sam and Gabriel the groom both don't like the too-clever remarks of the arrogant-speaking butler in the jacket, and are satisfied hearing the landlady's remark.

"We could not do much anyway," says Sam.

Then both of them, trying to look smart in the madam's eyes, start talking about the fire, using many religious words, appealing for God's help, "Look, this is how God is punishing us people for our sins. That's it! A man sins and does not know what he is doing, but God, you know, he knows everything . . ."

The sight of this glow has the same effect on all of them. The landlady and the servants alike feel inner cold—the kind of cold where the hands, the head, and the voice start to tremble. The fear is great, but their impatience is even greater. They want to get to a higher elevation to see the fire, its smoke, and the people better. Their desire to experience this emotional situation and its stress becomes stronger than their compassion for the misfortunes of others.

When the glow becomes pale, seemingly smaller, Gabriel happily proclaims: "It looks like they have put the fire out. God helps them!"

However, a note of disappointment can be heard in his voice. When the glow in the sky grows, becoming larger, he sighs and desperately waves his hand in the air. From the loud breaths he is making while trying to stand up on his tiptoes, it is obvious that he is expressing some sort of pleasure.

They all know that they are observing a terrible disaster, but they are not satisfied with their vantage point, wanting to get a better view. This dubious feeling is a natural one, and it should not be reproached.

No matter how frightening it is, it was a beautiful sight, people have to admit.

They hear the sound of thunder, someone making heavy steps on the iron roof of the house.

"Ivan, is it you?" asks Sam.

"Yes, I am here with Anastasia."

"You can fall down from the roof, boy! Can you see better from over there?"

"Yes, I can. It is in the Kreshensky village, brothers!"

"We can probably see it better through the top window in the attic, right under the roof," says Maria Sergeevna. "Maybe we can go there and have a look?"

The sight of the disaster brings people closer together. Sam and both Gabriels go into the house. With pale faces, they tremble all over, waiting to get a better glimpse of this sight. They maneuver though the rooms and climb the stairs to the top, headed for the attic. It is dark there. The candle held by Gabriel the butler does not light this darkness, but only allows dim spots to be seen around them. The landlady sees the attic for the first time. Its beams, the dark corners, the chimney pipes, the smell of the spiders' webs and dust, and the floor covered with a layer of soil—all this looks like a stage designed for a fairy tale.

"Is it the place where the house sprite lives?" she thinks.

They can see the fire better. A long and bright golden line stretches along the horizon. It moves and flows like a liquid.

"Look, it seems that more than one house is on fire."

"Yes, brother, at least half of the village is burning," says Gabriel the groom.

"Listen! The church bells have stopped! It means that the church must be on fire!"

"Their church is made of wood," says the landlady, suffocating from the heavy smell coming from the Sam's sheepskin coat. "What a misfortune!"

They all look for as long as they can, and then head down. Soon, the landlord, Nikolai Alexeevich, has returned home. He has had quite a few drinks while visiting his friends, and now drunk, he snores loudly, his body slumped in the carriage. As they wake him up, he looks at the glow with a blank expression on his face, and says,

"Give me a saddled horse! Faster! F-a-a-aster!"

"Please, don't go there!" his wife says vehemently. "Tell me, how can you go anywhere in your state? Go back to sleep!"

"A horse," he orders, ignoring her as he turns around. He is brought a horse. He climbs into the saddle, shakes his head, and then disappears into the darkness.

The dogs continue to howl and bark incessantly, as if they sense a wolf or danger. Women and young boys begin to gather around Sam and both Gabriels. The people keep making loud exclamations and sighs, making the sign of the cross regularly.

A horse rider rushes into the yard.

"Six people burned alive," he mumbles, out of breath. "Half of the village is burned. Carpenter Sam's mother has burned."

The landlady's impatience has reached its limits. The constant movements of people around her and loud conversations have excited her. She orders a carriage and goes off to see the fire in person. The night is cold and dark. The soil is slightly hardened by the early-morning frost, and the horseshoes make a knocking sound against it, like hitting a carpet. Gabriel the butler sits next to the groom, impatiently moving in his seat. He constantly turns his head, looking back and mumbling something, as if the fate of the Kreshensky village depends solely on him.

"The most important thing is not to let the fire grow bigger," he mutters. "They should know this, but how could those peasants know anything?"

After they go for five or six miles, the landlady sees something so awful—something which not everyone should see more than once in their lifetime, if at all. The whole village is alit, as if it's a huge bonfire. The constantly moving massive flame blinds her. Everything is completely immersed in this fire, as if in fog: the houses, the trees, and the church. The bright light, as bright as noon, is mixed with clouds of smoke and transparent vapor. These golden tongues slide along the black carcasses, licking them, and flickering joyfully. The clouds of red and golden dust fly up into the sky and, as if made on purpose, give the stronger impression of a flock of alarmed doves diving into these clouds of smoke and fire. A strange mixture of sound is filling the air—the terrible noise of cracking wood; the flickering of the flame in the wind, which reminds of thousands of bird wings—mixed with human voices, animal sounds, and the squeaking of wheels.

The church is a terrible sight. Flames and clouds of dense, dark smoke fly from its windows. The church tower hangs above the massive flame, as if it's a dark giant; it is completely burned, but the bells still hang. No one knows why they have not yet fallen.

Swarms of people are pushing each other, reminiscent of a village fair, or the first ferry after the river floods in spring. People, horses, carriages, piles of belongings, barrels—all this moves, stumbles, and makes noises. The landlady looks at this chaos and hears the piercing cry of her husband:

"Send him to the hospital! Pour some water on him!"

Gabriel the butler stands on the cart, waving with his hands. He is well lit, and with his long shadow appears much taller than in real life.

"It is obvious that someone set this on fire," he cries,

moving about. "Hey, you! You should have stopped the fire, and not let it grow! You should not let it grow!"

All around her, the landlady could see pale, stupid, motionless faces, as if carved from wood. The dogs are howling, the hens shrieking in fright.

"Let me pass! Let me pass!" cry the neighbors, who have just arrived.

What an unusual picture! Maria Sergeevna does not believe her eyes, and if not for the great heat, she would have believed that this was all a dream.

IGNORAMUS

———— ❦ ————

A young man, blond and broad-faced, in a torn sheep-skin and big, black felt boots, waited until the local doctor, having completed his appointments, left the hospital to go home, and approached him hesitatingly.

"My dear sir," he began.

"What do you want?"

The young man passed the palm of his hand upward along his nose, looked at the sky, and then answered:

"To your grace. . . . You've got my brother Basil, the black-smith from Varvarino, in the ward of convicts here, your lordship."

"Yes, so what?"

"Well, I mean to say, I'm Basil's brother. . . . Our father has the two of us: he is Basil, and I am Kirila. And three sisters apart from us, and Basil's a married man with a child now. . . . A big family, and no one to work. . . . See, we haven't heated the fire in the forge for two years now. I'm at the cotton factory, I'm no blacksmith, and father—there isn't any use for him as a worker, I should say, when he can't get his spoon to his mouth right."

"So what do you want from me?"

"Do me a favor, sir, let Basil go!"

The doctor looked at Kirila with surprise, and, without saying a word, walked on. The young man ran in front of him and fell down at his feet.

"Doctor, gracious master!" he implored, blinking and passing the palm of his hand along his nose again. "Reveal heavenly grace, let Basil go home! You'll make me pray to God for you forever! Your lordship, do let him go! The family is dying of hunger! Mother's wailing all day long, Basil's wife's wailing, it's terrible! I wouldn't see the light of day, if I could. Do me a favor, gracious master, let him go!"

"Are you a fool or are you out of your mind?" asked the doctor, looking angrily at him. "How possibly can I let him go? He is a convict."

Kirila started to cry. "Let him go!"

"Oh dear, what an odd man you are! What right do I have to do it? I'm not a jailer, am I? They brought him to the hospital for me to treat him, but I have no more right to let him go than to put you in prison, you silly man!"

"But they put him in prison for nothing! He spent a whole year there before trial, and why should he stay there now, is all I'm asking. It would've been a different thing if he'd murdered someone, or, say, stole horses; but it's just for nothing at all."

"I still don't see what I can do about it."

"They sent him to prison for no reason. He was drunk, your lordship, he didn't remember anything, and he even stroked father on the ear, he cut his own cheek through on a branch, and two of our villagers—see, they wanted some Turkish tobacco—told him to break into the Armenian man's shop at night to get tobacco. And drunk as he was, he agreed, the fool. They broke the lock, you know, got in, and made a complete mess. Everything upside down, windows broken, flour all over the floor. They were drunk, in short! Well, the constable turned up . . . this and that, and they took him to the investigator. They've been in prison the whole year, and a week ago, it was Wednesday, they were tried in town, all three of them. A soldier with a gun stood behind them . . . people swore an oath. Basil is less guilty than anyone, and so the gentlemen decided that he was the mastermind behind the whole thing. The two fellows went to prison, and Basil to a convict battalion for three years. And what for? Judge it yourself as it should be!"

"I've nothing to do with it, I tell you. You'd better go to the authorities."

"I've been there already! I was in court, I wanted to submit a petition—they wouldn't take it. I went to the sheriff, and I saw the investigator, and everyone I spoke to just said, 'It's not my business!' Whose business is it, then? And in the hospital, there's no one above you. You do whatever you like, your lordship."

"What a fool you are," sighed the doctor. "If the jury found him guilty, neither the governor, nor even the minister is in any position to change anything, let alone the sheriff. There's no use in your bustling about!"

"And who judged him, then?"

"Gentlemen of the jury . . ."

"There's no way they're gentlemen, they were folks from our village. Andrew Guryev was there, and Alexander Huk."

"Well, I am getting cold standing around and talking to you. . . ."

The doctor waved his hand and walked quickly to his door. Kirila wanted to follow him, but, seeing the door slam, he stopped.

For about ten minutes he stood motionless in the middle of the hospital yard, and standing without his cap on, stared at the doctor's flat, then he took a deep breath, scratched himself slowly, and went to the gate.

"Who shall I go to?" he muttered as he went out on the road. "One says it's not his business, another says it's not his business. Whose business is it, then? Yeah, that's true, you won't get nothing till you grease their palms. When the doctor talked to me, he kept looking at my fist all the time, as if I'd give him a five. Well, brother, I'll go to the governor himself, if I have to."

Shifting from one foot to the other and looking around him every now and then without any purpose, he dragged himself lazily along the road, apparently making up his mind about where to go. . . . It was not cold and the snow crunched faintly under his feet. Not more than half a mile away, the small town lay on a hill in front of him, where his brother had been tried not long ago. The dark spot of the town prison under the red roof with sentry boxes at the corners was on his right; on his left was the central park, now covered with hoarfrost. It was quiet, there was just an old man walking ahead, wearing a lady's jacket and a huge cap. He coughed and yelled at a cow that he was driving into town.

"Hello, grandfather," said Kirila, overtaking him.

"Hello . . ."

"Will you sell it in town?"

"No, it's just here with me," the old man answered lazily.

"Are you from town?"

They got to talking. Kirila told him what he had been to the hospital for and what he had talked about with the doctor.

"Sure, the doctor doesn't know these things," the old man was telling him as they came into town. "He's a gentleman, that's right, but all he knows is how to cure things with drugs. But to get real advice, or, say, write a statement for you—he has no understanding of it. For this, there are special authorities. You've seen the magistrate and the sheriff—they are of no help to you in this affair."

"Where should I go, then?"

"The most important man who is placed to settle all the peasants' affairs is a permanent member of the council. You should go to him, Mr. Sineokov."

"Is he in Zolotovo?"

"Yes, in Zolotovo. He is the most powerful man. If it's something to do with you peasants' affairs, even the sheriff has no full right against him."

"It's a long way to go, old fellow. . . . About twelve miles or even more, I'd say."

"When you need something badly, you'd go a hundred."

"True. . . . Shall I give a petition to him, or what?"

"You'll find out there. If it's a petition, the clerk will easily write it for you. The permanent member has a clerk."

Having parted from the old man, Kirila stood in the middle of the square, thought it over and went away from the town. He decided to go to Zolotovo.

Five days later, as the doctor was walking home after seeing his patients, he saw Kirila in his yard again. This time he was not alone but with a thin and very pale old man who kept nodding his head like a pendulum, and mumbled with his lips.

"Your lordship, I've come to see you," Kirila started. "This is my father; please do us a favor, let Basil go! The permanent member didn't want to talk to me. He said: 'Go away!'"

"Your lordship," the old man hissed with his throat, raising his trembling brows. "Be gracious! We're poor people, we cannot thank your honor properly, but if you so wish, Kiriushka here or Basil can work for you. Let them work."

"We'll work for you," said Kirila, and raised his hand as if wishing to take an oath. "Let him go! They're dying with hunger, crying their eyes out, your lordship!"

The young man glanced quickly at his father, pulled him by the sleeve, and both of them, as if on command, fell down at the doctor's feet. The latter waved his hand hopelessly, and, without looking back, walked quickly to his door.

TASK

⸻

The strictest measures are taken to keep the Uskovs' family secret within the walls of their house. One half of the servants have been sent to the theater and the circus, and the others are sitting in the kitchen and not allowed out. It has been ordered that no visitors be received. The wife of the uncle, the Colonel, her sister, and the governess, although initiated into the secret, pretend they do not know anything; they are sitting in the dining room and do not show up in the drawing room or the hall.

Sasha Uskov, a young man of twenty-five, the cause of the turmoil, arrived long ago and, advised by his defender, his uncle on his mother's side, Ivan Markovich, a kind man, he is now sitting humbly in the hall next to the study's door, getting ready for a sincere, open explanation.

Behind the door a family council is taking place. The subject is highly disagreeable and delicate. Sasha Uskov sold a false promissory note to a bank, and three days ago the note became due for payment. At present, his two uncles on his father's side, and Ivan Markovich, his uncle on his mother's side, are considering whether they should pay the note and save the family honor, or wash their hands of it and let the case go to court.

To outsiders with no personal interest in the issue, such matters seem simple; meanwhile, for those who have the misfortune to resolve them in a serious way, they turn out to be exceedingly difficult. The uncles have been talking for a long time, but they have not come a single step nearer to the solution.

"Gentlemen!" says the uncle Colonel, his voice sounding tired and bitter. "Gentlemen, who says that family honor is a mere prejudice? I don't say that at all. All I want is to warn you against a false opinion and reveal the possibility of a fatal mistake. How can you not see it? I am not speaking Chinese, after all, I am speaking Russian!"

"We do understand it, my dear," Ivan Markovich states gently.

"How do you understand it then, when you say that I deny family honor? I repeat it once again: fa-mi-ly ho-nor is a prejudice when false-ly un-der-stood! Falsely understood! That's what I say! It is against the law to conceal a swindler and help him get away with it for whatever reasons you may have and whoever he may be. It is unworthy of a gentleman, it is not saving family honor; it's civic cowardice! Take the army, for example. We value the honor of the army above all else, yet we don't conceal the army's guilty members, but send them to trial. And does the honor of the army suffer because of it? Quite the opposite!"

The other paternal uncle, a Treasury official, a taciturn, narrow-minded, and rheumatic man, either keeps silence or has only one subject on his mind: if the case goes to court, the Uskov name will certainly get into the newspapers. In his opinion, the case should be hushed up from the very beginning and not made known to the public. Apart from referring to the newspapers, he has no other arguments to support his position.

The maternal uncle, kind Ivan Markovich, speaks smoothly, softly, and with a tremor in his voice. He starts by saying that youth has its rights and that passion goes hand in hand with it. Is there anyone among us who has not been young, and has not been carried away? Even great men fall prey to temptation and errors in their youth, let alone simple mortals. Take the biographies of great writers, for example.

Was there one among them who, when he was young, did not gamble, drink, or enrage his elders? If Sasha's mistake borders on crime, then they must take into account that Sasha has received practically no education, as he was expelled from fifth grade in secondary school. As a little boy, he lost his parents, and thus, has known no supervision and good, benevolent influences from a tender age. He is a nervous, easily excitable young man, who has no firm ground underneath his feet and, above all, who has known no happiness in life. Even if he is guilty, he still deserves the indulgence and sympathy of all compassionate souls. He should be punished, of course, but he is already punished by his conscience and the suffering that he is going through now, while waiting for the decision of his relatives.

The comparison with the army made by the Colonel is delightful and proves his elevated intelligence; his appeal to the feeling of civic duty speaks of the nobility of his self, but still, we must not forget that the citizen side in each individual is closely linked with his Christian nature. . . .

"Will we go against our civic duty," Ivan Markovich exclaims with inspiration, "if instead of punishing a mistaken boy we give him a helping hand?"

Ivan Markovich talks further of family honor. He himself does not have the honor of belonging to the outstanding family of the Uskovs, but he is well aware of the fact that the family's history goes back to the thirteenth century; he also does not forget for a minute that his cherished, most beloved sister was the wife of one of the representatives of that family. In short, the family is dear to him for many reasons, and he will never believe that, for the sake of a mere fifteen hundred rubles, a shadow should be cast on the priceless heraldic tree. If all the above lines of reasoning do not sound convincing enough, in conclusion he proposes to clarify what the word 'crime' actually means. Crime is an immoral act based on evil intentions. But can human intentions be considered free? Science has not yet given a positive answer to this question.

Scientists have different views on the subject. The latest school of Lombroso, for instance, does not believe in free will, and every crime is considered to be a product of the anatomical characteristics of the individual.

"Ivan Markovich," says the Colonel in a pleading voice, "we are talking seriously about the important matter at hand, and you bring in Lombroso. You are an intelligent man; give it some thought: why are you going into this stuff? Do you really believe that all this empty chatter and your rhetoric can provide us with the answer to the question?"

Sasha Uskov is sitting at the door listening. He is neither afraid, nor ashamed, nor bored, he just feels tired and empty inside. It seems to him that it makes no difference whatsoever whether they forgive him or not; the only reason he has come here to sit and wait for the decision was because the very kind Ivan Markovich talked him into doing so.

He has no fear for the future. It is all the same to him whether he is sitting here in the hall, or in prison, or sent to Siberia.

"If Siberia, then let it be Siberia, to hell with it!"

He has grown sick of life and feels it is all unbearably hard. He is hopelessly weighed down with debts, not a penny in his pocket, he is disgusted with his family, and he understands he will have to part sooner or later from his acquaintances and ladies, as they have started to treat him with contempt in his role as a sponger. The future looks gloomy. Sasha is indifferent; there is only one circumstance that troubles him: that they are calling him a scoundrel and a criminal behind that door. Every minute he is ready to jump to his feet, burst into the study, and shout in reply to the detestable metallic voice of the Colonel: "You are lying!"

"Criminal" is a frightful word. This is how murderers, thieves, robbers, and, on the whole, wicked and immoral people are called. And Sasha has nothing to do with all that. . . . Well, he is involved in debts and does not pay the money he owes. But debt is not a crime, and very few people can do without debts. The Colonel and Ivan Markovich both have debts. . . .

"Is there anything else I've done wrong?" Sasha ponders.

He has cashed a false note. But all the young men he knows do the same. Say, Handrikov and Von Burst always sell the false notes of their parents or acquaintances when they are short of money, and then, after receiving the money from home, they buy the notes back before they are due. Sasha did the same, but could not buy the note back as he had not received the money that Handrikov had promised to lend him. It is not he who is to blame but the circumstances. Well, it is no good to use another person's signature, but, still, it is not a crime; it is a generally accepted tactic, an unpleasant formality that offended and harmed no one, and in forging the Colonel's signature Sasha never meant to cause anybody trouble or loss.

"No, it doesn't mean that I am a criminal . . ." Sasha thinks. "And one has to have a different character to commit a crime. I am too soft and sensitive . . . as soon as I have money I help the poor . . ."

Sasha ponders along these lines while the discussion goes on behind the door.

"Gentlemen, this is endless." The Colonel flies into passion. "Imagine we have forgiven him and paid the note. But this doesn't mean that after that he'll give up that dissipated life he leads, or that he'll never squander and make debts again, or go to our tailors to order clothes at our expense! Can you vouch that this will be his last fraud? As for me, I do not in the least believe that he'll mend his ways!"

The Treasury man mutters something in reply, and after him Ivan Markovich starts talking smoothly and softly. The Colonel moves his chair impatiently and drowns out Ivan Markovich's words with his disgusting metallic voice. Finally, the door opens and Ivan Markovich walks out of the study, red spots visible on his lean shaven face.

"Let's go," he says and takes Sasha by the hand. "Come in and explain everything open-heartedly. No pride, my dear boy, humbly and candidly."

Sasha goes into the study. The official of the Treasury is seated; the Colonel, his hands in his pockets, one knee on a chair, is standing in front of the table. It is smoky and stuffy in the study. Sasha looks neither at the official nor at the Colonel. Suddenly, he feels ashamed and terrified. He looks anxiously at Ivan Markovich and mutters:

"I'll pay it . . . I'll give it back. . . ."

"What did you hope for when you cashed the promissory note?" he hears a metallic voice.

"I . . . Handrikov promised to lend me the money before it is due."

This is all Sasha can say. He walks out of the room and again sits down on the chair near the door.

He would have been happy to go away altogether, but hatred is choking him and he ardently desires to stay to cut the Colonel short and say something cheeky to him. He is sitting at the door trying to think of something impressive and momentous that he could say to the hateful uncle, and at the same time a woman's figure, cloaked in the twilight, appears at the door of the drawing room. It is the Colonel's wife. She beckons Sasha toward her, wringing her hands and weeping:

"Alexander, I know you don't like me, but . . . listen to me, listen, I beg you. . . . My dear, how could it happen? Why, it's awful, awful! For goodness' sake, implore them, defend yourself, entreat them."

Sasha looks at her quivering shoulders, at the big tears rolling down her cheeks, hears the muffled, nervous voices of the tired, exhausted people behind him, and shrugs his shoulders. He had never expected that his aristocratic relatives would make such a fuss over a mere fifteen hundred rubles! He cannot come to terms with the tears or with the quiver of their voices.

An hour later he hears the Colonel take the upper hand: the uncles finally incline to let the case go to court.

"It's settled now," says the Colonel with a sigh. "Enough."

It is clear that after the decision all the uncles, even the insistent Colonel, lose their confidence. Silence follows.

"Oh, goodness!" Ivan Markovich sighs. "My poor sister!"

And he starts to say quietly that it is likely now that his sister, Sasha's mother, is present invisibly in this study. He feels with his heart how this unhappy, holy woman is weeping, grieving, and begging for her boy. They should forgive Sasha so she can sleep in peace in the other world.

Sobs can be heard. Ivan Markovich is weeping and muttering something that one cannot make out through the door. The Colonel gets up and paces from corner to corner. The long conversation starts over again.

At last, the clock in the drawing room strikes two. The family council is over. The Colonel walks out of the study and goes not to the hall but to the entrance to avoid seeing the man who has occasioned him so much trouble. Ivan Markovich comes out into the hall. He is agitated, he rubs his hands and looks contented. His tearful eyes are cheerful and his mouth twists into a smile.

"Excellent," he says to Sasha. "Thank God! My dear friend, you can go home and sleep tight. We've decided to pay the note, but on condition that you repent and tomorrow you'll go with me to the village and get work."

A minute later Ivan Markovich and Sasha, wearing their coats and caps, are going downstairs. The uncle is muttering didactically. Sasha ignores him as he feels something heavy and frightful dropping gradually off his shoulders. He is forgiven, he is free! Like a fresh wind, happiness bursts into his chest and splashes his heart with a sweet chill. He is willing to breathe, to move, to live! Glancing at the street lamps and the black sky, he remembers that today, in the "Bear" restaurant, Mr. Von Burst is giving a birthday party, and again happiness fills his heart. "I'm going!" he decides.

But then he remembers that he does not have a penny and

that the friends he wanted to see despise him for his lack of money. He must get some money, whatever it may cost him!

"Uncle, lend me a hundred rubles," he says to Ivan Markovich.

His uncle looks into his face with surprise and backs toward a lamppost.

"Give it to me," says Sasha, shifting impatiently from one foot to the other and starting to lose his breath. "Uncle, I beg you, I need a hundred rubles."

His face has distorted, he is trembling and advancing menacingly towards his uncle. . . .

"Won't you?" he asks, seeing that his uncle is still surprised and does not understand what is happening. "Listen, if you don't give me the money, tomorrow I'll denounce myself! I won't let you pay the note! I'll cash another false note tomorrow!"

Stupefied by terror, muttering incoherently, Ivan Markovich produces a hundred-ruble note from his wallet and gives it to Sasha. The latter takes it and quickly walks away.

In the cab, Sasha calms down and feels happiness breaking into his chest again. The "rights of youth" referred to by kind Uncle Ivan Markovich at the family council have awakened and spoken for themselves. Sasha is imagining the forthcoming bash, and a small thought flashes through his mind in between the bottles, women, and friends:

"Now I see I'm a criminal. Yes, I am a criminal."

DREAMS

Two police deputies: one is black-bearded and stocky, with legs so short that if you looked at him from behind you would think his legs began much lower than in other people; the other is long, thin, and upright as a stick, with a sparse beard of a dark, reddish color. They are escorting a tramp who doesn't remember his name into town. The stocky deputy struts, looking from side to side, and chewing now a straw, now his own sleeve; at times he slaps himself on the hips and hums a tune. He appears completely unconcerned and flippant. The other, despite his gaunt face and narrow shoulders, looks reliable, serious, and thorough. The way he is built and the expression of his whole body reminds one of the Old Believers or the warriors painted on icons. "For his wisdom God has added to his forehead"; in other words, he is bald, which only increases the above likeness. The first is called Andrei Ptaha, the latter Nikolai Sapozhnikov.

The appearance of the man they are escorting does not cor-
respond in the least to the standard conception of a tramp. He
is a small, frail man, feeble-bodied and sickly, his features faint,
colorless, and extremely indefinite. His eyebrows are sparse, his
eyes submissive and pale, and he has hardly any facial hair,
although he is over thirty. He walks timidly, with his shoulders
bent forward and his hands thrust into his sleeves. The collar of
his threadbare wool overcoat, too nice for a tramp, is turned up
to the very edge of his cap, so that nothing but his little red nose
dares to peep out into the big, wide world. He has an inaudible,
ingratiating tenor voice, and he coughs lightly now and again.
It is exceedingly difficult to take him for a tramp who won't
reveal his own name. He looks more like a penniless priest's son,
a God-forgotten loser, a scribe fired for drinking, or the son or
nephew of a merchant, who, having tried his scanty talent in
the theatrical world, is now walking home to play the last act of
the parable of the prodigal son; or, perhaps, judging by the dull
patience with which he struggles through the thick autumn
mud, he could be a fanatic crawling from one monastery to
another, endlessly seeking a life that is peaceful, holy, and free
from sin, and never finding it . . .

The travelers have been walking quite a while now but they
never seem to advance beyond the same small patch of land.
About thirty feet of the blackish-brown muddy road still lies
ahead of them, about the same is seen behind, and farther
ahead, as far as your eyes can see, there is an impenetrable wall
of white fog. They march on and on, but the land remains the
same, the wall will not move closer, and the same patch of
ground is forever there. From time to time they glimpse a
craggy white stone, a gully, or a bundle of hay dropped by a
passerby. A large, dirty puddle will glimmer, or a shadow with

vague outlines will suddenly come into view ahead of them; the nearer they come to it the smaller and darker it becomes; still nearer, and there in front of them stands a leaning milestone with its illegible number, or a miserable birch tree, drenched and bare, like a wayside beggar. The birch tree will whisper something with its last yellow leaves, and one leaf will break off and float lazily to the ground. And then again the same fog, mud, the brown grass along the edges of the road. Dim tears are hanging on the grass. These are not the tears of tender joy that the earth sheds when welcoming and parting from the summer sun, and that she gives at dawn for the quails, corncakes, and slender, long-beaked curlews to drink. The travelers' feet get stuck in a heavy, sticky mud. Every step takes effort.

Andrei Ptaha is somewhat excited. He keeps examining the tramp, trying to figure out how on earth a man, alive and sober, could happen to forget his name.

"Are you Christian at all?" he asks.

"I am," the tramp answers timidly.

"Hmm . . . then you've been baptized?"

"Well, to be sure! I'm no Turk. I go to church and I observe the fasts, and I don't eat meat when not allowed. And I do exactly what the pastor says. . . ."

"So what's your name, then?"

"Call me whatever you like, chap."

Completely at a loss, Ptaha shrugs his shoulders and slaps himself on the hips. His partner, Nicholas Sapozhnikov, maintains a significant silence. He is not as simple-minded as Ptaha and apparently knows very well the reasons that could induce an orthodox Christian to conceal his name. His expressive face remains cold and stern. He walks a little bit apart from the others and does not condescend to idle chatter. He seems to be trying to demonstrate to everyone, the fog included, his gravity and reason.

"God knows what to make of you," Ptaha keeps nagging. "Common man you are not, and gentleman you are not, you are sort of in the middle or so. . . . I was washing a sieve in the pond the other day and up comes this viper, you know, long as a finger, with gills and a tail. First I thought it was a fish, and then I had a good look at it—and, plague upon it! The thing had legs. Maybe it was a fish, or something else, deuce only knows. So that's like you. What's your calling?"

"I'm a common man and of a peasant family," sighs the tramp. "My mother was a house serf. I don't look like a serf, I don't, as my family were of a different kind, good men. They kept my mamma as a nurse with the gentlemen, and she had every comfort, and I being of her flesh and blood, I used to live with her in the master's house. She petted and pampered me, and did her best to take me out of my humble condition and make a gentleman of me. I'd sleep in a bed and eat a real dinner every day, and I wore breeches and half-boots like any other gentleman boy. What my mamma ate she'd give me to eat, too; they gave her money to buy herself new clothes, and she'd buy clothes for me. A good life it was! So many sweets and cakes I was eating as a boy that if I'd sold them all now I could've got a good horse. Mamma took me in hand in my learning, and taught me fear of God from my early days."

The tramp bares his head, and the hair on it looks like a toothless old brush; he turns his eyes upward and crosses himself twice.

"Grant her, dear Lord, a place plenteous and benevolent." He pronounces this in a drawl, sounding more like an old woman than a man. "Teach Thy servant Ksenia Thy justifications. My beloved mamma had such a good heart that without her I would've been the most commonest sort of man with no understanding. And now, chap, you can ask me about whatever you wish and I know it all: scriptures secular and holy, and prayers of all kinds, and catechism. And I live accordingly. I don't harm anyone, I keep my flesh clean and chaste, I observe the fasts, I eat at the appropriate time. Another man may be the slave of vodka and fish, and I—whenever I have some time—I'd sit in a corner and read a book. I'd read and I'd weep and weep."

"And why would you weep?"

"They write most pitiful! You can give just a five-kopeck piece for a book, and yet you'll weep and sigh uncommonly over it."

"Is your father dead?" asked Ptaha.

"I don't know, fellow. I don't know my father; I shall be sincere with you. I think I was Mamma's illegitimate child. My mamma lived with the gentry all her life and didn't want to marry a muzhik."

"Aye, and got mixed up with the master," Ptaha grins.

"She gave in to temptation, she did. She was very good-hearted, and God-fearing, but she didn't keep herself chaste. It is vicious, of course, very vicious, but now maybe I have some genteel blood in me and maybe they only call me a muzhik but in nature I am a noble gentleman."

This speech is delivered by the "noble gentleman" in a quiet and sugary little tenor, his narrow forehead wrinkled up and his chilled little nose emitting squeaking sounds. Ptaha listens to what he is saying, looks at him with surprise, and continually shrugs his shoulders.

Having walked nearly four miles, the police deputies and the tramp sit down on a little hill to have a rest.

"Even a dog knows his name," Ptaha mutters. "My name's Andryushka, his is Nikandr; every man shall have his own holy name, and it ain't to be forgot. No way."

"Who'd have any need to know my name?" sighs the tramp and sets his cheek on his fist. "And what good will it do me? If they allowed me to go where I want, but it would be even worse than now. I know the law, my Christian brethren. Now I am a tramp who-don't-remember-his-name, and at the very least they will send me to Eastern Siberia and give me thirty or forty lashes; but if it happens that I tell them my real name and calling they'll send me back to hard labor, I know it!"

"You have been in hard labor, have you?"

"I was, my friend. I had a shaved head and irons on my legs for four years."

"What for?"

"Murder, good fellow! When I was still a boy of eighteen or so, my mamma had an accidental oversight. She dropped some arsenic into the master's glass instead of soda and acid. There were all sorts of boxes in the storeroom, lots of them; it was very easy to have made a mistake over them."

The tramp sighs, shakes his head, and says:

"She was very good in her heart, but—who knows?—another man's soul is always dark. She mayn't have know'd, or she may've had this insult in her heart that the master preferred another servant. . . . She may've put it in on purpose, God knows! I was so small at that time as I didn't understand it all . . . now I remember it, our master did reveal a favor to another mistress and Mamma was very much upset. And then they sent us to trial for two years or so. . . . Mamma was condemned to hard labor for twenty years, and I, being a infant, only for seven."

"And why did they condemn you?"

"As an accomplice. You see, it was I that handed the glass to the master. It's always been that way: Mamma'd prepare the soda and I handed it to him. But look here, brothers, I tell it all to you now as a good Christian, like before the Lord. You don't tell anybody."

"Well, nobody's gonna ask us, be sure," says Ptaha. "So you've run away from the labor, right?"

"I have, my friend. It was about fourteen of us. Those folks—Lord bless them!—ran away themselves and took me with them. Now you tell me, good man, in all honesty, is this a fair reason for me to hide my calling? They will send me back to hard labor in the blink of an eye, you know! And I am no hard laborer! I am timid and given to sickness, and I have a preference for eating and sleeping in a tidy place. When I pray to God I like to light a little icon-lamp or a candle, and not to hear noise around me. And when I bow down before Christ I want the floor be clean and not spit upon. And I do forty bows for my mamma every morning and evening."

The tramp takes off his cap and crosses himself.

"And let them send me to Eastern Siberia," he says "I am not afeared of that."

"You think it's better?"

"That's pretty much a different thing. You are like a crab in a basket at the labor: it's all crowd and crush, no room to catch your breath there; it's absolute hell, such a hell as may the queen of heaven spare us from it! You are a bandit and they treat you like a bandit, worse than a dog. You don't eat, you don't sleep, you don't even pray to God. But the settlement ain't like that at all. The first thing I'll do in the settlement is that I make myself a member of society like all other folks. The chiefs must give me a piece of land as the law says, that's exactly how it is! And they say the land there don't cost anything, no more than snow; you can take as much you like! So they'll give me my field land, and my garden land, and my house land. I shall plough my field like other people, and sow seed, and I shall have cattle and stock of all kinds, and bees, and sheep, and dogs. A Siberian cat so rats and mice don't spoil my goods. I'll put up a house, and buy all sorts of icons, and get married and have children, God willing."

The tramp is muttering, looking sideways. Although his dreaming appears unrealistic, the tramp's voice sounds so sincere and affectionate that it is hard not to believe in what he is saying. The tramp's little mouth is distorted in a smile, while his whole face, his eyes, and his little nose have become frozen still and blank with blissful anticipation of distant happiness. The police deputies are listening to him, their faces quite serious and rather sympathetic. They, too, believe him.

"I ain't afeared of Siberia," the tramp is muttering on. "Siberia is the same Russia as here, with the same Lord and tsar, and they talk there in the same orthodox way like you and me. But it's more easier there and folks are better off. Everything's better there. Take the rivers there, they are so much better than ours here. And astonishing crowds of fishes and all sorts of game. And I, dear brothers, I'm particularly fond of fishing. Sit me down with a hook, and I ask no more. Yes, indeed! I fish with a hook and a reel, and I set traps, and on ice I fish with a net. See, I ain't got that strength to fish with a net, so I'd hire a man for a fiver. And, Lord, how wonderful it is! You catch an eelpout or a chub of some sort and you are so happy like you've met your own brother. And, you won't believe it, there's particular wisdom for catching every fish: you catch one with a little fish, you catch another with a worm, and for the third you prepare a frog or a grasshopper. And you ought to understand it all!

Take the eelpout for example. The eelpout has no particular respect, it can even take a ruff; and the pike loves to have gudgeon, the snapper likes butterfly. If you fish for a chub in a quick river it is no trout pleasure. You throw the line for, like, twelve meters without a sinker, with a butterfly or a beetle, so that the bait floats atop; you stand in the water without pants and let it go with the current, and here comes the pull! But here you need to be tricky so that he, the cursed thing, won't tear off. Once he pulls at your line you strike right away; no time to wait. Unbelievable how much fish I've caught in my time. When we were on the run, the other convicts would sleep in the woods, but I wouldn't, the river lures me! And the rivers there are wide and fast, and the banks are steep—astonishing! It's all slumbering forests along the bank. The trees are so high so that if you look at their tops it makes you giddy. Every pine would cost, like, ten rubles by the prices here."

Pressed by the confusion of disorderly daydreams, of artistic representations of the past and a sweet presentiment of happiness, the poor man falls silent, merely moving his lips as if he were whispering to himself. The stupid blissful smile won't leave his face. The police deputies are silent. Absorbed in reflection, they have lowered their heads. In the autumn stillness, when a cold, stern fog rises from the earth and covers your heart, when it stands before your eyes like a prison wall, and reminds man of the limits of his liberty, it feels so sweet to think of broad, rapid rivers with wild steep banks, of primeval forests and endless steppes. Slowly and peacefully the imagination pictures an early morning with the flush of dawn still on the sky and a man—like a tiny spot—making his way along a steep deserted bank; the ancient mast pines that tower in terraces on both sides of the torrent watch the free-willed man gravely and grumble gloomily; roots, huge stones, and thorny bushes lie in his way, but the man is strong in body and good in spirit and fears neither pines nor stones, nor his solitude, nor the reverberating echo that repeats the sound of every step he takes.

The police deputies are imagining the images of the life happy and free, the one that they have never lived; God knows whether they are vaguely recalling what they heard long ago or whether the notions of liberty have been passed down to them by some distant free-willed ancestor along with their flesh and blood.

Nikolai Sapozhnikov, who has not uttered a word so far, is the first to break the silence. He may have envied the tramp's illusory happiness or he may have felt deep in his heart that daydreaming of happiness has nothing to do with the gray fog and the blackish-brown mud; anyhow, he casts a stern eye on the tramp and says:

"It's all very well, to be sure, only that you won't make it to those benevolent locations, old fellow, you won't. Before you go two hundred miles you'll yield up the ghost. Look how very puny you are! Here, you've hardly gone five miles and you can't get your breath."

The tramp turns slowly toward Nikandr, and the blissful smile vanishes from his face. He stares with fear and guilt at the man's sedate face, apparently recalls something, and lowers his head. Silence falls again. All the three are reflecting. The minds of the police deputies are straining to embrace in the imagination what can be grasped by God alone, that is, that awful expanse separating them from the land of liberty. Meanwhile, images that are quite clear and distinct, and even more awful than that vast expanse, are filling the tramp's mind. Pictures of legal procrastination, of transit and convict prisons, of weary stops on the way and bitter-cold winters, of the illnesses and deaths of his companions all stand vividly before his eyes. The tramp blinks guiltily, wipes the tiny drops of sweat from his forehead with his sleeve, and takes a deep breath as if he has just leaped out of a very hot bathhouse, then wipes his forehead with the other sleeve and looks around with fear.

"Sure, you'll never make it there!" Ptaha agrees. "You ain't much of a walker! Look at yourself—nothing but skin and bones! You'll die, old fellow!"

"Of course he'll die! What else could he do?" says Nikandr. "And now, too, he'll go to a hospital. That's for sure!"

He-who-doesn't-remember-his-name looks in awe at the strict and passionless faces of his sinister companions and, keeping his cap on, his eyes open wide, hurriedly crosses himself. . . . He trembles, his head shakes, and his whole body starts twitching like a caterpillar when it is stepped upon.

"Well, it's time to go," says Nikandr, getting up; "we've had a rest."

A minute later the travelers are marching on along the muddy road. The tramp is more bent than ever, his hands thrust deeper into his sleeves. Ptaha keeps silence.

A CRIME: A DOUBLE MURDER CASE

A terrible crime was committed over there, in that ravine behind the woods.

It happened on the day when my father had to deliver a large amount of money to the landlord; he had fifty thousand rubles on him. Several of the local farmers were tenants, and my father had to collect and deliver the payment for their leases of this land for the last six months.

He was a God-fearing man who respected the law, never stole so much as a kopeck in his life, and never cheated anyone. So, everyone knew that he was an honest man, and the local farmers always sent him as their representative whenever anyone had to send something into the city: money, documents, whatever.

However, my father did have one weakness—he liked to drink, and every time he saw a pub or a tavern, he could not pass it by without stopping for a glass of wine. He was aware of this weakness of his, and so, whenever he had to carry other people's money, he used to take a companion with him—either me or my little sister Anna.

To tell you the truth, this habit runs in our family. People say that vodka is the blood of Satan. Look at me—my face is always red from my own constant drinking, and I slur my words, and even though I had a pretty decent education, I have to work as a cabbie, like some sort of ignoramus.

So, my dad carried the money and my little sister Anna went with him, sitting beside him in his cart. She was seven or eight years old at the time, and she was very short and not all that bright. They got about halfway to the city without any difficulty, but as soon as he spotted Moses' Pub, he dropped in, had a few glasses of wine, got himself drunk, and started to brag:

"Hey, you guys, look at me! I'm just a little guy, a nothing farmer, but I have a ton of money with me—all in cash. If I wanted to, I could buy this whole tavern, including Moses, his wife and kids, and the cat. I can buy anything with this money, you name it!"

He made all kinds of jokes, boasting about the money he had, and at the end he complained,

"Listen boys, it's not so easy being rich. If you have no money, you have nothing to worry about. But if you have a lot of money, you have to take care of it, and you've got to be careful that nobody steals it from you."

The pub was filled with people at the time, and most of them were drunk, but they all heard what he said. There were all kinds of people, including bums, tramps, and robbers, in this pub on that highway. All of a sudden, my dad realized that he had said too much, and he got scared. He left the pub in a hurry and went on his way. As he was reaching the forest, he could hear the sounds of a chase—several horses were galloping behind him.

"They're after me," my dad said to little Anna. "I should have held my tongue in that pub. I think I'm in trouble."

He thought for a while and then he said, "They are definitely after me, that's for sure. Here dear, Anna, take this bundle with the money and go hide in the bush. If something bad happens to me, give this money to your mother, and tell her to give it back to the farmers. Go, child, go, right across the forest, and don't talk to anybody."

So he gave her the money, and she hid herself in a thick bush. She saw that shortly, three riders came to her dad. One of them was a big-faced tall man in a red silk shirt, and the other two were day laborers from the railroad, the local bandits. They stopped their horses, and spoke roughly to my dad:

"Hey you, wait! Where's the money?"

"What are you talking about? What money? Let me go!"

"The money that you're bringing to your landlord for the leases. Give us the money, or we're going to kill you!"

And so they started tormenting my father, and instead of asking for mercy, he was laughing and mocking them,

"Hey, you bums, get out of here! You're a bad lot. You don't deserve any money, just a good beating, enough to make your back ache for the next three years. Let me go, or I'll defend myself. I have a revolver in my pocket!"

The robbers lost their patience when he said this, and they started beating him as hard as they could.

They searched him and the whole carriage, and they even took his boots; when my father went on scolding them after this, they started to torture him in other ways. Little Anna was so scared that she ran away through the thick forest. She ran for several hours, and it got dark. All by herself, deep in the forest, she was very frightened.

Suddenly she saw a little light in the distance. She went closer and saw that it was a forest ranger's hut. She knocked at the door, and a woman opened it and let her in.

Little Anna gave her the money to keep and told her the whole story.

The old woman put her to bed to sleep.

In the middle of the night, a man came into the house.

Anna saw that this was the same tall robber in the red shirt. He said,

"Listen, wife, I think that we killed a man needlessly. We murdered him, but there was no money on him."

My sister understood that the man in the red shirt was the forest ranger, and the woman was his wife.

"We just killed a man for nothing," his two rugged friends said. "We have sinned, killing that guy for no reason at all."

The forest ranger's wife looked at them and smiled.

"Why are you laughing, you stupid old woman?"

"I'm laughing because I have not sinned, and I have not killed anyone, and yet I got all the money."

"What money? You are a liar!"

"Look here, and then you can say whether I am a liar or not."

The woman untied the bundle, and showed them the money, and then she told them how little Anna came to her, and what she said and all that. The killers got happy and started arguing about how to share the money; they almost started a fight, but then they sat down at the table to eat.

Little Anna lay in bed. She heard everything that they said to each other, and she was very scared. What could she do? She had learned from their conversation that her father was already dead; he was lying in the middle of the road, and she imagined that the wolves and wild dogs were eating him, and that their only horse had escaped far into the forest and was also being eaten by the wolves, and that she too would be punished and beaten by the police because she did not save the money.

When the robbers finished eating, they sent the woman for vodka and wine. They had a lot of money now, and they could afford it. So they drank and sang songs and then they sent the woman for more wine. One of them said,

"We can drink all night, until morning. We have lots of money now, and we don't have to count our kopecks. Go ahead, drink like a fish!"

By midnight, they were thoroughly trashed. The woman had just been sent to fetch more wine, for the third time. The forest ranger stood up and paced across the room, trying to keep his balance.

"Listen, boys, we have to deal with that little girl somehow. We've got to get rid of her. If we leave her here, she'll be the first one to turn us in."

Their discussion was short. Anna could not be allowed to live. She should be stabbed. And yet, it is not so easy to take a butcher knife to a sleeping child—only a drunk or a madman can do this. The argument about who should kill her lasted for almost an hour. They almost started another fight; no one would agree to do it, and they ended up casting lots. It fell to the forest ranger. He downed another glass of vodka, heaved a deep sigh, stood up, and went outside to find his axe.

But little Anna was not so stupid. Maybe she was a bit slow at that age, but this time she did a smart thing. Maybe it was God who gave her this idea, or maybe you just get smart if your life depends on it.

She stood up quietly from the bed, took the fur coat that the forest ranger's wife had given to her, and covered their daughter who lay next to her on the bed with this coat. Quietly, she took the other girl's cardigan and put it on. Then, she pulled the hood over her head and face and walked across the room, past the two drunken labourers, and outside. They thought that she was the forest ranger's daughter and they never gave her a second glance. She was lucky that the woman was out at the moment—she had gone for more wine; she would have known whether it was her daughter or not.

As soon as little Anna got outside, she started running as fast as she could into the forest. She wandered all night, but in the dawn's gray twilight, she found the highway and started running along the edge.

She was lucky this time—George, the town clerk, God bless his soul, was going fishing, walking the other way with his fishing rods. Anna told him everything that she had seen that night. Without a moment's hesitation, he turned around and ran back to the village. He gathered a group of farmers, and they hurried to the forest ranger's hut.

When they got there, they found all four of them passed out drunk, lying on the floor asleep, including the woman. First, the farmers searched them all and retrieved the money—but when they looked at the little bed behind the fireplace—oh, Holy God!

The forest ranger's daughter was lying there on the wooden cot, covered with a fur coat, but her head was splattered with blood—they had killed her with an axe. The farmers woke up the three drunken men and the woman, tied their hands behind them, and brought them to the police station.

The woman was crying out loud and moaning, and the

forest ranger's head was nodding and bobbing wildly; he kept saying,

"What a hangover, boys! Can I have a drink? I have a headache."

There was on open court session in town, and they all got heavy sentences, exactly what they deserved, according to the law.

That is the story of what happened in the ravine behind that forest. You can hardly see the spot now, with the sun going down.

DRAMA

"Pavel Vasilich, a certain lady is asking for you," reported Luke, his butler. "She has been waiting for nearly an hour."

Pavel Vasilich had just finished his breakfast. When he heard about the lady, he wrinkled his nose as he said,

"Tell her to go to hell. Tell her that I am busy right now."

"Pavel Vasilich, this is the fifth time she has come to see you already. She says that it is very important for her to see you. She is on the verge of bursting into tears."

"Fine, invite her into my office."

Pavel Vasilich put on his jacket, slowly took a pen in one hand and a book in the other hand, and, pretending to be very busy, entered his office.

His visitor was already there, waiting for him. She was a big, chubby lady with a fleshy face, wearing glasses, dressed more than decency required. She had a sophisticated hat, the top of which was a gray bird with a design of four ribbons around it. As soon as she saw the master of the house she clasped her hands together as if in prayer and lifted her eyes to the ceiling.

"Certainly, you do not remember me," she started in a deep, male-sounding, tenor voice, obviously showing her excitement. "I had the pleasure of meeting you at the Krutsky party. My name is Mrs. Grasshopper."

"Oh, I remember. Well, please take a seat. What can I do for you?"

"You see . . . um . . . I . . . well," the lady muttered as she tried to continue. "I am Mrs. Grasshopper. I am a great admirer of your talent and I always read your articles with great pleasure. Do not think that I am flattering. God forbid! I am just saying what you deserve. I always read your work, always! I, too, am an author. Actually, I do not dare calling myself a female writer but I have a little drop of honey in the general beehive of liter-ature, so to speak. I have had published, at different times, three stories for children. I have also done a lot of translating, and my brother worked at the *Business Review Newspaper*."

"So what is it exactly that I can do for you today?"

"You see," Mrs. Grasshopper lowered her glance and blushed as she began, "I know your talent, and I know your views, but I would like your opinion, or, to be exact, your advice. As you know, pardon my French, I have an outline in the form of a the-atrical drama, and before submitting it officially, I would like your opinion."

Mrs. Grasshopper, with an expression of a bird caught in a net, rummaged nervously in the folds of her dress and pulled out a thick notebook.

Now, Pavel Vasilich loved only his own writing. Pieces written by others, which he had to listen to often, reminded him of a cannon being aimed at his head. On seeing the note-book, he became fearful, and hastily said,

"Please leave it here. I will read it later."

"Pavel Vasilich," Mrs. Grasshopper said dramatically, standing up and again folding her hands, as if in prayer. "I know you are busy. I know that every minute counts for you, and I know that you, in the depths of your soul, are sending me to hell, but please be so kind and let me read my drama to you now. Please," she implored.

"It was a pleasure to meet you." Pavel Vasilich now felt bewildered. "But my dear lady, I am very busy at the moment. I have somewhere to go."

"Pavel Vasilich." The lady groaned as her eyes filled with tears. "I must insist. I know I am an impudent, saucy, impertinent, cheeky creature, but please, please help me! Tomorrow I am going to the remote town of Kazan, and before I go I would like to know your opinion. Just give me half an hour of your time, just one half hour, I implore you!"

Pavel Vasilich was a weak person, and he could not refuse her request.

When he saw the lady begin to cry and to kneel in front of him, he became even more confused and murmured, seemingly at a loss, "Well, then. . . All right, all right, please read it, I will listen. Keep in mind, though, that I only have half an hour for you."

Mrs. Grasshopper gave a shriek of joy, took off her hat, sat down, and started reading.

First she read about a butler and a cleaning lady tidying up a luxurious parlor, discussing a landlady, Anna Sergeevna, who built a school and a hospital in their little town out of charity. After the butler left, the maid gave a lengthy monologue that education is good and ignorance is bad for you.

Then Mrs. Grasshopper brought the butler back to the parlor and gave him a lengthy monologue that the landlord, who was a general, did not tolerate the liberal views of his daughter and wanted her to marry a rich officer of the Guard, and who said that common people could be saved by keeping them in ignorance.

After the servants left, the landlady appeared by herself and announced to the spectators that she had not slept the whole night and had been thinking about Valentine Ivanovich, the poor son of a village teacher who was supporting his sick father. Valentine studied at the university, but he did not believe in love and he had no purpose in life. He was expecting his death, and the landlady was going to save him.

Pavel Vasilich half listened to the reading of the drama, and thought of his bed with great longing.

He looked angrily at Mrs. Grasshopper and could not follow a single word she was reading. He thought the following:

"You were brought here by the devil himself. Why should I listen to your nonsense? Why should I suffer sitting through your drama? Oh my God, her notebook is so thick! This is torture of the highest degree!"

Pavel Vasilich looked at the portrait of his wife on the wall and suddenly remembered the list of things his wife had asked him to bring up to the cottage: five meters of braid, a pound of cheese, and a pack of toothpaste.

"I hope I did not lose the sample of the braid," he thought. "Where did I put it? Oh, I think it is in the pocket of my blue jacket. Look how those mean flies have managed to put little dots on my wife's portrait. I should ask Olga, the cleaning lady, to clean the glass. She is reading Scene 12. This means soon it will be the end of the first act. How can she do this in this heat, with her complexion and bulk—how can she have any inspiration? How is it possible? Instead of writing dramas, she would be better off having a soft drink, and sleeping in her basement in this heat.

"Do you believe that this monologue is a little bit too long?" Mrs. Grasshopper asked, lifting her eyes from her reading.

Pavel Vasilich had not been listening to the monologue. He got confused and said in such a guilty tone, as if it were not the lady but he who had written this monologue,

"Not at all! It is very nice!"

Mrs. Grasshopper beamed with happiness and continued with her reading.

Anna: You are too deeply involved with logical analysis. Too early you stopped living with your heart and started living with your head.

Valentine: What is heart? Heart is a medicinal term for those who want to describe their emotions, and I do not care for it.

Anna: And love? Tell me, what is love? Is it the product of an association of ideas? Have you ever loved before?

Valentine (bitterly): Let us not touch old wounds that have not yet healed. *(Pause)*

Anna: It seems to me that you are unhappy.

In the middle of Scene 16, Pavel Vasilich yawned, and then snapped his teeth, a noise much like the sound made by dogs when they catch flies or insects. He instantly feared that this bad-mannered noise had been heard by her, and quickly put an expression of friendly attention on his face.

"Scene Seventeen," she read out loud.

"Where is the end of all this?" he thought. "Oh, my God! If this torture continues for ten more minutes, I will scream for help! This is unbearable!"

Finally, reading faster and louder, the lady raised her voice and read,

"The end of Act One. The curtain falls."

Pavel Vasilich made a small movement and sighed with relief. He made to stand up from his chair, but Mrs. Grasshopper quickly flipped the page and started reading very fast,

"The scene in the country. There is a school to the right, and the hospital to the left. You can see the local people sitting on the steps of the hospital, talking to each other quietly."

"Excuse me," Pavel Vasilich interrupted her. "How many acts do you have altogether?"

"Five acts. The play consists of five acts," Mrs. Grasshopper repeated, and then continued quickly, as if afraid that her listener would leave.

"Valentine is looking out of the school window. You can see in the background the local farmers bringing their belongings into the pub to pawn them and spend the money on drink."

With the feeling of being slowly executed, or no possibility of parole, Pavel Vasilich hopelessly waited for the end of her reading. He could hardly keep his eyes open and keep up the expression of attention on his face. Sometime in the future, the lady would stop reading and leave. That time seemed so remote that he dared not even think about it.

"Tru-du-du," Mrs. Grasshopper's voice rang suddenly in his ears. "Buzz-buzz. Tru-tu-tu. Buzz."

"I forgot to take some soda and medication for my stomach," he thought to himself.

"What was I thinking about? Oh yes, baking soda. I must have some irritation in my stomach. Isn't it strange that Mr. Smirnovsky drinks vodka all day long, and has no irritation. Look, a little bird on the windowsill outside. A sparrow."

Pavel Vasilich made an effort to open his heavy eyelids, yawned without opening his mouth, and looked at Mrs. Grasshopper. She began to sway and rock in his eyes, then she became three-headed, and one of her heads started growing and pushed against the ceiling.

Valentine: No. Let me go!

Anna (scared): Why?

Valentine (talking to himself): She is so pale. *(Addressing her)* Do not try to find out why. I would better die. You will never learn my reasons for leaving.

Anna (after a small pause): You cannot leave like this.

Mrs. Grasshopper started to swell and to grow, and turned into a huge monster. Then she blended with the gray air of the office. He could only see her talking mouth. And then she became very small, as small as a perfume bottle. After that she swayed from side to side and, together with the desk, moved into a remote corner of the room.

Valentine (holding Anna in his embrace): You brought me back to life; you showed me the purpose of life! You revived me as a spring rain revives the wakening earth. But it is too late, too late! I am sick with terminal tuberculosis.

Pavel Vasilich trembled and looked through cloudy eyes at Mrs. Grasshopper. For a minute, he looked at her, motionless, without understanding anything.

"Act Two. The same actors together with the baron, the police officer, and the witnesses."

Valentine: Take me! I am yours.

Anna: Take me, too! I am his. Finally! And you can take me. I am yours. I love him more than life!

Baron: Anna, you forgot that you are killing your father with this news, this kind of behavior.

Mrs. Grasshopper again began to swell.

Looking around him with the desperation of a wild animal, Pavel Vasilich stood up from his chair, cried out in an unnatural voice, grabbed a very heavy file from his desk and, without understanding what he was doing, hit Mrs. Grasshopper on her head.

"You can take me to the police station. I killed her!" he said a minute later to the people who ran into his office.

The jury found him not guilty, under the circumstances.

AN AMBULANCE

———— ❖ ————

Hey, people, let them pass through! The police sergeant and the town clerk are coming!"

"Good day, George Alpatych," the crowd greets the sergeant. "We hope you are fine, and that everything will be all right."

Several give him happy wishes for the future. The drunken local police sergeant tries to say something, but he cannot. He makes a vague gesture with his fingers in the air, bulges his eyes, and pumps his thick red cheeks with such force as if he were playing the highest note on a trombone. The city clerk, a tiny man with a short red nose and a jockey's hat, puts an energetic expression on his face as he moves through the crowd.

"Where is the person who was drowning?" he asks. "Where is he?"

"Here he is," someone yells in answer.

A tall and very thin elderly man dressed in a long robe and peasant's shoes has just been pulled out from the water by local farmers, and he is soaked from head to toe. He stretches his hands and legs to his sides, and sits in a puddle, at the edge of the river, mumbling to himself.

"Oh, my friends! I am from the Ryazan region, from Zaraisk County. Both my sons work, as do I. I work for Mr. Prokhor Sergeev in construction, painting houses. He pays me seven rubles and tells me, 'Now, Fyodor, you should respect me as if I am your son.' Hey, get out of here!"

"Where are you from?" the town clerk asks him.

"He says that I should respect him like a son! Hey, get out of here! Do I have to work for him for seven rubles?"

"He has been mumbling like this for quite some time, and we cannot understand a word," the local police deputy Anisim is yelling in a high, excited voice. His face is beaded with sweat, and he seems very excited by the ongoing events.

"I will tell you everything, Egor Makarych! Quiet down! He comes from Kurnovo, a neighboring village. So he comes—Listen up! So, he comes from Kurnovo and he decided to take a short cut and cross the river here. He was very drunk, and he could not control himself. It was dumb of him to get into the water. He then fell down and the current began to carry him around like a twig. He was crying for help at the top of his lungs, when I was coming by with Alexander. 'Who is yelling? What's happening?' I asked. Taking the situation in quickly, I said, 'Alexander, throw away your accordion, for we have to save this man!'

"The water was coming fast. The current was very strong. One of us pulled him by the shirt, and the other grabbed his hair. Then others ran to the bank of the river, making a lot of noise, and everyone wanted to save him, but they couldn't decide who should go! So we are tortured, George Makarovich, and if you had not come, he really could have drowned."

"What is your name? Where are you from? Who are you?" the town clerk asks loudly as he bends down to look the old man in the face.

The man glances around blankly with his empty eyes and keeps silent.

"He is a bit crazy," Anisim says. "His lungs are full of water. My dear man, tell us who you are? Look, he is silent! I wonder if there is much life left in him? Probably his soul has almost escaped from his body. Look at what can happen over a weekend to a man. He could die any minute now. God save us from this! Look, his face is all blue!"

"Hey, you." The town clerk is shaking the man by his shoulder. "Hey, you! Answer me! Where are you from? Is your brain filled with water? Hey, you!"

"Only for seven rubles?" the man mumbles. "Get out of here! I don't want to work for you anymore! I don't want to!"

"Speak clearly, man. What exactly is it that you do not want? Tell us!"

The drowned man shakes his head in the air, teeth shattering.

"It only looks as if you are alive. You do not look like a man in his right mind," Anisim says. "We should give him some drops."

"You and your drops," the clerk says in a mocking tone. "What drops are you talking about? The man here has nearly drowned. We should revive him, bring him back to life properly, and you want to give him drops! Have you no feelings? Quickly! Run to the town hall, grab a blanket, and we will be able to get him dry as fast as possible. Do it, fast!"

Several people rush to the village to fetch a blanket.

The clerk gets inspired. He folds up his sleeves, touches the sides of his body with both hands, and makes numerous small movements with his body, showing that he is filled with energy and decisiveness.

"Hey, everyone! If you don't belong here, get going! Have you sent for the police? You had better go home, dear George Alpatych! You are drunk today, and the best thing you can do is to go home and relax."

The sergeant waves his fingers in the air again, trying to say something, getting redder and redder as he fails to speak.

"Put it down here!" the clerk commands as they bring the blanket. "Take him by his arms and legs, like so. And now, put him in the middle of the blanket."

"Hey, get out of here!" the old man mumbles, without resisting their efforts, seemingly unaware that they had lifted him up on a blanket. "I do not want it, your job!"

"It's all right, my friend," the town clerk says. "Don't be afraid! We are going to throw you up in the air a little. You will feel better. In a little while, a village policeman will come and write a report. Now, let us bundle him up and get ready to throw him."

Eight strong and tall farmers, including the sheriff Anisim, pick up the folds of cloth. First they throw the man up tentatively as if they are not certain of their strength.

But then, getting the hang of it, with a cruel and concentrated expression, they do it faster and stronger, eagerly throwing the man up. They try to straighten their bodies, standing up on their tiptoes, and hop, as if they would like to fly in the sky together with the man on the blanket.

"One, two, three! One, two, three!"

The very short town clerk is trying to stand up on his tiptoes, as if he is trying to touch a little bit of the cloth with his hands. He yells instructions in a voice that does not seem to be his normal voice.

"Faster, faster! All together, now! One, two, three! Keep going! Anisim, I am asking you to do it faster! Go! Go!"

They take a short break, and for a moment they can see the old man's pale face surrounded by messy hair, wearing an expression of puzzlement, horror, and physical pain.

The next second, the face disappears again as the cloth is thrown up and to the right, then quickly goes down and then is thrown up and to the left.

The crowd of spectators cheers,

"That's it, boys. Good job! You are doing great! Keep it up!"

"Good, Egor Makarovich, you are doing a great job, we will not let him go. In a minute he will be on his feet, and he will buy us a drink of vodka."

"Hey you, I will whip you!" someone cries from behind the crowd.

"Look, neighbors, here comes the local lady with her estate manager." The cart stops near the crowd, and they see a rather fat, old woman in fashionable eyeglasses, with an umbrella shielding her from the sun. Next to her sits her property manager. The landlady looks frightened.

"What has happened? What are you doing?" she asks.

"We are trying to revive a drowned man. How are you? We are a little bit drunk, because it's such a nice day. We were walking across the village celebrating, as today is a holiday!"

"Oh my God!" the old landlady says in horror. "They are trying to revive the drowned man! Anthony," she addresses the manager, "go, for God's sake, and tell them not to do it. They'll kill him. You cannot revive a drowned man by tossing him up in the air. You need to rub him with alcohol, and resuscitate him. Go, I order you!"

Anthony goes down and pushes through the crowd toward the men throwing the drowned man in the air. He looks strict.

"What are you doing? You cannot revive a drowned man by throwing him up!"

"So then, how are we to revive him?" the town clerk asks. "He has nearly drowned recently."

"So what? I know that. People who are drowned should not be thrown up, but rubbed with alcohol. It is written in the calendar of wisdom. Stop doing this, and start doing what I tell you to do."

The clerk is confused. He shrugs his shoulders and steps aside. The people throwing the old man place him on the ground and stare at the landlady with surprised looks, glancing either at her or at her manager, Anthony.

The drowned man is already lying with his eyes closed, breathing heavily.

"Hey, you drunks!" Anthony becomes angry.

"My dear sir!" The clerk, out of breath, comes closer and puts his hand to his heart in respect. "Why use this tone? Do you think we are animals, and we do not understand?"

"Men, do not throw him up. Take his clothes off. We will rub him with alcohol."

"Men! We should rub him with alcohol, so do it!"

The drowned man is removed from his clothes, and under the guidance of Anthony they begin rubbing him. The landlady, who does not want to see the naked man, moves off to the side.

"Oh, Anthony," she moans. "Anthony! Come here. Do you know how to do rescue breathing? You need to roll him from side to side, and then push on his chest and his stomach."

"Hey, guys, roll him from one side to another," says Anthony, coming back to the crowd. "Then, push him in his stomach, but not very hard!"

The town clerk, who after his previous energetic activity feels a little tired, comes closer through the crowd to the old man and begins to push his chest and rub him.

"Help me, boys," he implores. "I need assistance!"

"Anthony," the lady asks, "come over here. Give him some burned feathers to breathe and tickle him. Tell them to tickle him well. Do it!"

Five minutes passes, then ten. The lady looks at the crowd and watches all this activity.

All that can be heard is the sound of the busy farmers breathing heavily, and Anthony and the town clerk giving commands. The smell of burnt feathers and alcohol fills in the air.

Finally, another ten minutes later, the crowd moves to the sides and Anthony steps out, completely red and soaked with sweat. Anisim follows him.

"We should have rubbed him from the very beginning," Anthony says. "Now we can do nothing."

"What could we do? We started late, far too late!" Anisim agrees.

"What now?" the landlady asks. "Is he still alive?"

"No, he is dead, God bless his soul." Anisim sighs deeply. "When we had pulled him out of the water, his eyes were open, but now his body is completely cold."

"It is a pity."

"This was his unlucky day. His destiny is to accept death not on firm land, but in the chilly water. Can we have some tips for our efforts, dear lady?"

Anthony jumps on the cart and looks disgustedly at the crowd that now is moving away from the corpse. The cart shudders, and begins to move away . . .

BAD BUSINESS

———— ✦ ————

Who is out there?"

There is no reply. The security guard cannot see anything in the darkness of the cemetery; however, through the noise made by the wind and the trees, he can hear someone walking in front of him along the alley.

The foggy and cloudy March night covers the earth. It seems to the guard that the earth, the sky, and himself, together with his thoughts, are united in something huge, impossible to penetrate, and dark. Walking is only possible through taking a guess and a small step, it is so dark.

"Who is out there?" the guard repeated. He thought he could hear a whisper and subdued laughter.

"It is me, father," the voice of an old man answers him.

"And who are you?"

"It's me. I am just a passerby."

"What kind of passerby are you?" shouted the guard, trying

to mask his fear with his shouts. "The devil must have brought you here. You are wandering in the middle of the night in a cemetery."

"Is it true that there is a cemetery here?"

"What do you think? This is a cemetery! Can't you see?"

"Ooh! Holy God!" The old man makes a deep sigh in the darkness. "I cannot see anything, dear sir, in this pitch darkness, nothing at all. It is pitch dark out here, dear sir. Ooh."

"And who are you, then?"

"I am wandering, just a traveler."

"What the heck? Why are you wandering at midnight? A drunk and a bum, that's who you must be," mumbles the guard, calming down as he listens to the sighs and quiet tone of voice of the passerby. "It's a sin. You drink alcohol all day long, and then wander at night. But somehow it seems to me that you are not alone, but you are two or three people talking."

"I am alone, dear sir, all by myself, here I am. Ooh!"

The guard bumps into a man and stops.

"So how did you get here?" the guard asks.

"Really, I got lost, dear man. I was going to the Dimitry Mill and got lost."

"Hey, do you think this is the road to the mill? You must be nuts. If you're going to the mill, you have to turn left and go along the major highway, as soon as you cross the town line. You must be drunk, as you have made a long trek of about three miles. Were you drinking there, in the city?"

"Yes, dear sir, you are right and I am wrong. Truly, I have sinned, I've done wrong. So where should I go now?"

"That way, all the way straight, along the alley to its end. When you come to a dead end, turn left until you cross the whole cemetery, all the way to the gate at the end. Open it and go. Good luck! God blesses you on your way. But watch out; do not fall into the ditch. And then go along the field until you reach the highway."

"Thank you so much, sir. Could you show me that way a little bit more, dear sir? Show me to the gate, please."

"I don't have time. Go by yourself."

"Please, help me; I would be so grateful to you. I cannot see a thing. It's pitch dark. Please show me to the gate, old man."

"As I told you, I do not have time for you."

"Please, please. I cannot see a thing. I am scared to walk through the cemetery. I am scared, scared, dear sir, I'm scared!"

"Why me?" The guard sighs deeply. "All right, I will help you out. Let's go."

The guard and the wanderer start walking together. They walk next to each other, shoulder to shoulder, keeping silent for a while.

The damp, piercing wind is blowing in their faces, and the trees throw drops of water at them. The whole alley is covered with big pools of mud.

"However, I cannot understand one thing." says the guard after a long silence. "How did you get in here? The gates are closed with a lock. Did you climb over the fence or what? If you climbed the fence, it would not have been nice for an old man like you."

"I don't know, dear sir, I don't know anything at all. It is a kind of obsession, a devil's trick. And you, are you a guard down here, dear sir?"

"Yes, a security guard."

"Is there only one for the whole cemetery?"

The wind blows so strongly that they both stopped for a

moment. The guard waits until the wind abates a little, and answers, "There are usually three of us, but one has a fever, and the second one is asleep. So I am taking turns with him."

"Yes, yes, dear sir, I see, I understand. What a loud wind, a strong wind! Probably, dead men can hear its howling. It howls like a wild animal. Ooh."

"And where do you come from?"

"Really, I come from far from here. I am from the Volga district. I am wandering, like a pilgrim, and praying for others."

The guard stops for a while to light his pipe. He bends behind the other man's back and burns several matches. The matches shine light for a few moments on an alley to the right, and several tombstones and an iron fence around one grave to the left.

"They are all fast asleep, our dear dead!" mumbles the wandering man, making another deep sigh. "The rich and poor, the wise and stupid, the kind and evil, all are asleep. All have the same price, and come to the same end."

"Now we are walking along the alley, but one day we will lie beside ones like them," says the guard.

"Yes, yes. We all will die sooner or later. Ooh. We all do bad things in this life, have bad thoughts."

"We sin. My soul is filled with sins. I have enraged the Lord, and will be punished both in this world, and in the next."

"Yes, and we all will die anyway."

"Yes, truly, that's true, you are right."

"A wanderer has an easier end than we common folk," the guard says.

"There are different wanderers, different pilgrims. There are those who do it for God's sake, and those who do the devil's business, walking late at night across the cemetery.

Such a wanderer can hit you on your head with an axe and you could be dead in an instant."

"Why are you saying this?"

"Just so . . . Here, it seems to me that here is the gate. Open it up, dear sir."

The guard opens the gate by touch, takes the wanderer by his sleeve, and shows him the way out of the gate.

"This is the end of the cemetery. Now, you should walk along the whole length of the field, and then you will end up at the major highway. But there will be a ditch there, so watch out and do not fall in it. And when you are on the road, turn right and you will soon get to the mill."

"Ooh." The wanderer lets out another deep sigh and then is silent for a while. "But now I think that I do not have to go to the mill. Why should I go there at this hour? I would better stay with you right here, dear sir."

"Why would you want to just stand around with me?"

"Just because . . . it is more interesting for me."

"Hey, you are a funny man! I can see that you like jokes."

"Yes, I like jokes," said the passerby with a hoarse giggle. "And you, dear sir. You will remember the wanderer for a long time now."

"Why should I remember you?"

"Well, I played a trick on you. I am neither a wanderer nor a pilgrim."

"Who are you then?"

"I am a dead man who has just been raised from the grave. Do you remember the turner Gubarev who committed suicide recently? I am that man, back from the dead."

"You just lied to me!"

The guard does not believe the man, but he feels a dark fear spread throughout his body as he rushes to try and relock the gate.

"Wait, where are you going?" the wanderer asks, holding the guard by the sleeve. "Where are you going? Do not leave me here all by myself."

"Let me go!" shouts the guard, trying to free his arm.

"Stand still! If you want to live, be quiet, stand here until I tell you to move. I do not want to shed blood, otherwise you would have died right in front of me, a long time ago, you dog. Stand still!"

The guard's knees begin to tremble. He closes his eyes and rests against the fence, filled with fear. He would like to shout out very loudly, but he knows that there is no one to hear him. The wanderer stands next to him, holding him by his sleeve. Another three minutes pass in silence.

"One guard has a fever, the second one is asleep and the third is off seeing to wanderers," the man whispers. "What kind of guards are you? How do you earn your salary? No, brother, criminals have always been faster than guards. Wait, stand still, do not move!"

Another five minutes and then ten minutes pass in silence. Suddenly, the wind brings them the sound of someone whistling.

"Now you can go. Go home, and thank God that you are alive," says the wanderer, finally releasing the guard's arm.

He whistles back, running from the gate, and one could hear as he jumped across the ditch. The guard, still anticipating something bad and trembling from fear, closes the gate and turns into the big alley. As he does, he hears someone's fast footsteps, and someone asks him in a whispering voice,

"Is it you, Tim? Where is Mike?"

He keeps on running along the big alley, and then notices a small flickering light in the darkness. The closer to the light, the more scared he becomes. "It seems to me that that light is coming from the inside of the church," he thinks. "Why do I see a light there? Oh, God! It is true!"

For a minute or so, the guard stands in front of a smashed window and looks at the altar in horror. A little wax candle that the thieves forgot to extinguish is still flickering in the gusts of the wind, and throwing dark shadows on the items lying on the floor of the church—the garments of the priests, the fallen boxes, and the footprints around the altar.

After some time passes, the howling wind blows the warning chimes of the church bells across the cemetery.

MISFORTUNE

〜✦〜

The director of the town bank, Peter Semenych, the accountant, his assistant, and two members of the board were sent to prison in the night. The day after the turmoil, the merchant Avdeyev, a member of the bank's auditing committee, was sitting in his shop with his friends, saying:

"So it must be God's will. There's no way to escape your destiny. Today we eat caviar, and tomorrow—beware of that—it can be prison, poverty, or even death. Things happen. Take Peter Semenych, for example . . ."

He was talking, narrowing his tipsy eyes, while his friends went on drinking and eating caviar, and listened to him. Having described the disgrace and helplessness of Peter Semenych, who just a day before was powerful and generally respected, Avdeyev went on with a sigh:

"If you steal money, beware of the sting. Serves them right, the swindlers! They knew how to steal, filthy scum, now time for them to answer!"

"Look out, Ivan Danilych, that you don't catch it, too!" one of his friends observed.

"What has it to do with me?"

"Well, they were stealing, and where was the auditing committee looking? You must have been signing the reports."

"Yeah, it's easily said," Avdeyev grinned. "See, I signed them! They used to bring the reports to my shop, and so I signed them. As if I understood it! I'll scribble my name on whatever I get. If you wrote I murdered someone, I'd sign that, too. I don't have time to make it out; besides, I can't see without my glasses."

Having discussed the ruin of the bank and the destiny of Peter Semenych, Avdeyev and his friends went to an acquaintance whose wife celebrated her birthday with a party. At the birthday party everyone was discussing nothing but the bank ruin. Avdeyev was excited more than anyone else and assured everyone that he had had a presentiment long before that the bank would soon be ruined, and as long as two years ago he knew there were big problems at the bank. While they were eating the pie, he described a dozen illegal operations that were known to him.

"If you knew it, why didn't you report on them?" an officer who was present at the party asked him.

"It wasn't just me who knew it: the whole town knew it . . ." Avdeyev grinned. "Besides, I have no time to waste in courts, to hell with them!"

He had a rest after the pie, then had dinner, and had another rest, and then went to his church, where he was a warden; after the vespers he went back to the birthday party and played Preference till midnight. Everything seemed all right.

But when Avdeyev returned home after midnight, the lady cook, who opened the door for him, was pale and trembling so much that she could not utter a word. His wife, Elizabeth Trofimovna, a well-fed, flabby woman, was sitting on the couch in the drawing room, her gray hair hanging loose. She trembled with her entire body and, like a drunk, rolled her eyes senselessly. Her oldest son, Vassiliy, a schoolboy, as pale as she was and extremely agitated, was fussing around her with a glass of water.

"What is it?" asked Avdeyev, and looked angrily at the stove (his family was often poisoned by its fumes).

"The investigator and the police have just been here," answered Vassiliy. "They've made a search."

Avdeyev looked around him. The cupboards, the chests, the tables—traces of the recent search could be seen everywhere. For a minute, Avdeyev stood still, not understanding a thing, then his whole inside quivered and grew heavy, his left leg went numb, and, unable to endure the trembling, he lay prone on the couch. He felt his insides were turning over and his left leg, which he could not control, was tapping against the back of the couch.

In the course of just two or three minutes he recalled the whole of his past but could not remember any guilt that would deserve the attention of judicial authority.

"It's simply nonsense," he said, rising. "They must have slandered me. Tomorrow I'll file a complaint so that they don't dare . . . you know."

Next morning after a sleepless night Avdeyev, as always, went to his shop. His customers told him that during the night the prosecutor also sent to prison a friend of the bank director and the chief clerk of the bank. This news did not upset Avdeyev. He was sure he had been slandered, and that if he filed a complaint today, then the investigator would get into trouble for yesterday's search.

After nine o'clock he rushed to the town council to see the secretary, the only educated person there.

"Vladimir Stepanych, what's it all about?" he said, bending down to the secretary's ear. "People have been stealing, and what have I to do with it? How come? My dear fellow," he whispered, "my house was searched last night! Indeed! Have they gone crazy? Why would they bother me?"

"Because you shouldn't be a muttonhead," the secretary answered calmly. "Before signing the papers you should've looked at them."

"Look at what? Even if I looked for a thousand years at those reports I wouldn't understand a thing! It's all Greek to me! I am no accountant. They used to bring them to me and I signed them."

"Excuse me. Apart from signing the papers, you—as well as all your committee—are seriously compromised. You borrowed nineteen thousand from the bank on no security."

"Oh goodness!" exclaimed Avdeyev, surprised. "Am I the only one who owes money to the bank? The whole town owes it. I pay the interest and will repay the debt. I assure you! And besides, to be honest with you, was it me who borrowed the money? It was actually Petr Semenych who made me take it. 'Take it,' he said, 'take it. If you don't take it,' he said, 'it means you don't trust us and remain an outsider. You take it,' he said, 'and build your father a mill.' So I took it."

"Well, you see, who else could reason like that but children or muttonheads. In any case, signor, you shouldn't worry about it. You won't escape trial, of course, but, very likely, they'll discharge you."

The secretary's indifference and calm tone set Avdeyev's mind at ease. Having returned to his shop and seeing his acquaintances there, he again drank, ate caviar, and philosophized. He almost forgot the search, and there was only one thing that troubled him that he could not help noticing: his left leg strangely grew numb and his stomach for some reason did not work properly.

That evening destiny fired another deafening shot into Avdeyev: at an extraordinary session of the town council, all the members of the bank's board, Avdeyev among them, were fired from the board, as they were on trial. In the morning he received a paper requesting him to give up immediately his duties as a churchwarden.

After that, Avdeyev lost count of the shots fired by destiny into him. Strange days flashed rapidly by, one after another, each bringing an experience he had never known and some new unexpected surprise. Incidentally, the investigator sent him a summons, and he returned home after the interrogation insulted and red-faced.

"He bothered me like hell with that question of his: 'Why did you sign it?' I did sign it and that's it. I didn't do it on purpose. They brought the papers to the shop and I signed them. To tell the truth, I'm no great reader of those written things."

Some young people with indifferent faces sealed up the shop, and made an inventory of all the furniture in the house. Suspecting there was some intrigue behind these actions and, as before, feeling no guilt whatsoever, the insulted Avdeyev started to run to different authorities and institutions filing complaints. He waited in the lobbies for hours on end, he composed long petitions, he wept, he swore. The prosecutor and investigator replied to his complaints in an indifferent, rational way: "Come here when you are summoned: now we have no time for you." Others said: "It's not our business."

The secretary, an educated man, who—as it seemed to Avdeyev—could help him, merely shrugged his shoulders and said:

"It's all your fault. You shouldn't have been a muttonhead."

The old man bustled about, while his leg continued to grow numb and his stomach functioned even worse than before. When he got tired of being idle and poverty was at the door, he decided to go to his father's mill, or to his brother to start a flour business, but he was not allowed out of town. His family went to his father's and he was left alone.

The days flashed by, one after another. Left without his family, without his shop and money, the former churchwarden, an honored and respected man, spent whole days wandering about his friends' shops. He drank, ate, and listened to advice. Every morning and evening he went to church to kill time. Looking at the icons for hours, he did not pray but reflected. His conscience was clear, and he thought of his current situation as being a mistake and a misunderstanding. In his opinion, this all happened only because the investigators and officers were too young and inexperienced; he believed that if he managed to talk to some elderly judge openheartedly and in detail, everything would be set right again. He did not understand his judges, and he believed that his judges did not understand him.

The days rushed by one after another, and finally, after a long and tedious protraction, came the day of the trial. Avdeyev borrowed fifty rubles, made sure he had some alcohol for his leg and herbs for his stomach, and set off for the town where the court chamber was located.

The trial went on for a week and a half. During the court hearings, Avdeyev remained among his fellow sufferers, listened attentively, but did not understand a word. As it becomes a respectable man and an innocent victim, he maintained corresponding dignity and self-worth. He was in a hostile mood. He was angry that he was detained in the court for so long, that he could not get any vegetarian food, that his lawyer did not understand him and, it seemed to him, was saying everything wrong. He believed the judges were not judging the way they should. They took hardly any notice of Avdeyev, addressed him once in three days, and the questions they asked were such that every time he answered them, Avdeyev made the audience laugh. As soon as he tried to speak of the losses he had suffered and of his wish to recover the court costs, his lawyer turned around and made a strange grimace, the public laughed, and the court president declared strictly that it had nothing to do with the case. In his last statement, he was not talking of the things his lawyer taught him but of something completely different, which, too, raised a laugh in the courtroom.

During the terrible hours when the jury was deliberating in its room, he sat angrily in the bar and did not for a minute think of them. He did not understand why they were deliberating for so long when everything was absolutely clear, and what they wanted of him.

As he grew hungry, he asked the waiter to bring him something cheap and vegetarian. He brought him some cold fish with carrots for forty kopecks. Avdeyev ate it and at once felt the fish falling into his stomach like a heavy lump; then followed belching, heartburn, and pain.

Later, as he listened to the foreman of the jury reading out the questions point by point, his entrails were turning over, his whole body was covered with a cold sweat, his left leg grew numb; he did not listen, he understood nothing, and suffered to the utmost because he could not sit or lie down while listening. Finally, when he and the other accused were allowed to sit down, the prosecutor of the court chamber got up and said something incomprehensible. At the same moment, as if out of nowhere, there appeared some policemen with bared swords and surrounded the accused. Avdeyev was ordered to get up and go.

Now he realized he had been found guilty and was placed under guard, but he was not scared nor surprised; there was such a revolution going on in his stomach that he could not care less about the guard.

"So we won't be allowed back to the hotel?" he asked one of his companions. "And I have three rubles and some untouched tea left in my room."

He spent the night at a private house; the whole night he felt disgusted by the fish and thought of his three rubles and the tea. Early in the morning, as the sky began to get blue, he was ordered to dress and go out. Two soldiers with bayonets took him to prison. Never before had the streets of the town seemed to him so long and endless. He did not walk on the sidewalk but in the middle of the street covered with the melting dirty snow. His insides were still fighting with the fish, his left leg was numb; he had forgotten his rubber boots either in the court or in the private house, and now his feet were cold.

Five days later all the accused were brought to court again to hear the sentence. Avdeyev learnt that he was sentenced to exile in Siberia, in the province of Tobolsk. And that did not scare nor surprise him. Somehow it seemed to him that the trial was not over yet, that the protraction still went on, and the real decision had not been made so far. He lived in prison and waited for the real decision every day.

Only six months later, when his wife and son Vassily came into prison to say good-bye to him, and when he hardly recognized his once well-fed and stout Elizabeth Trofimovna in this thin woman dressed as a beggar, and when he saw his son wearing a short, shabby jacket and light cotton trousers instead of his school uniform, only then did he realize that his fate was already decided, and that whatever new "decision" there might be, he would never be able to return to his past. And for the first time since the trial and imprisonment, he wiped the angry expression off his face and wept bitterly.

THE MAN WHO WANTED REVENGE

⊷ ⚊⚌⚊ ⊶

Fyodor Fyodorovich Sigaev—shortly after he'd caught his wife "in flagrante delicto"—was standing at the counter of the Shmuck and Co. gun store, choosing a handgun suitable for his needs. His face expressed anger, woe, sadness, and absolute resolution.

"I know what I must do," he thought. "The foundations of my family life are shattered, virtue has been ground into the dirt, and vice rejoices. As an honest citizen and a decent man, I must have revenge. First, I will kill her and her lover, and then I will kill myself."

He has not picked up any of the guns, and he has not yet killed anyone—not yet; but his imagination already pictures three bloodied corpses, the skulls blown to pieces, the splashing brains, the excitement of the crowd, the group of passersby watching the scene, and the autopsies to follow.

With all the joy of the offended innocent who achieves

239

justice, he imagines the horror of the public, the terror of the insulting and annoying woman who'd cheated on him, and in his imagination he reads already the editorial article about the shattered foundations of his family.

The French shop assistant, who makes a comically odd figure with a small potbelly and a white vest, is placing various handguns before him on the counter, smiling respectfully and rubbing his hands.

"I must recommend to you, my dear sir, this wonderful handgun made by the company Smith and Wesson. This is the finest achievement of the handgun industry. It has three different switches, an extractor for the next cartridge; it can hit any target from six hundred paces, and it is very easy to aim. I would like to draw your attention, my dear sir, to the beautiful and very clean finish of this particular piece. This is the most fashionable handgun nowadays. Every day, we sell at least ten of them to robbers, wolves, and lovers. It has a very powerful and precise performance, and uncompromising quality. With one shot you can kill both your wife and her lover, and for suicides, I do not know of a better system."

The shop assistant touched the triggers and breathed on the barrels, evincing an attitude of complete immersion in delight and joy. Looking at his face, so filled with admiration, one might imagine that he would gladly have put a bullet in the middle of his own forehead, if only he could be the owner of the handgun made by the wonderful Smith and Wesson company.

"And what is the price?" Mr. Sigaev asked.

"Forty-five rubles, sir."

"Well, this is kind of expensive for me."

"Then, my dear sir, I will show you a handgun made by

another company, a bit cheaper. Let me see—we have a wonderful selection here, all different price ranges. For example, this handgun made by the Laforchet Company costs only eighteen rubles, but (the shop assistant wrinkled his face in disgust) this system is so old-fashioned for today. Only complete losers or psychopathic ladies buy this one. To kill your wife with a Laforchet is such bad taste. Good taste and good manners are only for the guns made by Smith and Wesson."

"I am not going to shoot anyone or commit suicide," Mr. Sigaev lied gloomily. "This is for my summer cottage, to scare off thieves."

"We do not ask why our customers wish to purchase a handgun," the shop assistant said humbly, lowering his glance. "If we were to ask why people bought guns, we would soon go out of business. But with the Laforchet gun you cannot even scare a crow, because when it shoots, it makes only a very quiet, subdued little pop. Instead, I will recommend to you another line of nice guns made by the Mortimer Company. Here it is, these are called duel guns."

"Should I challenge him to a duel?" a quick thought appeared in Mr. Sigaev's head. "But this is too much honor for him. People like him should be killed like animals, like the rats they are."

The shop assistant turned to another counter with a few mincing steps, and talking and smiling nonstop, placed another pile of handguns before him. The Smith and Wesson guns looked the most appealing and respectable. Mr. Sigaev picked up one of the revolvers made by this company, looked at it dully, and was lost in his thoughts again.

In his imagination, he pictured how he would smash their skulls, how the blood would flow in a river on the area rugs and the parquetry tiles, and how the legs of his cheating wife would twitch as she died.

But this was not enough for his indignant soul. He was trying to find something more terrible.

"I've got it—I will kill only him and myself," he decided. "And I will leave her to live. Let her be destroyed by her conscience and by the contempt of her neighbors. For a woman as nervous and sensitive as she is, this would be far more torture than a quick death."

And then he imagined his funeral. Hurt feelings and all, he would lie in a coffin, with a humble smile on his lips, and like Niobe in the ancient Greek stories, she would be tortured by her conscience, and she would not know where to hide herself from the scornful glances of the indignant crowd.

"I can see sir, that you do like the guns by Smith and Wesson," the shop assistant interrupted his dreams. "If you think that they are too expensive, I can come down by five rubles. But we also have guns made by other companies, a bit cheaper."

The graceful French figure of the shop assistant turned, and he pulled out another dozen handguns in their boxes.

"Here, my dear sir, this goes for just thirty rubles. The foreign currency exchange rate has fallen again, and the customs taxes are going up, dear sir, up every hour. I swear to God, my dear man, I am not a conservative man, but even I become angry with all this. You see, these exchange rates and these customs taxes put us in such a crazy situation that a good gun can only be bought by a rich man. Poor guys can only buy these locally made guns from Tula, and sulfur matches, but these local guns are a complete disaster. When you attempt to shoot your wife with one of these, you hit your own shoulder blade."

Suddenly it occurred to Mr. Sigaev that if he were dead, he would not be able to witness the torment of the woman who had cheated on him. Revenge is only sweet when you can taste its fruits. And what would the point of all this be, if he were lying in a coffin, unable to see or hear anything?

"Or should I do it this way?" he thought. "I will kill him and then stay for his funeral and see everything, and then afterward I will kill myself, too. But no, they would arrest me and take away my gun.

"Then, I should kill him, and leave her alive. I would not kill myself for some time, so I could watch how things develop. First, I would be arrested. Later on, I would have enough time to commit suicide. The arrest is good, because during the preliminary investigation, I would have plenty of opportunity to reveal to the police and society all those cheap, rotten things that she did. And if I did kill myself, she would accuse me of everything, with her ability to tell a low and dirty lie, and people's opinion would excuse her actions and they would probably laugh at me, unless I were to stay alive . . ."

In a minute he considered her again.

"Yes, if I kill myself, they will believe her and her dirty lies. Why should I kill myself at all? This is one good reason not to. But secondly, to kill oneself is the act of a coward. Therefore, I must kill him, and would leave her to try to lie her way out, and as for me—I shall go to court. There will be a trial, and she will be called to the witness stand. She will be so embarrassed when my lawyer interrogates her in front of the crowd. The judge, the public, and everyone present will sympathize with me!"

As he was thinking along these lines, the shop assistant put more guns in front of him and decided that his duty was to keep the customer busy with conversation.

"Here is a British handgun, made by another company. But I would assure you, dear sir, that this one is not as good as the Smith and Wesson. Recently, you may have read in the papers that an officer bought a gun made by Smith and Wesson at our store. He was going to shoot his wife's lover—and what do you think? The bullet went through the lover's body, then it hit the bronze lamp, and then it hit the grand piano, and ricocheted off the grand piano, killed the lady's little dog, and even slightly wounded his wife. This is a brilliant handgun! It has brought honor to our company. The officer was just arrested recently; it is certain that he will be sentenced to hard labor." He paused.

"First of all, my dear sir, our law is too old-fashioned. Secondly, our law is always on the side of the lover. Why, you may ask? It is all very simple, dear sir: all of them—the judge, the jury, the prosecutor, and the defense lawyers—they each live with the wife of some other man, and they would all feel better if we had one husband less in the country. It would be nice for them if all the husbands could be sent to eastern Siberia, to the Sakhalin Island Prison.

"My dear sir, you should know how indignant I become when I see virtue destroyed in our society. To love another man's wife is seen as no worse than to smoke his cigarettes, to read his books. And our trade grows worse and worse—this does not mean that there are fewer lovers, no! This means that more husbands are deciding to ignore their situation. They do not seek revenge, they are afraid of the sentences, afraid of their long prison terms."

The shop assistant looked around and whispered,

"And who is to blame for all this, sir? The Russian government."

"I am not going to go to Sakhalin Island for the sake of some dirty swine. That doesn't make any sense at all." Mr. Sigaev was lost in his thoughts. "If I go to prison, it would just give my wife another opportunity to get married again and to cheat on her second husband. She would win. Therefore, I will leave her to live, I will not commit suicide myself, and as for him—I am not going to kill him. I have to think up something more logical and sensible. I shall torture them with my contempt, and start a scandalous court case against her."

"And over here, my dear sir, there is another line of wonderful shotguns. I would like to draw your attention to the very original design of the trigger."

After making his decision, Mr. Sigaev did not need a gun anymore, but the shop assistant was getting more and more inspired, and the pile of guns on the counter had grown into a great heap. The husband felt ashamed that the poor little man had spent so much time in vain, that he had wasted so much time smiling, talking, and admiring his guns.

"All right," he mumbled, "in this case, I will come back later, or I will send someone over."

He did not see the facial expression of the shop assistant, but to ease the situation, he decided to buy something. But what should he buy? He looked at the walls of the store trying to pick something cheap and his glance stopped at a green net hanging from the wall next to the entrance door.

"And this? What is this?" he asked.

"This is a net for catching small birds, quail and the like."

"And how much does it cost?"

"Eight rubles, sir."

"Wrap it up for me then please, I will purchase this."

The hurt husband paid eight rubles, took the net and, feeling even more hurt, left the store.

THIEVES

❉

A medical nurse, Mr. Ergunov, a simple-minded man, believed to be one of the greatest boasters and drunks in the county, was returning one evening on Christmas week from the little town of Repino, where he had made some purchases for the hospital. The local doctor had loaned him his best horse so that Ergunov might return on time and not be late.

At first the weather was fine and still, but by about eight that night, a violent snowstorm began. By the time he realized he only had four more miles to go, Ergunov was completely lost. He was an inexperienced rider who was unfamiliar with the road, and so he hoped the horse could find the way on its own. Two hours passed; the horse grew exhausted, Ergunov was chilled to the bone. By now he had figured out he would not make it home and he should return to Repino.

At last, through the sound of the storm, he heard a vague barking of a dog, and a blurred red spot appeared ahead of him.

Little by little, he could discern a high gate, a long fence with protruding pointed nails, and then a crooked roof came into view beyond the fence. The wind drove away the mist of snow from before his eyes, and where before there had been a red blur, there now appeared a sturdy little house with a steep cane-covered roof. One of three windows, curtained with something red, was lit up.

What kind of place was it? Ergunov recalled that on the right side of the road should be Andrei Chirikov's inn, three or four miles from the hospital. He also remembered that Chirikov had recently been killed by some robbers. He left behind an elderly wife and a daughter named Lyubka, who had been in the hospital two years earlier for treatment. The inn had a bad reputation, and it was believed quite dangerous to stay there overnight, especially with someone else's horse. However, Ergunov knew he had no choice. He felt for his revolver in his saddlebag and, after coughing boldly, knocked on the window frame with his whip handle.

"Hey! Anybody there?" he shouted. "Granny, please let me in to get warm!"

A black dog, barking hoarsely, rolled under the horse's feet, then another, this one white. Then yet another black one, until there must have been at least a dozen of them. Ergunov noticed the biggest, swung his arm and lashed out at the dog with all his force. A small long-legged dog raised his pointed muzzle upward and howled in a high-pitched, piercing voice.

Ergunov had been standing at the window knocking for a long time, until the frost glowed red on the trees next to the house, the gate creaked open, and a muffled female figure appeared holding a lantern.

"Dear granny, let me in to get warm," said Ergunov. "I was

going to the hospital, and I've lost my way. It's such weather, Lord forbid. Don't be afraid, granny, we're not strangers, right?"

"All the strangers are at home by now, as they are not invited," said the figure sternly. "Why did you feel the need to knock? The gate was not locked."

Ergunov drove through the gate into the yard and stopped at the porch, requesting that the stable boy take his horse from the old granny.

"I'm no granny." And indeed, she was not a granny. When she blew out the lantern, her features came to light and the doctor recognized Lyubka.

"What helpers are you talking about?" she said as she went into the house. "Those who are drunk are asleep, and the rest left for Repino in the morning. The holiday's coming. . . ."

As the boy fastened his horse up under the shed, Ergunov heard a whinny, and distinguished another horse in the dark, with a Cossack saddle on. It meant there was someone else in the house apart from the owners. Just in case, Ergunov took the saddle off his horse, and on his way to the house, he took both his purchases and the saddle with him.

The first room he entered was spacious, well heated, and smelled of freshly washed floors. A short, lean peasant of about forty, with a small, light brown beard, wearing a blue shirt, was sitting at the table under the icons. It was Kalashnikov, an arrant knave and horse-stealer, whose father and uncle kept an inn in Bogalyovka, who traded in stolen horses at any opportunity. He, too, had been to the hospital more than once, but he would come not for medical treatment, but to negotiate with the doctor about horses: whether there was any for sale, and whether the dear doctor, his honor, wished to trade his chestnut mare for a lovely dun gelding. Now, with his hair greased back and a silver earring glittering in his ear, he looked quite festive. Frowning, with his lower lip pulled down, he was attentively examining a big book with pictures, frayed and dog-eared. Another peasant lay stretched out on the floor near the stove, his face, shoulders, and chest covered by a sheepskin as he slept. There were two dark pools of melted snow near his new boots, with shining pieces of metal on the soles.

Seeing the doctor, Kalashnikov greeted him.

"Yeah, the weather's awful," said Ergunov, rubbing his chilled knees with the palms of his hands. "The snow's gone down my neck; I'm soaked through, I'd say, like a rat. And I think my revolver is also, well. . . ." He took out his revolver, looked at it all over, and put it into his bag again. But the revolver produced no reaction whatsoever; the peasant kept his eyes on his book. "Yeah, the weather. . . . I lost my way, and had it not been for the dogs here, I'd have been dead, I believe. Yeah, there would have been something to talk about. And where's the hostess?"

"The old woman has gone to Repino, so the girl is cooking dinner," answered Kalashnikov.

Silence followed. Shivering, Ergunov blew on his hands, huddling, and pretending he was extremely warm and well rested. The dogs were still heard barking outside. It was getting boring.

"You are from Bogalyovka, aren't you?" Ergunov asked the peasant strictly.

"Yes, I am."

As he did not have anything better to do, Ergunov started to think about that village of Bogalyovka. It was a big village that lay in a deep ravine, so that when one drove along the big road on a moonlit night, and looked down into the dark ravine and then up at the sky, it seemed that the moon was hanging over a bottomless abyss and it was the end of the world. The road down to the village was steep, serpentine, and so narrow that when one drove to Bogalyovka for any reason, one had to scream at the top of one's voice, or whistle loudly, to ensure safe passage through the pass, as there was only room for one to travel.

The peasants of Bogalyovka had the reputation of being good gardeners and horse-stealers. Their gardens always yielded large crops. In spring time, the whole village drowned in white cherry blossoms, and in summer, you could pay three kopecks and pick a pail of cherries for yourself. The peasants' wives were well groomed and well fed, they were fond of lovely clothing, and did nothing even on workdays. They would sit on the ledges of their houses, and gossip.

At that moment someone's steps were heard. Lyubka, a girl of twenty, entered the room in her bare feet, wearing a red dress. She looked swiftly at Ergunov and walked from one corner of the room to another a few times. She did not move simply, but with little steps, holding her head up high. She obviously enjoyed walking barefooted on the freshly washed floor, and had taken off her shoes for exactly that reason.

Kalashnikov grinned at something, beckoning her with his finger. She went over to the table, and he showed her a picture of the prophet Elijah driving three horses rushing up to the sky. Lyubka leaned her elbows on the table; a long reddish plait tied with a red ribbon at the end fell across her shoulder and almost touched the floor. She also grinned.

"That's a remarkable picture," said Kalashnikov. "Remarkable," he repeated, and made a movement with his hands as if he wanted to take the reins instead of Elijah.

The wind droned in the stovepipes; something growled and squeaked as if a big dog had strangled a rat.

"Hear that? That's the sound of evil forces," said Lyubka.

"That's the wind," said Kalashnikov; then, after a pause, he raised his eyes to Ergunov and asked: "And what's your expert opinion, Osip Vasilich—are there devils in this world or not?"

"What shall I say, young fellow?" answered Ergunov, shrugging one shoulder. "If we reason scientifically, then of course, there are no devils, it's just a prejudice. If we talk about it simply, as we are doing right now, then they do exist, to put it briefly. I've experienced many things in my lifetime. After I finished school, I served as medical assistant in the army in a regiment of dragoons. I was in the war, of course. I was awarded a medal and a decoration of the Red Cross. After the peace treaty of San Stefano, I returned to Russia and began working for the county government. And I should say, having been around, I've seen many things that others could not even imagine. I have seen devils; I don't mean the kind with a tail and horns, for that's rubbish but, some kind of devil . . ."

"Where?" asked Kalashnikov.

"Different places. Not long ago. Last summer. You know, it's not good to speak of him at night. I came across him right here, near this very inn. Well, I was going to Golyshino; I remember it, to vaccinate against smallpox. You know, it's always like that, racing the horse, carrying all the necessary stuff besides my watch, and so I was riding and on the alert. Tramps are always around, you know. So I headed down into the Zmeinaya gully, when, well, this thing approached me! Black hair, black eyes, even his whole face looked blackish, too, as if completely covered in smoke! He came up to my horse and took hold of the left rein right away, commanding us to: 'Stop!' He looked at the horse, then at me, and then dropped the rein. Without saying a bad word, he asked, 'Where are you going?' as he bared his teeth, with a malicious glint in his eyes. 'Well,' I thought to myself, 'you must be the devil!' 'I'm here to vaccinate against smallpox,' I answered, 'And what difference is it to you?" He replied: 'If that's the case, then vaccinate me, too,' as he thrust his arm right into my face. Of course, I didn't go on talking with him, just immediately vaccinated him to get rid of him. And then I looked at my lancet and as I said 'Here we go' I realized that it had gone all rusty."

The peasant who was sleeping near the stove suddenly turned and threw off his sheepskin. To his great surprise, Ergunov recognized that very stranger he had once met at Zmeinaya gully. The peasant's hair, beard, and eyes were as black as soot; his face was swarthy; and, on top of it all, there was a black lentil-sized spot on his right cheek. He looked at the hospital assistant sarcastically and said: "I did take hold of the left rein, that's true, but about the smallpox—here you've told lies, sir. We never discussed the smallpox."

Ergunov was confused and scared. "I was not referring to you, sir." He did not know who the swarthy peasant was or where he had come from. Now, looking at him, he decided the man must be a gypsy.

The peasant got up, stretching and yawning loudly, and came up to Lyubka and Kalashnikov, sitting down next to them. He, too, looked into the book. His sleepy face softened as a look of envy came over it.

"See, Merik," Lyubka said to him; "get me such horses and I'll ride them to heaven."

"Sinners can't go to heaven," said Kalashnikov. "It's reserved for saints."

Then Lyubka laid the table for the meal with a big piece of

lard, salted cucumbers, a wooden plate of cubed boiled meat, and finally a frying pan still sizzling with sausage and cabbage. A decanter of vodka also appeared on the table, filling the room with the aroma of orange peels as it was poured.

The medical assistant was annoyed that Kalashnikov and Merik were talking to each other, ignoring him completely, as if he were not in the room. He wanted to chat, to boast, to have a drink and a filling meal, and—if he could, flirt with Lyubka. She kept sitting beside him briefly throughout the meal, and as if by accident, kept bumping him with her beautiful shoulders or elbows as she swiveled in her place and stroked her broad hips with her hands. She was a healthy, restless girl, who laughed easily as she was constantly in motion.

Ergunov also found disconcerting the fact that the peasants stopped drinking after only one glass of vodka each, making him feel uncomfortable continuing to drink alone. Eventually he gave in and drank a second glass, then a third, as he ate all the remaining sausage. He now decided to flatter the men so that they would accept him instead of continuing to avoid him.

"You're a bunch of good guys over there in Bogalyovka!" he commented, as he shook his head.

"Good at what?" asked Kalashnikov.

"Well, with horses, for example. Good at stealing!"

"Hah, good guys, you say. There's only drunks and thieves left."

"Yeah, those days are over," said Merik, after a pause. "There's just old Filya left, and he, too, is blind."

"Right, just Filya left," sighed Kalashnikov. "He must be about seventy now; the German colonists put out his one eye, and now he can barely see out of his remaining one. In the good old days the police officer would see him and shout: 'Hey, you

Shamil!' until everyone called him that. Now that's the only name he goes by, One-eyed Filya. He was a nice guy, indeed! One night he, along with Andrei Chirikov, Lyuba's father, got into Rozhnovo—some cavalry regiments were stationed there at that time—and they stole nine of the soldiers' horses, the very best ones. They weren't afraid of the sentry or anything. That same morning they sold them all to the gypsy Afonka for twenty rubles. Yeah! Nowadays, people steal horses when the master is drunk or asleep, having no fear of God, but will take the boots off the man, too. He'll then head a hundred and fifty miles away to sell that horse at the market, negotiating the price like a wretched Jew, until the police track him down, the idiot. It's no longer fun, which is such a shame! Lousy people, I must say."

"And what about Merik?" asked Lyubka.

"Merik is not from our area," said Kalashnikov. "He is a Kharkov guy, from Mizhirich. And yes, he is a nice fellow. Nothing can be said to the contrary, he is a fine fellow."

Lyubka turned a playful eye toward Merik, and said: "Yeah, there was a good reason why the folks bathed him in an ice hole."

"What do you mean?" asked Ergunov.

"Well," answered Merik, grinning, "Filya stole three horses from the Samoylovka tenants and they accused me. There were ten tenants in Samoylovka—with their hired hands, about thirty altogether, all of them Molokans. So one of them tells me at the market: 'Come to our place, Merik, we've bought new horses from the fair, come take a look.' Of course, I was interested. When I arrived, they—the thirty of them—tied my hands behind my back and dragged me to the river. 'Now, we'll show you the horses, man,' they said. There was one ice hole already, and they cut another one about seven feet away. They then took a rope, put a loop under my armpits, and tied a crooked stick to the other end, long enough to reach both holes. Well, they thrust the stick in and dragged it through the holes. And I, dressed as I was in my fur coat and boots, went plop! into the ice hole. They stood on the ice, pushing me along with their feet or the stick as they dragged me under the ice and pulled me out through the other hole."

Lyubka shuddered and grew tense.

"At first I got all hot from the cold," Merik went on, "but when they pulled me out, I could only just lie down in the snow. The group of them was standing around me beating my knees and elbows with sticks. It hurt like hell. So they beat me up and left me there. I was entirely covered in ice, and freezing to death. Thank God, a woman drove by and gave me a lift."

Meanwhile, Ergunov had drunk five or six glasses of vodka; everything seemed brighter. He, too, wanted to tell some extraordinary story to prove to them that he, too, was a very nice fellow, who wasn't afraid of anything.

"Now, let me tell you about what happened once in our province of Penza," he began. Because he was quite drunk, and maybe in part because they had already caught him lying, the peasants completely ignored him, even refusing to answer his questions. Their discussion turned so frank in his presence that he grew terrified and chilled, which meant that for now they took no notice of him.

Kalashnikov had the respectable manners of a mature and sensible man. He talked about everything in detail, and covered his mouth every time he yawned. Nobody would have thought he was a heartless thief who robbed the poor, who had already been in prison twice, and who had been sentenced by the community to exile in Siberia, had it not been for his father and uncle, rascals just like him, buying his freedom.

Merik behaved like a sharp guy. He understood that Lyubka and Kalashnikov admired him, and he himself believed he was beyond all praise. He would periodically put his arms askew, puff up his chest, and stretch himself so that the bench would creak . . .

After dinner Kalashnikov stayed in his seat as he prayed to the icon, then shook hands with Merik. The latter, too, prayed, and shook Kalashnikov's hand. Lyubka cleared the table and then brought out some peppermint cakes, roasted nuts, pumpkin seeds, and two bottles of sweet wine.

"The kingdom of heaven and eternal peace to Andrei Chirikov," toasted Kalashnikov, clinking glasses with Merik. "When he was alive we used to visit him here, or at brother Martyn's. Oh, my God! What a company it was, and what conversations we used to have! Remarkable conversations with Martyn, Filya, and Fyodor Stukotey. . . . And all was done so fine, how it should be. . . . And what fun we had! We really enjoyed ourselves!"

Lyubka went out and returned after a while with a green kerchief, wearing a necklace. "Merik, have a look at what Kalashnikov brought me today," she said. She looked in the mirror and shook her head several times to make the beads jingle. She then opened a chest and started to take items out. First, a cotton dress with red and blue spots on it, then a red one with frills that rustled and crackled like paper. She next pulled out a new blue kerchief with an iridescent shimmer. She showed off these items, laughing and tossing up her hands as if stunned at all her treasures.

Kalashnikov tuned the balalaika and began playing it. Ergunov could not make out what kind of song he was playing, whether it was joyful or sad, because at one moment it sounded so sad he wanted to cry, and the next it would turn quite jovial. Merik suddenly jumped on his feet and started stamping with his heels on the same spot. Suddenly he spread his arms wide, walked on his heels from the table to the stove, from the stove to the chest, then sprang up as if he had been stung, clicked the heels of his boots together in the air, then squatted down and went around in circles. Lyubka waved both her arms, shrieked desperately, and followed him. At first she moved sideways menacing, as if she wished to sneak up on somebody and hit him from behind. She tapped fast with her bare heels the way Merik had done with the heels of his boots, then she spun around and around like a top as she squatted down, her red dress blowing out like a bell. Looking at her fiercely and baring his teeth, Merik squatted down, then rushed toward her to crush her with his frightful legs. She jumped up, flinging her head back and waving her arms like an enormous bird flapping its wings, barely touching the floor, as she floated across the room. . . .

"That girl is hot!!" thought Ergunov, sitting down on the chest, watching the dance from there. "She makes my blood boil! Even if you gave her all you could, it still wouldn't be enough." He regretted that he was a medical assistant, not a common peasant, and that he was wearing a jacket and a chain with a gilded key, instead of a blue shirt with a rope belt. If he'd only just been a peasant. Then he could have sung bravely, danced, and gotten drunk, and could hug Lyubka with both arms the way Merik did. . .

A sharp noise, shouting, and whooping made the dishes clink in the cupboard and set the flame of the candle dancing. Lyubka's necklace thread snapped, scattering beads all over the floor, while her green kerchief fell off her head, until all that was left of her was a flashing red cloud with sparkling dark eyes. Merik's arms and legs seemed as if they would fall off at any moment.

Finally, Merik stamped his foot for the last time and stopped completely still. Exhausted and hardly breathing, Lyubka leaned against his chest. He drew her tight, hugging her as he looked into her eyes and told her tenderly, as though he were joking, "One day I'll find out where your old mother hides her money, I'll kill her, and cut your throat, sweetie. Then I'll set your inn on fire. People will think you were lost in the fire, and I'll take your money and head to Kuban, where I will drive herds and keep sheep."

Lyubka made no reply, only looked up at him and asked: "Is it nice in Kuban, Merik?"

He did not answer. Instead, he went over to the chest, where he sat down and started reflecting on something, most likely Kuban.

"Anyway, it's time for me to go," said Kalashnikov, getting up. "Filya must be waiting for me now. Goodbye, Lyubka."

Ergunov went out into the yard to make sure that Kalashnikov did not steal his borrowed horse. The snowstorm was still going strong. Everything was white, from the grass to the bushes to the open field where it looked like giants in white robes with wide sleeves were spinning round, falling down, and then getting up again to wave their arms and fight. And the wind! The bare birch and cherry trees, unable to endure its rude caresses, bowed low to the ground, crying, "Oh Lord, for what sin did you fasten us to the ground and not set us free?"

"Whoa!" said Kalashnikov, as he saddled his horse. Half of the gate was open, with a high snowdrift lying beside it. "Well, go!" shouted Kalashnikov to the little short-legged nag, who promptly set off and sank up to its stomach in the snowdrift. Kalashnikov appeared completely white from the snow, and soon he, together with his horse, vanished through the gate.

When Ergunov returned to the room, Lyubka was crawling along the floor picking up her beads; Merik was not there.

"She's a great girl!" thought Ergunov, as he lay down on the bench, putting his head on the sheepskin. "Oh, if only Merik weren't here." Lyubka made him nervous as she crawled near the bench. It occurred to him that if Merik had not been there, he would certainly have hugged her, with no one around to see what would happen next. Well, she was still a girl, of course, but not likely to be chaste. Even if she were chaste, who would care about that fact in a den of thieves? Lyubka picked up her beads and left the room.

The candle was fading as it flickered down near its base. Ergunov put his revolver and matches beside him and blew out the candle. The small icon lamp was twinkling so strongly that it hurt his eyes, causing spots of light to dance around the room, and on Lyubka, until it seemed as if she were dancing and spinning around again.

"Oh, if only the evil would take Merik away," he thought.

The icon lamp blinked for the last time, crackled, and went out. Someone, it must have been Merik, entered the room and sat down on the bench. He puffed away at his pipe, and a swarthy cheek with a black spot got lit up for an instant. The nasty tobacco smoke made Ergunov's throat itch.

"What nasty tobacco you've got, damn it!" commented Ergunov. "It makes me sick."

"I mix my tobacco with oat flowers," answered Merik after a pause. "It's easier to breathe." He smoked, spat, and walked away again. About half an hour later, a light gleamed in the hallway. Merik entered in a sheepskin jacket and cap, then Lyubka with a candle in her hand.

"Please stay, Merik," Lyubka was begging.

"No way, Lyubka. Don't hold me back."

"Listen, Merik," said Lyubka, as her voice turned tender. "I know you'll find mother's money, and will do away with both her and me, and will go to Kuban to love other girls. Whatever happens will happen. There's only one thing I ask of you, sweetheart: stay now!"

"No, I want to have fun . . ." said Merik, tying his belt.

"But you came here on foot, how will you travel now?"

Merik bent down and whispered something quietly in Lyubka's ear. She looked toward the door and laughed through her tears.

"And he's sleeping, that puffed-up villain . . ." she said.

Merik hugged her, kissed her forcefully, and went outside. Ergunov thrust his revolver into his pocket, jumped to his feet, and ran after him.

"Get out of the way!" he said to Lyubka, who hurriedly bolted the door in the hallway and stopped on the threshold. "Let me pass! Why are you in my way?"

"What do you want out there?"

"To check on my horse."

Lyubka glanced up at him coyly. "Why go look at your horse when you can look at me?" she said, touching the gilded key that hung on his chain with her forefinger.

"Let me pass, or he'll get away with my horse," argued Ergunov. "Let me pass, damn it!" he shouted, hitting her angrily on the shoulder. He thrust his chest against her with all his might to try and push her away from the door, but she grasped tightly at the bolt, with an iron grip.

"Let me go!" he shouted, exhausted. "I tell you, he'll get away."

"How could he? He won't." Breathing heavily and rubbing

her sore shoulder, she glanced up at him again, blushed, and laughed. "Don't go away, darling," she said. "I get so bored all alone."

Ergunov looked into her eyes, hesitating only for an instant before putting his arms around her. She did not resist.

"Well, come on, let me go by," he asked her. She kept silent.

"I overheard you just now," he said, "telling Merik that you loved him."

"That doesn't matter. . . . My heart knows who I love." She touched his key again, and said quietly: "Give it to me."

Ergunov took the key off the chain and gave it to her. She suddenly stretched out her neck, as if listening to something. Her face grew cold, stern, almost sly, to Ergunov. All of a sudden he remembered his horse, brushed past her, and ran out into the yard.

A sleepy pig was grunting contentedly in the shed, and the cow's bell could be heard. Ergunov lit a match. He was able to see the pig, the cow, and the dogs who rushed toward him at the sign of the light, but there was no trace of his horse. Shouting and waving his arms at the dogs, he stumbled through the snowdrifts and sank into the snow as he tried to get a glimpse of the road outside the gate. He strained his eyes but could only see the heavily fallen snowflakes and the shapes they made as they fell— a white laughing skull, a white horse ridden by an Amazon in a muslin dress, or a string of white swans flying overhead. . . .

Shaking with anger and cold, not knowing what else to do, Ergunov took a shot with his revolver at the dogs, missed, and angrily rushed back to the house.

As he entered the house he distinctly heard someone dart out of the main room and the door slam behind them. It was dark in the room. Ergunov pushed against the door and found tit was locked. Lighting match after match, he rushed back through the hallway, into the kitchen, and from the kitchen into a little dressing room filled with dresses and skirts, with a bed with a huge pile of pillows standing in the corner by the stove. The room smelled of cornflowers and dill; he figured it must be the old widow's room.

As he left the room, he passed into another little room, and there he found Lyubka. She was lying down, covered with a multicolored patchwork cotton quilt, pretending to be asleep. A little icon lamp was burning above the head of her bed.

"Where is my horse?" Ergunov asked firmly. Lyubka did not stir.

"Where is my horse, I ask you!" Ergunov asked again in a louder voice as he tore the quilt off her. "I'm asking you, witch!" he shouted.

She jumped up onto her knees, holding her nightgown with one hand and trying to grasp the quilt with the other, pressing her back against the wall. She looked at Ergunov with a combination of disgust and fear, her eyes darting like a trapped animal watching his every move.

"Tell me where my horse is, or I'll beat the life out of you," shouted Ergunov.

"Get away from me, you villain!" she said hoarsely.

Ergunov seized her gown by the neck and tugged at it. Immediately, unable to control himself, he embraced her with all his might. Hissing with fury, she slipped out of his arms. One arm was still tangled in her nightgown, but freeing the other, she reach up and struck him on the head.

He suddenly felt dizzy with pain, as his ears rang from the blow. He stumbled back just as she hit him again, this time on his forehead. Staggering and grabbing at the doorjambs to remain on his feet, he made his way to the main room where his things were and lay down for a minute. He took a matchbox out of his pocket and began to light match after match for no reason, which he did over and over until no matches remained.

Meanwhile the air was getting bluer outside as the roosters began to crow. His head still ached, and he felt as if he were sitting under a railroad bridge as a train passed overhead. Somehow he managed to put on his sheepskin jacket and cap. He could not find his saddle or his purchases, for his bag was empty. He now knew why he thought he had seen someone darting out of the room when he came in from the yard late last evening.

He took a poker from the kitchen to defend himself against the dogs and headed outside, leaving the door wide open. The snowstorm had begun to subside and it was quiet outside. As he went out through the gate, the white field looked barren, without a single bird in the morning sky. A small forest appeared blue along both sides of the road and far ahead off in the distance.

Ergunov began thinking about how he would be received at the hospital coming back empty-handed. What was the doctor going to say to him? He needed to prepare for any question they might throw at him. However, he could think of nothing besides Lyubka, and the robbers. He remembered how Lyubka looked at him, with her hair loosened from its plait right after she hit him the second time. He grew confused the more he thought. Why should there be a world filled with doctors, lawyers, businessmen, and peasants? Why shouldn't everyone live free to make their own choices, like the animals and birds do, and Merik—fearless and not dependent on anyone? Whose bright idea was it to make one get up in the morning, have lunch at noon, and go to bed in the evening? Why were doctors more important than medical assistants? Why should you only love one woman for the rest of your life? Why not have lunch at night and sleep during the day? Who said we can't? Oh, how nice it would be to jump on a horse without caring whose it is, riding like the wind, going wherever your fancy took you, loving many women and making fun of whoever you wanted to!!

Ergunov thrust the poker into the snow, pressed his forehead to the cold, white trunk of a birch, and continued to sink deeper in thought. His gray, monotonous life, filled with low wages, his lowly position, working in the pharmacy with the never-ending bustle with pots and blisters—it all seemed contemptible and loathsome.

"Who says it's a sin to have fun?" he asked himself, annoyed. "Those who say so have never lived a free life like Merik and Kalashnikov; have never loved a woman like Lyubka. They have been begging all their lives, never enjoying themselves, nor loving anyone but their froglike wives."

He realized that it was only due to his lack of opportunity that he had not become a thief or a cheat.

A year and a half passed. Late one evening that spring, Ergunov, long since fired from the hospital and out of work, left an inn in Repino, content to wander the streets with no real purpose. He headed into a field, enjoying the fresh spring air and the light wind blowing under a starry sky. My God, thought Ergunov, how deep the sky is and how it stretches over the world! If all was right in the world, then what made people divide themselves into those who drank and those who remained sober, those with jobs and those who were unemployed, etc.? Why do the sober and well fed sleep comfortably at home while the drunk and hungry must wander around the field without shelter? Why do the homeless have to go hungry, without decent clothing? Whose idea was it? Why do birds and beasts in the forest not go to work, yet all they need is provided for them?

Far away in the sky, open wide above the horizon, a beautiful crimson glow glittered. Ergunov stood gazing at it for a long time, realizing that something was on fire in the distance. He kept on reflecting: why is it a sin if yesterday someone stole someone else's samovar and sold it for the cost of a drink in a tavern? Why?

Two carts drove by on the road: a woman lay sleeping in one, and an old man without a cap sat in the other one.

"Grandfather, where is that fire burning?" asked Ergunov.

"Andrei Chirikov's inn," answered the old man.

Immediately Ergunov recalled what had happened to him a year and a half ago, that winter in that very inn, especially the threat Merik had made. He imagined the old woman and Lyubka, with their throats cut, burning, and he envied Merik.

As he headed back to the inn, looking at the houses of the rich land owners, cattle dealers, and blacksmiths, he reflected how nice it would be to break into some rich man's house!

MURDER

(Abridged)

———※———

Matthew was sitting in the kitchen, eating a bowl of baked potatoes. Near the stove, Aglaya and Dashutka were facing one another, winding yarn. An ironing-board, with a cold iron on it, was stretched between the stove and the table where Matthew was sitting.

"Sister," Matthew asked, "let me have a little oil!"

"Who would eat oil on a day like this?" asked Aglaya.

"I'm not a monk, sister, I'm a regular man. Due to my ill health, I may take not only oil but even some milk."

"Sure; if this were your factory, you could have anything you want."

Aglaya took a bottle of oil from the shelf and set it down angrily before Matthew. She was gloating, obviously very pleased to see that he was such a sinner.

"But I tell you, you can't eat oil!" shouted Yakov, startling Aglaya and Dashutka. Matthew, as if he had not heard the comment, poured some oil into the bowl and continued eating.

"I tell you, you can't have the oil!" Yakov shouted still more loudly, blushing at his own boldness. He suddenly yanked away the bowl, lifted it above his head, and dashed it to the ground with such force that the bowl broke into little pieces. "Don't you dare speak!" he shouted furiously, although Matthew had not said a word. "Don't you dare!" he repeated, and struck his fist on the table.

Matthew turned pale as he rose from the table. "Brother!" he said, while still chewing, "brother, come to your senses!"

"Get out of my house, NOW!" shouted Yakov. He was thoroughly disgusted by Matthew's wrinkled face, his voice, the crumbs on his moustache, and even his chewing. "Get out, I tell you!"

"Brother, calm down! Evil pride has seized you!"

"Shut up!" Yakov stamped his feet. "Get lost, you devil!"

"If you care to know," Matthew went on loudly, as he, too, began to get angry, "you are an apostate and a heretic. You've been cursed by having the light of truth hidden from you, and God is not pleased with your prayer. Repent before it is too late! The death of a sinner is cruel! Repent, brother!"

Yakov grabbed him by the shoulders and dragged Matthew away from the table. Confused, Matthew, who turned even paler, began muttering, "What's the matter? What's going on?" and, struggling in his effort to free himself from Yakov's grip, he accidentally tore the collar of Yakov's shirt, causing Aglaya to believe he was going to beat Yakov. She uttered a scream, snatched the bottle of oil, and with all her force smashed it down straight on the top of the hateful brother's head. Matthew reeled, and a moment later his face turned calm and indifferent.

Panting heavily, Yakov was excited and pleased by the crack made by the bottle as it struck Matthew's head. Yet, Yakov would not let him fall. Several times (he remembered it very well) he pointed to Aglaya and the iron with his index finger. It was not until the blood started trickling over his hands, and Dashutka let loose with a loud cry as the ironing board fell over when Matthew fell against it heavily, that the anger released Yakov and he finally realized what had happened.

"Let him croak, the factory stud!" Aglaya uttered with repulsion, the iron still in her hand. The white bloodstained kerchief slipped down onto her shoulders, allowing her gray hair to hang loose. "It serves him right!"

Everything was frightening. Dashutka was sitting on the floor near the stove with her yarn in her hands, sobbing and bowing, uttering "Gam! Gam!" with every bow. However, nothing was more frightening to Yakov than the boiled potatoes, sodden with blood. He was afraid to step on them. Yet something else was more sobering, depressing, and seemed to him most dangerous of all. It took him a moment to grasp that the barman, Sergey Nikanorych, was standing in the doorway with the abacus in his hands, very pale, and had watched in terror what had just happened in the kitchen. Only when he turned, walking quickly through the hall and outside, did Yakov realize who had observed them, and went after him.

Yakov wiped his hands on the snow as he walked, and reflected. The idea came to him that he could say their hired hand had asked to go to his village to stay there overnight and so wasn't around to be a witness. They had just butchered a pig the day before, and there were signs of blood from the slaughtering on the snow, the sleigh, and even on one side of the well cover. It would not seem suspicious to any outsider if even all of Yakov's family had bloodstains. It would be grievous enough to conceal the murder, but when Yakov thought about the policeman, whistling and smiling ironically, the local villagers coming together to gossip and stare at Yakov and Aglaya as they would be bound, and taken triumphantly to the police station, while everyone would point at them along the way cheering, "Ha, here come the preachers!" This seemed to Yakov the most grievous offense of all. He wished time could somehow stretch, so this disgrace would occur not now, but sometime in the future.

"I can lend you a thousand rubles," he said, catching up to Sergey Nikanorych. "There is nothing in it for you if you tell anyone . . . and there's no way to bring him back." He could hardly keeping pace with the barman, who refused to look at him as he tried to walk as far from Yakov as possible. "I could give you fifteen hundred as well . . ."

He stopped as he was out of breath. Sergey Nikanorych kept on walking as quickly as he could, probably afraid that he, too, would be killed. It was not until he had walked past the railroad crossing and halfway down the road to the railroad station, that he looked back quickly and slowed his pace. The red and green lights were already on at the station and along the tracks; the wind was dying but snowflakes were still falling, turning the road white again. Sergey Nikanorych stopped as far as the station itself, deep in thought, and then resolutely walked back. It was growing dark.

"Fifteen hundred rubles, Yakov Ivanych," he said quietly, trembling all over. "I agree."

Only part of Yakov Ivanych's money was in the town bank; the other part he had invested by offering mortgages in the village. He kept very little at home, just what he needed to run the household.

Entering the kitchen, he groped for a box of matches. Lighting one, he was able to make out the Matthew's corpse still lying on the floor where he had fallen, covered with a white sheet. Only his boots could be seen. A cricket was chirping loudly outside. Aglaya and Dashutka were sitting behind the counter in the tearoom, winding yarn in complete silence.

Holding a lamp in his hand, Yakov Ivanych went into his room and pulled the little chest holding the household money out from under the bed. There was only four hundred and twenty-one rubles in small bills, and thirty-five rubles in silver; the notes felt heavy and unpleasant. Yakov Ivanych put the money into his cap, heading first into the yard, then outside the gate. He walked, looking around, but could not find the barman.

"Hey!" cried Yakov.

A dark figure separated from the shadows near the railroad crossing and moved slowly toward him.

"Why are you still walking?" asked Yakov with annoyance, as he recognized the barman. "Here you are; it's a little less than five hundred, but that's all I had at home."

"Very well . . . I'm grateful to you," mumbled Sergey Nikanorych, grabbing the money greedily as he stuffed it into his pockets. He was visibly trembling all over, despite the darkness. "And you, Yakov Ivanych, don't worry about it. . . . Why would I tell? It's simple. I was there earlier, and then left. As the saying goes, I know nothing and I can say nothing . . ." And he added with a sigh, "This cursed life!"

They stood standing quietly for a minute without looking at each other.

"Yeah, but this all happened over a trifle, God knows how it could . . ." said the barman, trembling. "You know, I was sitting counting to myself when I heard that noise. . . . I looked through the door. . . . It was all because of the oil. . . . Where is he now?"

"Lying in the kitchen."

"You'd better take him somewhere. . . . What are you waiting for?"

In silence, Yakov accompanied him to the station, and then returned home. He harnessed the horse to take Matthew to Limarovo forest and leave him somewhere on the road, the plan being to tell everyone that Matthew had gone off to Vedenyapino and not returned, causing everyone to think he had been killed by some travelers. He knew he would not deceive anyone with these lies, but it felt less torturous to have something to do than just to sit and wait. He called Dashutka, and together they carried Matthew away. Aglaya remained in the kitchen to clean up.

When Yakov and Dashutka were returning, they were stopped by the lowered bar at the railroad crossing. Breathing heavily and letting shafts of crimson fire out of its ash pits, a long freight train was passing by, dragged by two engines. At the crossing, in sight of the station, the first engine let out a piercing whistle.

"Whistling . . ." said Dashutka.

The train had finally passed, and the watchman took his time lifting the bar.

"Is that you, Yakov Ivanych?" said he. "You know that old saying, if I didn't recognize you, you'll be rich. Ha, ha, ha!"

It was very late by the time they made it back home. Aglaya and Dashutka made themselves a bed on the floor in the tearoom and lay down side by side. Yakov went to sleep on the counter. Before going to bed none of them prayed to God, or lit the icon-lamps. None of them slept a wink that night, nor spoke a single word. The entire night, they all felt like someone was walking in the bedroom above them.

Two days later, a police officer and an investigator came from town to conduct a search, first in Matthew's room and then throughout the whole inn. They questioned Yakov first of all, and he told them that on Monday evening Matthew went to Vedenyapino to fast, and that he must have been attacked and killed by the woodcutters working on the train track.

The investigator asked him how Matthew was found on the road, while his cap was found in his room at home—could he have gone to Vedenyapino without his cap?—Why not a single drop of blood was found on the road near Matthew, although his head was fractured, and his face and chest were black with blood. Yakov was confused and taken aback, and answered: "I don't know how."

And everything happened just as Yakov had feared: the policeman came, the investigator smoked in the prayer room, Aglaya swore and was rude to the officers; and while Yakov and Aglaya were led in handcuffs from their yard, the peasants happily crowded at the gates and said, "They are taking away those religious nuts."

During the investigation, the policeman testified without hesitation that Yakov and Aglaya killed Matthew to avoid sharing their inheritance with him, and since Matthew had apparently had money of his own, none of which could be found in the police's search of his property, that Yakov and Aglaya must have stolen it.

Dashutka was interrogated as well. She said that Uncle Matthew and Aunt Aglaya quarreled and nearly beat each other up every day over money, and that Uncle Matthew was rich, because he had given his "sweetheart" nine hundred rubles.

Dashutka was left alone at the inn. No one came now to drink tea or vodka, leaving her to either clean up the rooms or eat pastries with honey. A few days later, they interviewed the watchman from the railroad crossing, who said that late Monday evening he had seen Yakov and Dashutka return from Limarovo. As a result, Dashutka, too, was arrested, taken to town and put in prison.

Soon word spread that Sergey Nikanorych had been present at the murder. A search was conducted at his place, where money was found in an unusual place, in his boot under the stove. The money was all in small bills, three hundred one-ruble notes. He swore he had earned this money at work and that he hadn't been to the inn for over a year, but witnesses testified that he was poor and had lately been short of cash, and how he used to go to the inn every day to borrow money from Matthew. The policeman described how on the day of the murder he himself had been at the inn twice accompanying the barman to help him borrow some money. It was also noted that Monday evening Sergey Nikanorych did not meet the freight and passenger train as he usually did, and his whereabouts were unknown. He, too, was arrested and sent to the town.

Eleven months later the trial occurred.

Yakov Ivanych looked much older and thinner, and spoke in a sickly, quiet voice. He felt weak, miserable, and smaller than anyone else. His soul, tortured by his conscience and dreams, his constant companions in prison, had grown old and thin like his body. When it came to the point that he was not attending church, the chief justice asked him: "Are you a dissenter?"

"Not that I know of," he answered.

He had no faith at all now. He knew and understood nothing. His former faith was disgusting to him, it seemed unreasonable and dark. Aglaya had no peace, and continued to blame Matthew for all their misfortunes. Sergey Nikanorych now had a beard instead of stubble. At the trial he blushed and perspired, obviously ashamed of his gray prison robe and sitting on the same bench with common peasants. He justified himself awkwardly, and when he kept trying to prove he had not been at the inn for a year, he was continually proved to be there by every witness, to the amusement of the audience. While in prison, Dashutka had put on weight. At the trial she did not understand what she was being asked. All she could say was that when Uncle Matthew was killed, she was very scared, and then it felt better.

All four were found guilty of murder and given lengthy sentences. Yakov Ivanych was sentenced to penal servitude for twenty years; Aglaya for thirteen and a half; Sergey Nikanorych for ten; Dashutka for six.

Late in the evening, a foreign steamer stopped in Sakhalin and requested coal. The captain was asked to wait till morning, but did not want to wait even one hour, saying that if the weather got worse throughout the night he would have run the risk of leaving without coal. In the Strait of Tartary the weather can change dramatically within half an hour, becoming dangerous for those near Sakhalin's shores. The water was growing colder and the waves were gaining height.

A group of prisoners was driven to the mine from Voevod-skaya prison, the gloomiest and most severe of all the prisons on the island. They had to load barges with coal and then to tow them using a small steamboat to the waiting steamer anchored more than a quarter of a mile from the coast. There, the coal had to be reloaded, a most exhausting task. The barge kept bumping into the steamer, and the workers, weak with sea sickness, could hardly stand on their feet. The convicts, still sleepy and not quite awake, stumbled along the shore in the dark, clanking their shackles.

A steep and extremely gloomy bank was barely visible on the left, while on the right there was a thick, impenetrable mist; the sea was monotonously repeating, "Ah! . . . Ah! . . . Ah!"

Only when the overseer lit his pipe were the faces of the gun-carrying guard and two or three of the closest coarse-faced convicts lit for an instant, and the white crests of the foremost waves could be discerned.

Yakov Ivanych—nicknamed Broom by the convicts for his long beard—was a part of this group of convicts. He was now called simply Yashka. He had a bad reputation. Three months after coming to Siberia, feeling incredibly homesick, he had escaped. He had quickly been caught, given a life sentence and forty lashes. He was later punished by caning twice more for losing his prison clothes, although each time they had been stolen from him. His homesickness had begun the very moment he had been brought to Odessa, and the prison train had stopped at Progonnaya station. Yakov, pressing against the window, could see nothing, especially not his home, in the darkness.

He had no one to talk to about home. His sister Aglaya had been sent to the other side of Siberia, and nobody knew where she was now. Dashutka was in Sakhalin, too, but she lived in a faraway settlement with a former convict. The only gossip he had heard from another transferred prisoner was that Dashutka had three children. Sergey Nikanorych was serving as footman to an officer who lived not far from the prison, in Dui, but there was no hope of seeing him due to his revulsion at peasant convicts.

The group reached the mine and stopped at the quay. They were told there would be no loading, as the weather was getting worse and, supposedly, the steamer was set to leave. Three lights could be seen. One was moving: the light from the steamboat that had been near the steamer and was now coming back to say whether the loading would occur or not. Shivering in the autumn cold and the damp from the sea, wrapping himself in his short, torn sheepskin coat, Yakov Ivanych looked intently without blinking in the direction where his home lay. Since coming to live in the prison together with men from all over Europe—Russians, Ukrainians, Tatars, Georgians, Chinese, Finns, Gypsies, Jews—he began to listen to their conversations and watched them suffering, his faith began to grow again, as he felt that finally he had learned the true faith, the very faith that his whole family had longed for and for which they had searched in vain. He knew now where God was, and how He was to be served. There was only one thing now that he did not understand: why did one person's destiny differ so much from another's? Why did this simple faith, that some got for free while living their lives, come at such a price, with his limbs trembling like a drunk's from all the horror and suffering that apparently would go on without end until his death.

Yakov peered intensely into the darkness. It seemed to him that through a thousand miles of that mist he could see his home, his village, and the railroad station. He could see the ignorance, savagery, heartlessness, and indifference of the people he had left behind. His sight grew dim with tears, but he kept gazing into the distance where the steamer's pale lights were shining vaguely. His heart ached with longing for home. He wanted to live, to return home and share his new faith with all, in the hopes of making a difference to one man, and to live without suffering, if only for a day.

The small steamboat arrived. The overseer loudly announced that the coal loading was canceled.

"Step back! Atten-tion!" he commanded.

They could hear the anchor being raised on the steamer. A strong, piercing wind was blowing now, with the sound of trees creaking somewhere above, up on the steep shore. Most likely, a storm was coming.

CRIMINAL INVESTIGATOR

T he county doctor and the criminal investigator were riding to perform an autopsy one wonderful spring day.

The investigator was a man in his mid-forties. He thoughtfully looked up and said to his companion, "There are many mysterious, dark forces in the world. But even in our everyday life, dear doctor, you can stumble on events that cannot be explained. For example, I have come across several very mysterious and strange deaths, which can only be explained by mysticism or spiritualism, things that a person with a logical mind would only shake his head at in disbelief. To give you an example, I once knew a very intelligent woman who managed to foretell her death, without any visible reason. She told many others that she would die on a particular day, and she died on that very day."

"There is no action without a reason. If there was a death, then there was a reason for it," the doctor replied. "And if we are to talk about predictions in general, that is not very strange. People often talk about this, especially women in the local villages. A lot of them think they have some sort of gift, like premonition,"

"This is true, dear doctor, but the lady I am talking about was a very special woman. In her prediction and in her death there was no psychic, magic, or any of those kinds of influences. She was very young and healthy, intelligent, and without any prejudice. She had clever, clear, and honest eyes, with a very light, completely Russian kind of smile on her lips. She possessed a true feminine beauty.

"She was kind and gracious, with fine eyes and gorgeous, lovely hair! To complete her portrait, I should add that she was a very optimistic woman, filled with a zest for life, infected with happiness and joy, so to speak. She had a contagious laugh, and was filled with that light carelessness that only very smart, simple, and joyful people possess. How can we speak about mysticism, spiritualism, psychics, or magic in this case, when in life she laughed at these very things?"

The doctor's horses stopped near the well. Both the investigator and the doctor got down and drank some water while waiting for the driver to finish watering the horses.

"So, what was the cause of her death?" the doctor inquired, as they continued on their way.

"She died in a very peculiar way. One day, her husband came to her and said that it would be nice to replace their cart and their old horses with stronger, younger ones, especially Out-Runner, their old horse, and Dobchinsky. The husband did not like this horse and so gave her a funny name. He wanted to get rid of the horse by giving it to the horse knacker [to convert to dog food and glue].

The wife listened to him and said,

"Do whatever you want. By the end of this summer, I'll be in the cemetery."

The husband shook his head and smiled.

"I am not joking in the slightest," she continued. "I assure you, I will die soon."

"How soon?" her husband asked her.

"Right after I will deliver the baby, I shall take one last look at the child, and then die."

Now the husband did not pay any attention to her words. He did not believe in premonitions and future-telling. We all know that when women are expecting, they can often be prone to depressing thoughts.

But the next day, his wife told him the same thing: that she would die on the day of her delivery, and she continued to say the same thing with each day that followed. He just laughed and called her a worried old woman.

However, his wife had developed a fixed idea about her upcoming death. The husband discovered when he went to the kitchen and spoke with the cook and nanny that his wife had repeated her belief to the staff, saying:

"I will not live long, for I will die soon, my dear nanny. As soon as I deliver, I will die, for this is my fate."

Both the nanny and the cook would cry when she spoke like this. Word of her situation spread across the area. Local ladies would come and try to speak to her about her future plans, but she only spoke of her upcoming death. She spoke very seriously, without hesitation or objection, with a sad, ill-looking smile on her face, and often with an angry expression. She had formerly been a very fashionable lady, but in the wake of her premonition she did not take any visible care with her appearance, which was now constantly untidy. She stopped laughing or dreaming aloud.

Even more, one day she went with her aunt to the cemetery

and purchased the plot of her future grave. Five days before the baby was due, she wrote out her will.

Please keep in mind that she was in perfect health, without any hint of illness. Giving birth is a difficult thing, and there can be medical problems, but the woman I am telling you about was completely happy and healthy, and there seemed nothing to worry about.

The husband was tired of the whole situation. One day, during dinner, he grew angry and asked her loudly, "Listen, Natasha, when are you going to stop this foolishness?"

"I am not being foolish. I am telling the truth," was her reply.

"Nonsense! Stop talking about these foolish things, otherwise later you will be embarrassed."

The day of the delivery finally came. The husband brought the best midwife in from the city. This was her first child, and everything went smoothly, without a problem. When the labor was over, the wife wanted to take a look at her newborn son. She glanced at him and said,

"Now, I can die."

She then said good-bye to everyone, closed her eyes, and half an hour later was dead.

Up until the last moment she was in good health, could see and hear everything, and she was in control of herself. When they brought her some milk during the delivery instead of water, she quietly whispered,

"Why do you bring me milk? I asked for water."

This is the end of the story. She predicted it in detail, and died exactly as she had predicted.

The investigator grew silent for a little while, then waved his hand in the air and asked,

"I can't figure it out. So, tell me, how do you think she died?

I give you my word that this is not a fictional story, but it is completely based on real facts."

Absorbing all he had heard, the doctor raised his eyes to the sky as he said,

"They should have done an autopsy."

"Why?"

"In order to determine the real reason of her death. She did not die because of her premonitions. Most likely she poisoned herself."

The investigator turned toward the doctor, squinted his eyes suspiciously, and asked,

"Why do you come to the conclusion that she poisoned herself?"

"It was not a conclusion, but an educated guess. Was she happy with her husband?"

"Well, not exactly. They had some misunderstanding right after they got married. There were some unpleasant circumstances. One day, the newlywed wife saw her husband with another woman, in a compromising position. However, shortly after, she forgave him."

"And what happened first, her husband's affair, or the first time she spoke about her future death?"

The investigator carefully looked at the doctor, as if trying to guess the reason for this question.

"Wait a minute, wait! Let me remember." The investigator took off his hat and wiped his forehead. "Yes, she started talking about her death right after this event. Yes!"

"So you see. Now, most likely it was then that she decided to poison herself, but because she did not want to kill the child she carried as well, she decided to postpone her suicide until after her delivery."

"You could hardly be right. That would be impossible. She forgave her husband right after the event."

"If she forgave so fast, it means that she intended on revenge. Young wives do not forgive very easily or so fast."

The investigator forced a smile to cover his very obvious excitement, halting all conversation while he smoked a cigarette.

"It can't be. I do not think so. This possibility never occurred to me. He did not cheat on her, and he did not plan to do that. One day he came home from work, a little bit drunk. He wanted to give a little love to someone, and then all of a sudden he met the lady who had been visiting them for a weekend, a stupid, completely silly and unattractive woman. You cannot even call it cheating. The wife looked at it the same way, and shortly after this incident, she forgave her husband. After that, there was no mention of the event at all."

"People do not die for no reason," the doctor responded.

"This is true, but I cannot believe she poisoned herself. It is so strange, no one even thought about it! Everyone was surprised that her prediction came true, but there was not even the slightest thought of this possibility. This cannot be possible, that she had poisoned herself, no!"

The investigator was lost in thought and was silent for a while.

The thought of this woman, who accurately predicted her own death, did not leave him while the doctor performed the autopsy. He was writing down what the doctor was dictating to him, frowning gloomily and rubbing his forehead.

"Are there any poisons that could kill a person in a quarter of an hour, quite easily and without any pain?" he inquired of the doctor when they were examining the skull.

"Yes, morphine, for example."

"Well, that is strange. I remember that she had something like that on hand, but it's hardly likely, hardly."

On the way back, the investigator looked very tired. He nervously bit his moustache, and stroked it without any enthusiasm.

"Let us take a little walk, doctor. I am tired of sitting in the cart."

After taking about a hundred steps, the police investigator looked completely drained, as if he had just finished climbing a steep mountain. He stopped, looked at the doctor with dull eyes, and said,

"Oh my God! If your suggestion is true, what she did was cruel and inhuman. She poisoned herself to torture another person! It was not such a great sin that her husband committed! Why did you give me that terrible suggestion? My dear doctor, you should not have suggested such a thing to me!"

The investigator held his head with both hands in despair and continued,

"I was telling you the story of my wife and myself. Oh my God! Yes, I am to blame, I hurt her. But is it easier to die than to forgive? She reasoned like a typical woman, in a very cruel and merciless way. Oh yes, she was very cruel when she was alive, now I remember everything. Now everything is clear to me!"

The investigator could not stop talking. At some points he waved his hands in the air, and held his head in his hands. He was either jumping from the cab or walking next to it. The new revelation by the doctor had completely stunned, overwhelmed, and poisoned his existence. He was completely at a loss, weakened in both body and soul, and when their journey ended, he did not say good-bye to the doctor, and, despite his earlier promise, declined the doctor's invitation to have lunch together.

THE DRAMA AT THE HUNT

From the Notes of a Police Detective

(Abridged)

<hr>

Chapter One
My First Meeting with Olga

Early in the morning, whistling happily and hitting the tops of cobblestones with my walking stick, I was on the way to the village of Tenev, where there was supposed to be a county fair.

What a beautiful morning! It seemed that happiness itself was floating over the earth, reflected in the diamondlike dewdrops that beguiled the traveler. At this early hour, the forest was quiet and motionless, as if it were listening to my steps. The chirping of little birds was inviting. The whole air was filled with the greenery of spring. I was breathing the fresh morning air and listening to the songs of the insects and the whispering of the wind in young birch trees and the grass.

In an hour, I was walking among the kiosks of the Tenev county fair. There were many sounds—the neighing of horses, the mooing of cows, children tooting on toy trumpets, carousel music, and the babble of many conversations. So many new different types of people, so much beauty and movement in this crowd, dressed in bright colors, made luminous by the morning sun. This was an amazing picture! (. . .)

Soon I was on my way back home from the town of Tenev. I ran into Olga, who was heading home in her heavy, old-fashioned cart.

"Please, can you give me a lift?" I cried.

"She is really nice-looking," I thought, observing her soft round neck and the curve of her cheek.

Olga had been shopping. She had several pieces of nice fabric, and an assortment of packages and bags.

"You've been on a spree," I said. "Why do you need so much fabric?"

"I will need even more," Olga answered. "What I've bought is only the tip of the iceberg. You cannot imagine how much trouble I've had with all this shopping. Today I spent an hour walking across the county fair and selecting stuff, and tomorrow I will have to go to the city to do some serious shopping for the whole day! And then we will have to sew all this to make a dress. You don't know of a good seamstress, do you?"

"I don't know anyone who does that. But why so much shopping? Why do you need a new dress? Your family is pretty small—just the two of you, as far as I know."

"You men are such strange creatures! You don't understand anything! Now, when it's your wedding day, you'll be the first to get angry if your wife turns up the next morning without a nice, fresh trousseau. I know that Peter Erogovich doesn't need the money, but I have no desire to show myself as a bad house-wife from the very beginning."

"What does Peter Erogovich have to do with it?"

"Hm, you're being a tease, acting as if you don't know any-thing," Olga said, blushing a little.

"My dear young lady, you are speaking in riddles."

"Hadn't you heard? I am going to marry Peter Egorovich!"

"Married?" I was startled. My eyes must have popped open. "To Peter Egorovich?"

"Oh, my! No, excuse me, that's Mr. Urbenin."

I looked at her smiling, flushed face.

"You . . . getting married? To Mr. Urbenin? You must be joking!"

"I am not joking at all . . . This is not the least bit funny."

"You are getting married . . . to Mr. Urbenin?" I mum-bled, getting pale for no reason. "If this is not a joke, then what is this?"

"What are you talking about—this is not funny! There is nothing unusual or strange in it," Olga said, pursing her little lips.

Several moments passed in silence. I looked at this beautiful young woman, at her fresh, almost childish face, and I was sur-prised that she could make such a terrible joke. For a moment, I imagined myself in the place of the old, decrepit Mr. Urbenin, with his huge pendulous ears and cracked, prickly skin, the mere touch of which would scratch this young and delicate female body. The picture frightened me!

"Yes, he is a little bit too old for me, he is over fifty." Olga sighed. "But he loves me anyway. His love is reliable."

"It is not that important to have a reliable partner, but it is important to have happiness."

"Well, well, he has enough money, he's no pauper, and he has some good connections. I am certainly not in love with him, but is happiness restricted to people who are madly in love? I know what these love matches can become!"

"My dear child!" I looked into her blue eyes, frightened and bewildered. "When did you manage to stuff your little head with all this terrible common sense? I'd rather believe that you are making jokes at my expense, but where did you learn to joke this way?"

Olga looked at me with surprise.

"I don't see what the problem is. It displeases you that a young woman should marry an older man. Is that it?"

Olga suddenly flushed, clenched her lower jaw, and didn't wait for my answer. The words all came in a rush:

"If you can't deal with this, then you go live deep in the forest in a hut with your crazed father, and you wait for a young man to come and marry you! Can you imagine those long winter nights when you pray for death to come and take you, can you imagine what it feels like, this horror in the middle of the forest?"

"This all is not sensible, my dear Olga. This is not mature, this is all foolish and wrong. If you are joking, I don't know what to say. You'd be better to be quiet, just stop talking now, don't pollute the air with your silly words. In your place, I would keep silent."

"At least he can afford to buy medicine for my father and take care of him," she whispered.

"How much money do you need to take care of your father?" I cried out. "Here, take the money from me! A hundred? Two? A thousand? You're lying to me, Olga. You're not marrying him to take care of your father."

The girl in red moved a little closer to me, and for an instant we were illuminated by dazzling white light. There was a huge crack somewhere above, and it seemed to us that something big and heavy fell from with a huge noise from the sky down to the earth. There was a crash.

"Are you afraid of thunderstorms?" I asked Olga.

She lowered her cheek to her shoulder and looked at me trustingly, like a child.

"Yes, I hate them," she whispered, thinking for a while. "My mother was struck by lightning. They even wrote about it in the newspaper. She was walking across a field, crying. Her life was very hard in this world. . . . God took pity on her and killed her with His heavenly electricity."

"How do you know what electricity is?"

"I studied it at school. You know that people who die during a thunderstorm or at war, and those who die during giving birth, they all go to heaven. This is not written in the Bible, but it's true. One day I'll be killed by a thunderstorm, and I will go to heaven. Are you an educated man?"

"Yes."

"Then you'll probably laugh at me. Here's how I want to die. I want to get dressed up in the most expensive and fashionable dress, the one I saw on Lady Sheffer. Then I will stand on top of the mountain, and let the lightning kill me, so everyone will see. A terrible thunderstorm, you know, and then the end."

"What a wild fantasy." I smiled, looking into her eyes filled with the sacred horror of an effective death. "And you don't wish to die in an ordinary dress?"

"No," Olga shook her head decisively, "And I want everyone to see me go."

"The dress you're wearing is better that all those expensive gowns. It suits you very well. You look like a red flower in a green forest."

"No that's not true, this is a cheap one. This dress is no good," Olga sighed.

I was so excited by Olga's news that I did not notice that we'd arrived in the front entrance area of the count's mansion and stopped in front of the manager's door. When I saw the manager, Mr. Urbenin, run out with his children joining him to help Olga with her purchases, I headed for the mansion's main entrance, without saying good-bye to her or greeting him.

Chapter Two
The Wedding

I was sitting at the table, hating the crowd of guests who gazed with curiosity and admiration at the vast, corrupt decadence of Count Korneev's inherited wealth. The walls were covered with rich mosaics, the rooms had sculptured ceilings, and the luxurious Persian rugs and Louis XIV–style rococo furniture aroused everyone's esteem.

A perpetual vain smile covered the count's mustachioed face. He accepted his guests' approbation as his due, but he'd never made the slightest effort to accumulate these riches; instead, he deserved scorn and opprobrium for his indifference to the riches created by his father, his grandfathers, and his great-grandfathers over many generations.

Many in the crowd were sufficiently rich and independent that they could afford to judge objectively, but no one said a single critical word—all admired and smiled at the Count.

Mr. Urbenin was smiling, too, but he had his own reasons for doing so. He wore the grin of a happy child, talking about his young wife and asking questions like these:

"Who'd have thought that a young beauty like this could fall in love with an old man like me, three times her age? Couldn't she find someone younger and better-looking? There's no understanding women's hearts!"

He even turned to me and remarked in passing,

"We're living in strange times. Ha-ha! An old man like me steals a fairy-tale creature right out from under the nose of a young man like you! What were you waiting for? Ha! Young men these days—they're not like we used to be."

Gratitude swelled his huge chest as he spoke, and he bowed and raised his wineglass to the Count:

"You know my feelings toward you, my lord. You have done so much for me—all your attention. Only aristocrats and oligarchs could celebrate a wedding in this fashion. All this luxury, and all these famous guests—what can I say? This is the happiest day of my life!" And he went on like this.

Olga, however, disliked his obsequious speeches; she forced a smile at the Count's jokes and left the delicacies on her plate untouched. As Mr. Peter Egorovich Urbenin became drunker and happier, she grew more and more unhappy.

During the second course of the banquet, I looked at her and was so surprised that my heart beat faster. She pressed a napkin to her mouth, almost crying. She glanced around, frightened that someone might notice that she was nearly in tears.

"Why are you so sour today, Olga?" the Count asked. "Peter Egorovich, you're to blame. You haven't pleased your wife. Ladies and gentlemen, let the groom kiss the bride! Yes, I demand a kiss. Not that she should kiss me—ha-ha-ha, no, they should kiss each other!"

"Let them kiss each other!" the judge Kalinin repeated.

Forced by the cheers of the guests, Olga rose. Mr. Urbenin also stood, listing a bit to one side. She turned her cold, motionless lips to him. He kissed her, and she quickly turned away and tightened her mouth into a line so that he could not kiss her again.

I watched her carefully. She could not stand my glance. She put a napkin to her face, slipped away from the table, and ran out of the living room into the back garden.

"Olga has a headache," I tried to explain. "She complained to me about it earlier this morning."

"Listen, brother," the Count joked. "Headache has nothing to do with it. It's that kiss that did it, and she's all confused. I may have to give a verbal reprimand to this groom. He hasn't broken his wife in to his kissing yet. Ha-ha-ha!"

The guests enjoyed the joke and laughed uproariously. But they should not have been laughing. Five minutes passed, and then ten, but she did not return. Silence fell. The jokes stopped. Her absence was profound because she had not excused herself as she left. She had simply stood up, right after the kiss, as if she were angry that they had forced her to kiss her husband. She did not seem to be confused, because one can only be confused for a moment; this was different— the bride stood up, walked out. It was a nice plot twist for a comedy of manners.

Mr. Urbenin glanced around nervously.

"My friends," he mumbled, "maybe something in her gown has come undone. It's a woman thing." But several more minutes passed, and he gazed at me with such unhappiness in his eyes that I decided to enter the scene.

I met his eyes. "Maybe you can find her and get me out of this spot. You're the best man here," his eyes said.

I decided to respond to his desperate need and to come to the rescue.

"Where's Olga?" I asked the waiter who was serving the salad.

"She's gone into the garden," he said.

"The bride has left us and my wine grows sour," I addressed the ladies at the table. "I must go and search for her, and bring her back even if all her teeth are aching. I am the best man at this wedding, and I have duties to fulfill."

I stood up, walked past the applauding count, and went out into the garden.

I looked in side alleys, little caves and gazebos.

Suddenly, off to the right, I heard someone either laughing or crying. I found the bride in a little grotto. She was leaning on a moss-covered wooden column and her face was shining with tears, as though a new spring had burst forth from the earth.

"What have I done? What have I done!" she cried.

"Yes, Olga, what have you done?" I said as she flung her head on my chest.

"Where were my eyes, where was my head?"

"Yes, Olga, this is a good question." I told her, "I can't explain this as just being spoiled."

"And now everything is ruined and there's no going back. Everything! I could have married the man I love, the man who loves me!"

"Who could you have married? Who is this man, Olga?" I asked.

"It's you!" she said, looking directly into my eyes. "I was so stupid! You're clever, you're noble, and you're young . . . You're rich, too—you seemed to me—so far from me."

"Stop it, Olga," I said. "Wipe your eyes, stop crying, stop it! Stop this, my dear, you've made a silly mistake and now you have to face it. Calm down; calm down, please!"

"You are such a nice man, such a beautiful man. Yes?"

"Let it go, my dear," I said, noticing to my terrible surprise that I was kissing her forehead, that I held her slender waist, that she was leaning on my neck. "Stop it, please!"

Five minutes later, tired by new impressions, I carried her out of the cave in my arms.

A short distance away, I saw the Count's manager Mr. Kazimir applauding quietly as he watched us go.

CHAPTER THREE
HORSEBACK RIDING

On a beautiful evening in June, when the sun had already set, but the wide orange line still covered the faraway west, I went to Mr. Urbenin's house.

I found Mr. Urbenin himself there, sitting on the steps of his porch with his chin resting in both hands, looking away into the distance. He was very gloomy; his small talk came only unwillingly, so I chatted instead with his daughter, Alexandra.

"Where is your new mother?" I asked her.

"She went horseback riding with the Count. She rides with him every day."

"Every day," mumbled Mr. Urbenin with a sigh.

There was a lot in his sigh. Olga's conscience was clouded, but I could not understand what was going on as I looked into her guilty eyes when she came secretly to see me, twice during the past week.

"I hope that your new mother is in good health?" I asked Alexandra.

"Yes, she is," answered the little girl. "But last night she had a toothache, and she was crying."

"She was crying?" Mr. Urbenin asked, puzzled. "You saw it? Well, you must have dreamed it, my dear."

I knew that Olga's teeth were fine. If she'd been crying, it was from something else.

I wanted to talk to Alexandra a bit more, but we heard galloping hooves, and we saw two figures, an awkward male rider and a graceful Amazon. I lifted Alexandra into my arms, trying to hide my happiness at seeing Olga, caressed her blond curly hair with my fingers, and kissed the little girl on her head.

"You're such a pretty girl, Alexandra," I said, "You have such lovely curls!"

Olga looked at me briefly, nodded politely, and, holding the Count by the elbow, went into the mansion. Mr. Urbenin stood up and followed her. A few minutes later, the Count stepped out. His face looked fresh, and he was joyful in a way I'd never seen before.

"Please congratulate me, my friend," he said taking my arm under the elbow.

"What for?"

"A victory!"

"One more ride like that, and I will—I swear it on the dust of my noble ancestors—I will pluck the petals from this flower!"

"You haven't picked them yet?" I asked.

"Not yet, but I'm almost there," the Count said. "Wait, my dear—will you have a swig of vodka? My throat is very dry."

I asked the butler to bring the vodka. The Count drank two shots in quick succession, sat down on the couch, and continued his chatter.

"You know, I've just spent some time with Olga, and I am starting to hate this Mr. Urbenin! This means that I am beginning to like Olga, you know I do. She's a damned attractive woman. I'm going make some serious advances before long."

"You should never touch a married woman." I sighed.

"Well, yes, but Peter Egorovich is an old man, and it's not such a sin to amuse his wife a bit. She's no match for him. He's a dog in the manger—he won't eat it himself, and he won't let anyone else near it either. The campaign will begin later today, and I'm not going to take no for an answer. She is such a woman, I'm telling you! This is first-class, brother. You're going to love hearing about it."

The Count downed a third shot of vodka, and continued,

"You know what? I'm going to throw a party. We'll have music, amateur theater, and literature—all for her, to invite her in and make it with her there. As for today, well, Olga and I were just out riding, and you know what? It was for ten minutes"—and then the Count started singing, 'Your hand was in my hand'—"and she didn't even try to take her little hand away. I kissed it everywhere. But just wait until tomorrow, and for now let's go in. They're waiting for me. Oh, yes! I need to talk to you, my good man, about one thing. Tell me, please, is it true what people are saying about you—that you have intentions for Nadine Kalinina, the daughter of the old judge?"

"What if it is?"

"Well, if this is true, then I won't get in your way. To be a rival in such affairs—this is not my game. But if you have no special interest in her, then it's different!"

"I have no plans for her."

"Merci, my dear friend!"

The count wanted to kill two sparrows with one stone, thinking that he would do this with ease. In the end, he did kill two sparrows, but he didn't get the feathers, nor the skin.

(. . .)

I saw how the Count secretly tried to take Olga's hand when she entered, and greeted him with a friendly smile. Then, to show that he had no secrets from me, he kissed her hand wetly in front of me.

"What a fool!" she whispered in my ear, wiping her wet hand with disgust.

"Listen Olga," I said as soon we were alone. "It seems to me that you'd like to tell me something. Am I right?"

I looked questioningly into her face. She blushed and started blinking her eyes, as frightened as a cat caught lapping the cream.

"Yes, I would like to tell you something," she whispered, pressing my hand. "I love you, I cannot live without you . . . but you mustn't try to visit me anymore, my darling. You must not love me anymore, and you cannot address me as a familiar. I can't go on like this anymore. We cannot do this. You must not even show that you love me."

"But why?"

"I want it to be this way. You don't need to know the reasons, and I'm not going to tell you. Well, for what it's worth, if I hadn't married Mr. Urbenin, I could've married the Count by now. And then the Count and I would live together in the capital, and you could pay us visits. Hush! They're coming. Step back from me."

I did not step back, I was furious; so she had to do it to stop our conversation. Then she took her husband by the hand as he passed, and with a hypocritical smile, she nodded her head to me and left.

Chapter Four
At The Count's House

Late at night I was sitting at the Count's house, drinking. I was a bit drunk myself, but the Count was deeply intoxicated.

"Today, I was allowed to touch her waist in passing." The

Count was mumbling. "Today, we will keep on moving even further."

"How about the other girl, Nadine? What about her?" I asked.

"We are moving along nicely with her as well. We are at the stage of conversation of our eyes at the moment. And my dear, I would like to read more in her dark, sad eyes. There is something there that you cannot express with words. You have to understand this with your soul. Will you have a drink?"

"So she must like you, if you can talk to her for hours. And how about her father, old judge Kalinin? Does he also like you?"

"Her father? You are talking about that stupid old man? Ha-ha-ha. This idiot presumes that my intentions are honest."

The Count coughed and had another drink.

"Do you think that I'm going to marry her? First, I cannot marry anyone at this point. And what's more, I honestly think that it's much more honest to just seduce the young lady than to marry her. Imagine her terrible eternal life with an old drunk like me, constantly coughing. She would either die or run away the next day. And—what is this noise—listen!"

We jumped to our feet. Several doors slammed loudly, and then Olga ran into our room. She was pale and out of breath, trembling like the string of a guitar that has been struck rather than plucked. Her hair was loose and uncombed, and her eyes were wide open. Her fingers fiddled nervously with her nightgown on her breast.

"What's happened to you?" I asked, totally bewildered, and took her by the hand. Perhaps the Count was surprised by this level of intimacy between us but he showed no signs of it. He sighed, and turned a questioning look at Olga, as though he were seeing a ghost.

"What's happened?" I repeated.

"He's beating me!" she said with a sob, as she fell into an armchair.

"Who is?"

"My husband! I can't live with him anymore! I've decided to run away."

"This is terrible!" the Count said, hitting the table with his fist. "He has no legal right to do this. This is tyranny. This is God knows what! To beat your wife—for what?"

"For nothing," Olga said, wiping her tears. "I took a hand-kerchief out of my pocket, and that little envelope with the letter that you wrote to me yesterday also fell out. He jumped toward me, snatched it up from the floor, read it, and started beating me up. He held me by the wrist—look—he held me so hard that I still have a bruise here—look, and then he asked for an explanation. And instead of giving an explanation, I ran here. I need your support and defense. He cannot treat me like this. I'm not his servant, I'm his wife."

The Count started pacing the room, mumbling some words that if you could translate them into the speech of a sober person would be "About the situation of women in Russia."

"This is wild—he is behaving like a barbarian! This is not New Zealand or those islands where they eat people alive. He thinks that his wife should be butchered during his funeral. You know, people in some countries, those savages—when they die they also take their wives with them."

As for me, I asked her no questions but tried to calm her down, and offered her a glass of wine.

"I was mistaken; I was mistaken," she continued, talking to me, as she took a sip of wine. "And you—you are such a quiet man; I thought that you were an angel, not a man."

"And did you think that he would like that letter?" I asked her, but the Count interrupted me.

"This is mean, this is really nasty. You do not treat women like this! I will beat him up, I will challenge him to a duel, I will have a talk with him. Look, dear Olga, he won't go unpunished."

The Count spoke like a bantam cock. I thought to myself that no one had asked him to interfere in the relationship of Olga and her husband, and I knew that nothing would happen except for a lot of talk.

"I will smash him into the dirt. I'll do it tomorrow, first thing tomorrow!" So spoke the perfect gentle knight. As he was talking, he invited her to dinner, and in a mechanical way, without thinking, she picked up a fork and knife and started eating. In another few minutes her fear had entirely dissipated, and there were no signs of what had happened beyond her red eyes and loose hair. In a while she was laughing like a little child who'd forgotten all about a recent tumble. The Count was laughing, too.

"You know what I've decided? he said, sitting closer to her. "We'll stage a nice little play with some good roles for women. What do you think?"

The time was passing. She was sitting and talking to the Count.

"It's getting late. It's time for me to go, dear Olga," I said.

"Where should I go?" she asked. "I cannot go to him."

"Yes, yes, you cannot go to him; he would beat you up again," I said as I paced the room.

There was silence. Olga and the Count exchanged glances, and I understood everything. I took my hat and put in on the table.

"Well, well," the Count mumbled, rubbing his hands

impatiently. Then he stood up, drew me close to him, and whispered in my ear.

"Listen, Sergey, you have to understand the situation, and these things."

"Cut to the chase. You can skip the introductory matter."

"You know what, my dear friend, you should go home. She will stay with me at my place."

"Excuse me, but you're the one who doesn't understand," I said as I came to her.

"Should I leave now?" I asked, waiting for her answer. "Yes? Should I go?"

With a tiny movement of her eyes she answered "yes."

I said nothing more to her. What was left to say? I took my hat, and without saying good-bye I left the room.

CHAPTER FIVE
THE MURDER

When I arrived at the scene of the crime, my friend Count Korneyev related the following:

"We were in the middle of our picnic, and we heard a terrifying, heart-piercing cry; it just froze the blood. It came from the forest, and the echo repeated it four times. It was so unearthly that everyone got up from the grass, the dogs started barking, and the horses pricked their ears. It was the cry of a woman in terrible, mortal danger. A group of servants ran off into the forest to see what happened.

"The old butler Elias was the bearer of bad tidings. He ran back to the edge of the forest, out of breath, and said,

'The young lady has been killed!'

'Which lady?' 'Who killed her?' But Elias did not answer these questions.

"The second messenger was the one person whom we did not expect. This was Mr. Peter Egorovich Urbenin, my ex-manager, and Olga's husband. First, we heard heavy footsteps in the forest, and the cracking of dry branches. We thought that perhaps a bear would emerge from the dark trees. As he appeared from the bush, he saw us; he took a step back and froze for a moment. His hair was stuck to his forehead and temples. His face, usually red, was extremely pale; his eyes were wide, and he looked a bit crazy. His lips and hands were trembling.

"Yet what caught our attention and what shocked us all were his hands: they were covered with blood. Both hands and shirt sleeves were thickly coated with blood, as if he had just washed them in a blood bath.

"After standing motionless for a long moment, Mr. Urbenin collapsed onto the grass and began to moan. Some of our dogs sensed that something was wrong, and they circled him, barking.

"Casting a dim, sidelong glance at us, Urbenin covered his face with his hands and froze again.

'Olga, Olga, what have you done!' he moaned.

"Suppressed sobs rushed from his throat, and his huge shoulders shook as he wept. When he dropped his hands from his face, we all saw the bloody handprints impressed on his face; his cheeks were covered with blood."

At this point, my friend the Count stopped, shrugged, downed a shot of vodka, and continued,

"After that, I do not really remember in detail what happened next—I was so shattered by these events that I had lost the ability to think logically. I remember only that some men brought a body dressed in torn clothes completely covered with blood out of the forest, and I could not stand the sight. They put the body on a carriage and left. I did not hear the moans and the crying of the others.

"They say she was stabbed repeatedly in the chest, between the ribs, with a hunting knife. She always carried it on her; I remember I gave it to her as a gift.

"It was as blunt as the edge of this shot glass. How in the world could anyone have stabbed her with it?"

The Count stopped, poured another shot of vodka, and continued,

"Listen, shouldn't this Urbenin stab me as well, since we were lovers?"

"How can you be sure that it was he who stabbed Olga?" I asked.

"Of course he did it! But what I do not understand is how he found her in the forest! He was not with our picnic party, so how could he have known about that particular spot, which I chose for the picnic at the last moment? How could he have known that she would be walking right there in the forest, all by herself?"

"You don't know anything about this," I said, "So please, if I take up this case as a local investigator, you must not give me your advice, or your ideas, but only answer my questions. Do you understand?"

I left the Count and went into the room where they had brought Olga.

A small blue lamp was lit, and it barely illuminated the faces of the people in the room. It was so dark that you could neither read nor write. Olga lay on her bed. Her breasts were naked, because they were applying ice to her wounds, trying to stop the bleeding.

Two doctors were in attendance. As I came in, the first

doctor, Pavel Ivanovich, who had been in the picnic party, was listening to her heart, his eyes twinkling, his lips pursed. The second doctor, who was from the local village, looked extremely tired and sick; he sat in an armchair next to her bed, lost in his thoughts, pretending to take her pulse.

I looked in the corner—Mr. Urbenin sat there on a small stool. I hardly recognized him; he had changed so much recently. The poor man sat motionless, his head cupped in both hands, without averting his glance from the bed. His hands and his face were still covered with blood. It had not yet occurred to him to wash himself. At that moment, I realized that I could not believe Olga, when she had told me earlier that her jealous husband was capable of murder.

"Was it him or not?" I asked myself as I looked at his unhappy face. And I did not know the answer to this question, in spite of the Count's direct accusations and the blood covering the man's face.

"If he had killed her, he should have washed off the blood a long time ago," I thought. I remembered a phrase that one of my colleagues, a criminal detective, had taught me: "Murderers can't bear the sight of their victims' blood."

In an hour, a male nurse came from the faraway hospital and brought all the necessary things. They gave her an injection.

"It is highly unlikely that she will come to her senses," Pavel Ivanovich said with a deep sigh. "She has lost a lot of blood, and she was hit on the head with a heavy blunt object, which has probably caused a concussion."

I don't know if there was a concussion or not, but she opened her eyes and said that she was thirsty. She began to speak in a muffled, weak voice, and the doctor said that she could not talk for long, just for a few more moments.

Olga was lying on the couch, with a big wound in her right side. She came to her senses and opened her eyes.

"You can ask her whatever you want now," Pavel Ivanovich pushed my elbow. "Quickly now."

I came to her bedside. Olga's eyes focused on me.

"Where am I?" she asked.

"Olga," I began. "Do you remember me?"

Olga looked at me for a second and closed her eyes.

"Yes," she moaned, "Yes!"

"My name is Mr. Zinoviev. I am a police detective. I met you earlier, I was best man at your wedding."

"Oh, it's you, my dear," she whispered.

"She is delirious," muttered the doctor.

"My name is Zinoviev," I repeated, "I am a police officer. I was present at the hunting party and the picnic that followed. How do you feel?"

"Get to the point." the doctor said. "I cannot promise you that she will be conscious much longer in her condition."

"Please, do not lecture me, dear sir," I said. "I know what to say and what questions to ask. Olga, please try to remember the events of the preceding day. You were at a hunting party. Then a picnic. Do you remember?"

"And you . . . and you . . . killed," she said.

"The crow?" I asked. "Yes, after I killed the crow, you were upset, left the picnic, and went for a walk in the forest. Someone attacked you there. I am asking you as a police officer, who was it?"

Olga opened her eyes and looked at me.

"There are three people in this room besides me," I said. She negatively shook her head.

"You have to tell me his name. He will be persecuted and will be sentenced to hard labor in prison. I am waiting. Tell us the name!"

Olga smiled again but did not say a word. The rest of my interrogation did not bring any results. She did not say another word, and she did not move. At quarter to five in the morning, she died.

At seven a.m., the witnesses I had requested from the village finally arrived. It was impossible to go to the crime scene; last night's rain was falling heavily. Little puddles had become lakes. It was of no use, because all traces of the crime, such as blood-stains, footsteps, etc., were most likely washed away by the night's rain. Even so, I was formally required to examine the crime scene; however, I postponed the trip until the other police officers arrived.

In the meantime, I set about writing the crime report, and I interrogated other witnesses.

I do not enclose here the complete report and interrogation from the police investigation. It would be too lengthy, and I have forgotten many of the details. However, I will tell you briefly the crime, as I understand it.

Her clothing gave us plenty of evidence. Her upper cloak, made of velvet, with a silk lining underneath, was still completely soaked with fresh blood. The right side had a large hole made by the dagger and lots of clots of blood. The left side of the cloak was also covered with blood. The left sleeve was torn in two places—at the shoulder and at the cuff. Her belt and the pockets of her pants were bloodstained. Her handkerchief and her glove were turned into two small red rags. Her entire skirt was covered with blood spots of various sizes and colors.

The personal belongings of Olga—her big gold and diamond brooch and a massive golden chain— were intact. It was clear that the killer did not do it with the motive of robbing her.

The doctors concluded that she died from a severe hemorrhage and, as a consequence, a considerable loss of blood. It was a complete shock for the doctors that she had not died immediately at the crime scene. However, I digress, and I do not want to postpone the picture of the murder as I saw it, which I will present to you, the reader.

Olga separated from the hunting party while they were having a picnic, and headed off for a walk in the forest. Lost in her thoughts, she ventured deep into the thick forest. There, she met her murderer. While she stood pondering under a tree, the man came to her and began the conversation. She was familiar with this person and was not suspicious of him; otherwise, she would have cried for help. After they had spoken for a while, the killer snatched her by her left arm so hard that he tore her upper clothes and left four of his fingerprints on her upper arm. It was most likely then that she made that terrifying cry from pain, the one that everyone had heard when she realized his intent.

To prevent her from further shouts for help, possibly in a fit of anger, he seized her by her collar, the evidence of which is supported by the two torn upper buttons on her upper dress and the red line across her neck. The killer pulled at the golden chain around her neck, which tightened and made another thin line. After this, the killer dealt a strong blow to her head with a blunt object, probably with a stick or the handle of the dagger that Olga always had on her belt. In his rage, he decided that this one wound was not enough, and so he pulled her dagger from its sheath and stabbed her in her side with a very fierce blow—I say fierce, since the dagger was so blunt.

It was evident that Olga did not name the killer because she knew him and because somehow he was still precious enough to her to make her want to save him from his punishment.

Among such people were her insane father, the husband she did not love but felt guilty about, and the count that she felt obliged to for his financial support. Her father, as the servants later witnessed, was at home writing a letter to the police to punish the imaginary thieves that were surrounding his house. The Count, before and during the time of murder, was with the hunting party; which left only one person—Mr. Urbenin. His sudden appearance from the forest and his strange behavior supported this theory.

If that were not enough, it appeared that Olga's life had become a complete romance novel that included a loving old husband, jealousy, beating, escape to her rich count/lover. If the beautiful protagonist of such a novel is killed, then you should not be looking for thieves, but rather study the principal characters of the novel.

Thus, Mr. Urbenin, the husband, was the main suspect from any point of view.

—·—

I had to begin the interrogation.

[Translator's Note: A lengthy interrogation of Urbenin and further investigation were complicated by the murder of a farmer who was the key witness and who was killed in his prison cell. Mr. Urbenin, whose cell was in the same hall, is accused in the second murder. The investigation becomes a well-known case across the country. The detective is forced to retire after a fight with one of the minor witnesses.]

I performed the preliminary investigation in the living room of Urbenin's house, where I once sat on the couch courting the local ladies. Urbenin was the first person whom I interrogated. They brought him to me from the Olga's room, where he had remained, sitting and staring at the empty bed

For a minute or so, he stood before me in silence, but then he understood that I meant to speak to him in my official capacity as a police detective, and he finally broke the silence and said rather tiredly,

"Please, Sergei Petrovich, could you interrogate other witnesses first. I cannot talk now."

At that moment, he still considered himself to be a witness, or at least he thought that we considered him a witness.

"No, I have to interrogate you at once," I said. "Can you please sit down."

He testified that he was Peter Egorovich Urbenin, fifty years old, and that he was the formerly the manager of the Count's estate. When he spoke about his marriage with the nineteen-year-old Olga, he said that he loved her madly, and that he knew that she had married him without love, and that he had decided to be satisfied with her friendship and loyalty.

When he mentioned his disappointment in life and his gray hair, he stopped, and then asked not to talk about this aspect of things for the moment.

"I can't. It is too hard for me now. You know."

"All right, let us leave this for later. Tell me, it is true that you used to hit your wife? They say that you beat her when you found a note from the Count."

"This is not true. I just took her by her hand, and then at once she burst out crying."

"Did you know about her relationship with the Count?"

"I have asked you to postpone this conversation. And why should we talk about this at all?"

"All right, let us talk about this the next time. Now, can you explain to me how you found yourself in the forest where Olga was killed? You said that you were in the city. How did you wind up in the forest?"

"Yes, I had been staying with my sister in the city since I'd lost my position. I was keeping myself busy by seeking another position, and I was drinking, upset by my misfortune. That last week I was drinking nonstop, and I do not remember anything. I was lost."

"You were going to tell me how you ended up in the forest."

"Yes, I woke up late. It was a sunny day, and I decided to go and see her, maybe for the last time. I was going to the Count's place. I wanted to return the hundred rubles that he had loaned to me. I went through the forest, which I knew so well."

"So, you did not expect to meet your wife there?"

Urbenin looked at me with surprise, thought for a little while, and answered,

"Sorry, but this is a strange question. You cannot foretell your meeting with a wolf in the forest, and meeting a terrible misfortune, this is even more unpredictable. Look at this terrible case. I was crossing the aspen forest, and suddenly I heard that strange cry. It was so sharp that it seemed to hit me right in the ear."

His mouth was deformed by a grimace, and his chin trembled. He blinked his eyes and began to cry.

"I ran in the direction of the cry and I saw—I saw Olga lying on the grass. Her hair and forehead were covered with blood, and her face looked terrible. I cried, called her by her name. She did not move. I kissed her, lifted her in my hands."

Urbenin stopped and mopped the tears from his face with his sleeve. In a minute he continued.

"I did not see the scoundrel. When I ran to her, I heard someone's distant steps. Probably, he was running away."

"This story of yours is wonderfully invented whole," I said, "but you know—the police detectives do not believe in the sort of coincidence that would bring you by chance to the scene of the murder that coincided with your random walk in the forest."

"What do you mean it is invented?" Urbenin asked me. "I did not invent it at all."

Urbenin suddenly blushed and stood up.

"It seems that you suspect me of something," he said. "Well, you can suspect everyone, but Sergey Petrovich, you have known me for a long time."

"I know, but this is not personal at all. Police investigators must take the circumstances into consideration, and there are a lot of circumstances in this case that tell against you, Peter Egorovich."

Mr. Urbenin looked at me with horror, shrugged his shoulders, and said,

"But—no matter the circumstances, you should understand that I could not do this. How could I? To kill a quail or a crow is one thing—it is possible, but to kill a person, a person who is more precious to me than my own life. The mere thought of Olga was like sunshine for me. And suddenly you suspect me. And you say this—you whom I have known for many years, Sergey Petrovich. Please, let me go."

"Yes, we can stop for now. I will continue the interrogation tomorrow, but for now, Peter Egorovich, I have to arrest you. I hope that tomorrow you will understand the importance of all of the insinuating circumstances against you that we possess, and stop wasting time and make a confession. As for me, personally I am sure that it was you who killed Olga. I cannot tell you anything more today. You can go for now."

At the interrogation was finished. Urbenin was put under guard and placed in one of the Count's buildings.

On the second or third day, the deputy prosecutor Mr. Polugradov arrived from the city, a man whom I cannot remember without disgust. Imagine for yourself a tall, thin man around thirty, nicely shaved, with curly hair resembling that of a sheep and very smartly dressed. His face was thin and expressionless, so that looking at him you could see only the emptiness of a fop; he spoke with a very soft, sweet, insincere, and repulsively polite voice.

About a year after my retirement, when I was living in Moscow, I received an invitation summons to be present at the court sitting of the Urbenin case. I was glad to visit the places in the countryside, which I liked, and the case gave me a reason to go there. The Count, who was then living in St. Petersburg, did not go, and sent instead a medical certificate outlining his bad health.

The case was to be heard in the local county court. The prosecutor was Mr. Polugradov, who cleaned his teeth five times a day with red English toothpaste; the defense lawyer was a certain Mr. Smirnaev, a tall and thin blond, with a sentimental face and long straight hair. The jury was drawn almost exclusively from the local farmers and residents of the town; only four of them could read, and the rest looked very confused when they were given Urbenin's letters to his wife as evidence.

As I entered the court building, I did not recognize

Mr. Urbenin; his hair had turned completely gray, and he had aged twenty years. I had expected his face to show only apathy and indifference to his fate, but I was wrong. Mr. Urbenin was passionate during the trial; he rejected three members of the jury; he gave lengthy and emotional explanations; he interrogated the witnesses; and he denied his guilt, and asked numerous questions of the witnesses who testified against him.

The witness Mr. KazimirPoshekosky testified that I had been intimate with Olga, the victim in this case.

"It's a lie," Mr. Urbenin cried out from his bench. "I do not trust my wife, but him I do trust!"

When I testified, the defense lawyer asked me what sort of relationship I had had with Olga, and presented the testimony of Mr. Kazimir Poshekosky, who had apprehended me in the garden pavilion. To tell the truth (that I had made love to Olga) would be to support the accused; the more dissipated the wife, the more sympathy you must have for Othello-the-husband, I understood this. On the other hand, if I were to tell the truth, I would hurt Mr. Urbenin, and he would be in terrible pain. I decided to lie.

"No," I said. "I was not in a relationship with her."

The prosecutor's darkly colored description of Olga's murder stressed the anger and hatred of the killer. "That old, worn-out dissipated man met an innocent, very young, and beautiful woman. He lured her from the path of virtue with the promise of luxury. She was young and she had grown up reading romantic novels, and sooner or later she had to fall in love. He reacted like a wild animal that sees his prey slipping out of his claws. He was enraged, like a beast whose nose is singed by a burning coal." The prosecutor ended with the words, "She brought out the animal in him, and he treated her like a dog."

The defense lawyer did not deny that Urbenin was guilty but asked the jury to take into consideration that he was in the state of maximum excitement, and to soften his sentence. He noted that the feeling of jealousy could torture people, and referred to the all-too-human Othello, and then went into such great detail about the play that the judge had to interrupt him to remark that "it is not necessary for the jury to know that classic piece of literature."

The last word went to Urbenin, who swore that was not guilty: neither in deed nor in thought. He finished with the words,

"I no longer care about my own fate. But I am worried about the fate of my two little children." He turned to the public, started to cry, and asked the public to take care of his little children. He had probably forgotten that the verdict was still forthcoming, being completely immersed in thoughts of his children.

The jury took very little time to reach a verdict. He was found guilty on all counts, lost all his rights and his estate, and he was immediately sentenced to fifteen years of hard labor.

That was the price he had to pay for his meeting with a "young woman in red," on a May morning a few years ago.

About eight years have passed since these events. Some of the players in this drama have died; some are serving sentences for their crimes, and some simply go on living their miserable lives, waiting for death.

Chapter Six
The Truth Is Revealed

It was three months after the day when Mr. Kamyshev brought me the manuscript. My secretary announced that there was a gentleman in uniform waiting for me outside. Mr. Kamyshev came in.

"Sorry for bothering you, for heaven's sake. Have you read my manuscript? What is your decision?"

"You'll have to make some changes to it, I hope with our mutual agreement." We waited for a few moments in silence. I was very excited; my heart was beating and my temples were pulsating. But I did not want to show my guest that I was agitated. I continued, "Yes, according to our agreement. You told me that your novel is based on a real story."

"Yes, and I am ready to affirm this. I can introduce myself, I am Mr. Sergey Zinoviev."

"Do you want to say that you were the best man at Olga's wedding?"

"Yes, the best man and a friend of the household. Do you think that I am a sympathetic character in the story?" Mr. Kamyshev smiled, teasing his knee and blushing. "Is it so?"

"Yes. I like your novel; it's better than many other crime stories. But we should make some serious changes to it."

"What would you like to change?"

"First and foremost, you never do tell the reader who is guilty, who committed the crime."

Kamyshev's eyes widened and he stood up and said, "If you really think that you know the person who stabbed his wife and then strangled the only witness, then I don't know what to tell you, nor what should we do next."

"But Mr. Urbenin did not kill."

"Then who did?"

"It wasn't Urbenin!"

"Maybe you're right. *Humanum est errare.* Even criminal investigators are not perfect. Judicial mistakes do get made in this world. Do you think we made a judicial mistake?"

"No, what I think is that you didn't just make a mistake; you made a mistake on purpose. If a criminal investigator makes a mistake, it's not an accident."

"Then who was the killer in this case?"

"You!!"

Mr. Kamyshev looked at me in surprise mixed with horror.

"So this is it." He went to the window.

"Sir, what kind of joke is this story," he mumbled. He breathed nervously at the window, trying to draw something in the condensation with his finger.

I looked at his hand, a very muscular, iron-hard hand, and imagined how he had strangled the servant in the prison cell, and how he had destroyed Olga's tender body. The figure of a murderer standing right in front of me filled me with horror. Not for myself, but for this giant, and in general for all mankind.

"You killed her!" I said.

"Then I can congratulate you with your discovery," he said. "How did you come to this conclusion, please tell me."

"Yes, you are the murderer." I said. "And you can't even hide it. It's between the lines in your novel, and you're a lousy actor, trying to act in front of me now. You might as well go ahead and tell me the truth—this is all very interesting, and I'd be very curious to know."

I jumped up and started pacing the room.

Mr. Kamyshev went to the door, looked outside, and closed it very securely. This precaution gave him away.

"Why did you close the door?"

"I'm not afraid of anything. I just thought that there might be someone behind the open door."

"And why do you need this? Tell me. Can I start an interrogation? I should warn you that I'm not a police detective and I may get tangled up in the interrogation, and mix up some things. But in any case, first of all—where did you disappear to, after you said good-bye to your friends, when the picnic was over?"

"I just went home."

"You know, in your manuscript, the description of your route was crossed out. Did you walk across the same forest?"

"Yes."

"And could you have met her?"

"Yes, I could."

"And did you meet her?"

"No, I did not."

"In the course of your investigation, you forgot to interrogate one important witness, namely, yourself. Did you meet the victim?"

"No. There you are, my friend," he said. "You are not an expert interrogator." At this moment I noticed that Mr. Kamyshev was smiling at me in a patronizing way, enjoying my inability to find the answers to the questions that were torturing me.

"All right then, you did not meet her in the forest. But it would have been even more difficult for Mr. Urbenin to have found her in the forest. He wasn't seeking her there, but you—on the contrary—being drunk and excited and angry with her—you could not escape looking for her. And why did you go through the forest and not along the country road?"

"Let us imagine that what you say is true," he admitted.

"How can we explain your crazy state of mind on the night of the event? It seems to me that it was connected with the crime that you committed earlier that day. Then, after coming to the Count's house, instead of asking the question directly, you waited for a whole night and a day until the police arrived. This can only be explained by the fact that the victim knew the murderer, and you were the murderer.

"Further, Olga did not name her murderer because she loved him. If it were her husband, she would have told you the name at once. She did not love him; she didn't even care about him, but she loved you and she wanted to save your life.

"And therefore, when she came to consciousness for a few moments, why did you procrastinate instead of asking her the one question that mattered, wasting her last few minutes with secondary questions that were not connected with the event? You were dragging the time out, because you did not want her to name you as the murderer. Also, you wrote in detail about the numerous shots of vodka that you drank, but the death of "the woman in red" is never described. Why?"

"Continue, continue."

"You didn't study the scene of the crime on the first day; you waited for the next day to come. Why? Because the night rain would wash away all your steps in the forest. Then you don't mention interrogating the caterers and the guests who were present at the picnic. They heard Olga yelling, and you should have interrogated them, but you didn't, because at least one of them would have remembered that you yourself had disappeared into the forest. They were interrogated eventually, but by then they would have forgotten all the details concerning you."

"You are smart," Mr. Kamyshev said, rubbing his hands. "Do go on."

"Isn't this enough? And to prove that you killed Olga, I must remind you that you were her lover: the lover whom she traded for a man she despised, the Count. If the husband could kill from jealousy, then the lover could just as easily have done it for the same reason.

"That's enough," Kamyshev said, laughing. "Enough. You

look so pale and excited that you don't have to continue. But you're right. I did kill her."

There was silence. I paced the room and he did the same.

"Very few people could have done this; most readers would not come to this conclusion. They're not as smart as you."

At that moment, one of my workers from the editorial board came to my study, looked carefully at Mr. Kamyshev, put some materials on my desk, and then left. Kamyshev came to the window.

"It has been about eight years, and I am still tortured by the weight of bearing this mystery. Not by my conscience. The conscience by itself is nothing—it can be dulled by logical explanations. But when logic fails, I try to kill it with wine and women. And I am still popular among women, by the way. It surprises me that for eight years, not a single person had the slightest idea that I bore this terrible secret. So I wanted to tell people about this secret of mine in a special way—can you believe it?—I did so in the form of a book. When I wrote this novel, I thought only a few people would discover the truth. Every page has a clue to the mystery, but I was writing it for an average reader."

My secretary Andrew came in and brought two glasses of tea.

"You are looking at me as a man of mystery, and now it's three o'clock and it is time for me to go."

"Stop. You haven't told me how you killed her."

"What else do you want to know? You know what? I killed her in a state of extreme stress; I was overcome with emotion."

"People smoke and drink when they're stressed. Right now, you have just seized my cup of tea instead of yours, and you smoke more often because of stress. Life is stressful."

"I did not intend to kill her as I was walking through the forest. I was only going to find Olga and tell her that she was behaving badly. But sometimes when I'm drunk, I can get aggressive. I saw her about two hundred steps from the edge of the forest. She was standing in front of a big tree looking into the sky. I called her name, and she stretched her hands out toward me. 'Please do not scold me, I am so unhappy,' she told me. I was drunk and I forgave her, and we embraced. She told me that she'd never loved anyone but me all her life. Then, in the middle of all this, she said the most dreadful thing: 'I am so unhappy,' she said. 'If I hadn't married Mr. Urbenin, then I could have married the Count. And we could meet secretly.' It was like a bucket of cold water. I was filled with disgust. I took this little creature by the shoulders and threw her on the ground, as you throw a ball in a game. And then, I was in a rage at that moment. I threw her on the ground, and then I killed her; yes, I killed her, I finished her off."

I looked at Mr. Kamyshev and saw that there was no shame on his face. His lips spoke the words 'I killed her, I finished her off' with no more expression than if he'd said 'I smoked a cigarette.' I had a feeling of disgust toward him.

"And how about Mr. Peter Urbenin? What happened to him?"

"They say that he died on his way to prison, but this is not known for sure, and how and why."

"What do you mean by 'and how and why'? An innocent person was suffering, and you are asking me 'and how and why.'"

"What was I supposed to do—go to the police and make a confession? They would like to me to do this—but they are all stupid."

"You are disgusting."

"And I am disgusting to myself. Perhaps I should go."

"And Count Korneev? Where is he?"

"He is my chauffeur and personal assistant now. Mr. Kazimir—his ex-wife took his estate from him, and became rich. Look outside, you can see him! Over there."

I looked outside and saw a small figure with a curved back, dressed in a worn-out hat and a shabby overcoat of no particular color. It was difficult to see the protagonist of the drama in this old man.

"I found out that Urbenin's son lives in the Andreev Hotel. I would like to make a set-up so that the Count could take some money from the son of Mr. Urbenin. Thus, he would be avenged. I really must say good-bye. Adieu!"

Kamyshev bowed his head and walked out the door. I stared at my desk, lost in thought.

I did not have enough air to breathe.